Pelican Bay

Mei-Ling Venning

Copyright © 2016 Mei-Ling Venning
All rights reserved.
ISBN: 1523964596
ISBN-13: 978-1523964598

DEDICATION

To all people with a learning disability of any kind.

ACKNOWLEDGMENTS

I would like to thank Kathryn Coughran for suggestions and advice at the planning stage and every stage thereafter. At the research stage, thanks to Irene Freeman-Smith and Sandra Powel for assistance with medical information and Liz Conners for help with information regarding social services. I would like to thank Wyong Writers for their support and feedback, and finally a huge thank you to Bob Venning for micro-editing, support and encouragement throughout the journey from finished manuscript to print.

Chapter 1

She saw them through the trees. Everything in her turned to lead. She couldn't outrun them. The shop. Maybe they wouldn't follow her there. She forced petrified legs to move. The trees gave way to pavement. Her tormentors loomed, their shapes made black against the midday sun.

Short thick legs ran till she reached the shop panting. She stumbled into the nearest aisle of close packed shelves. She caught at the nearest thing. Marmalade. The jar flew through the air. Michelle's stumpy fingers gripped the dismembered lid. She looked with horror at the broken jar and shiny orange jelly oozing onto the lino. Small rectangles of peel disbursed in orange. Jagged edges of glass thrust through the gelatinous mess.

Her eyes widened and her lungs beat like bellows. Her shallow breaths disturbed the silence which had descended on the shop. Her hands began to flutter, palms splayed towards the floor, fingertips pointing at the ceiling. Thumbs faced each other, and rapid sideways flapping movements followed. Hands crossed and uncrossed, as the sides of her thumbs beat off each other.

The bullies had arrived silently. Uneven voices drifted from the left.

"Look what The Dumbo's done now." Troy's half-broken voice rasped through the stillness.

Michelle felt a tear beginning. They always called her Dumbo. She'd seen and heard them at the caravan park. They'd started when she was a visiting child, too young to understand that they were making fun of her. When they thought no one was watching they pulled at the corners of their eyes, narrowed them, then stuck their tongues out to imitate her. Sometimes they muttered gibberish. They sought her out with taunts whispered from the corners of their mouths. Each time they laid innocent seeming traps and played small pranks which they called jokes. The girl had never told anyone of her humiliations. She shuddered, hoping they wouldn't come too close.

Suddenly, Darryl was at her shoulder, his voice deeper and harder than his brother's.

"Yeah, with luck they won't let her out anymore after this." He laughed, pushing her so that her foot slipped into the shiny orange stuff.

"Don't," her cry was soft and humble.

"Don't what? We haven't done anything. You're the clumsy one."

A kick sent her other foot into the slippery marmalade, and Michelle lost her balance. She struggled, trying not to fall over. Her hands sought the nearby shelves but missed. She could hear the boys' insults. Her foot slid through the marmalade. She began to fall, her calf catching and tearing on broken glass. She landed with a painful thump.

The voices receded and Michelle lay on the floor aware of faces above her. Someone had knelt beside her and was holding her shoulder gently. "Don't move. You've got one cut already and the rest of you is very near the broken glass."

The girl looked up to see a kindly face, sun wrinkled, surrounded by wispy white hair. Dark knowing eyes crinkled at the corners as the owner of the face smiled.

Michelle arrived back at the caravan park tearful, sobbing out parts of her story. Her mum, Trish, patched her up and listened with pursed lips. She suspected more than she knew but rarely pushed for more information, fearing that it would cause her daughter more discomfort. Without being carefully drawn out the girl could not find the words to say much more than that she had been pushed, had fallen and had been rescued.

Trish wondered whether she should try to find out more. Their visits to the caravan park in the past had usually been short, and she was afraid of dwelling on unpleasant aspects, fearing that doing so would taint Michelle's joy at visiting her grandfather. She assembled salad vegetables as she worried at the thought of their extended stay. *We've only been here a short while and already Michelle's encountered tormentors.*

"Would you lay the table Sweetie?" Trish tore at lettuce leaves, as her mind ripped through thoughts of slashing out at her daughter's persecutors, but she kept her thoughts to herself.

Mother and daughter ate lunch quietly, each wanting to say more but not knowing how. Afterwards Michelle retreated to her bedroom and looked around the small pink room she was forced to share with her older sister every time they came to stay. She knew her grandfather had decorated it specially for her but pleasure in its brash pinkness evaporated just a little more each time her sophisticated sister poured scorn on it.

Michelle eyed a black top folded neatly in her sister's half of the wardrobe. Her heart called out to stroke the smooth silkiness and little dangly beads. Short stubby fingers caressed the contrasting textures of embroidery and detail. Slowly she pulled the top towards her and held it against her face. She closed the bedroom door and took off her own blouse.

Trish looked up to see her youngest daughter silhouetted against the doorway.

"Michelle, are you wearing your sister's top?"

"Yes. Awesome isn't it?"

"It's Stella's top, Sweetie. Her new top. She won't want you borrowing it. It's an evening top. It's only the afternoon now. Stella wore it to a club in Sydney, remember?"

"You said it looked good. Gareth's friend whistled when he saw her in it. I want to look good too." Michelle's bottom lip stuck out in defiance.

"You do look good, but ... well maybe it's just not your style." Trish finished lamely. Michelle stood with hands on hips. "Stella looks good in it. I want to look good!"

"Take it off, young lady. I want it folded and on Stella's bed, or better still in the wardrobe where youfound it. Put your blouse back on." She paused before bellowing, "Now!"

Michelle shrank as the soundwaves from her mother's reprimand reached her. She walked with bowed head into the small bedroom and tugged at the black top. A tiny rip appeared under the armpit. Resentfully, she folded it, and laid it on the other bed. She put on her own blouse. Small discreet blue checks on white cotton looked tame after the excitement of the slinky back top. She walked back out of the bedroom.

Trish looked appreciatively at her. "That looks so much better Michelle. It really does."

Michelle shrugged.

"Come now, tomorrow's Saturday. Dad and Gareth will be here."

Michelle's expression was solemn. "I miss them."

"I know, Sweetie." Trish reached out for her daughter, drawing her close. Michelle wrapped her arms around her mother's neck.

Trish continued, "I know you don't like it, but we have to be here, at least for now—someone has to run the caravan park while Poppy's in hospital. At least Dad and Gareth can come up for weekends." She searched her mind for something to keep her daughter occupied.

"Would you do something to help me?"

Michelle nodded.

"Would you bring the washing in please? Take one of the baskets."

Michelle walked off. Trish didn't notice tears glistening in her eyes.

Michelle stood outside the camp laundry and looked at the ropes strung between trees. Four lines of assorted family washing. She wondered if they would be mixed with clothes of visiting tourists. Would she find the right washing? Would her mum be angry if she brought back the wrong washing? She thought back to her life in Sydney—a mere week earlier her life had been so safe, so sure. Her mum had never been angry then. The small tear escaped the corner of her eye and rolled down her cheek. Soon another joined it, and another. Not long after that the tears were coursing down, splashing, rushing, gushing till she could see no more.

Michelle didn't see a tiny stooped figure coming towards her. The small wrinkled lady carried an old fashioned wicker basket that resembled a baby's crib. She put it down next to Michelle. Very gently she prized the plastic basket from Michelle's hands.

Michelle felt arms around her shoulders. She felt herself propelled to a nearby chair. She was aware of a tissue being handed to her and the heat of a human body next to her.

"Tell me what makes you so unhappy on such a beautiful day?" The old lady leaned towards her.

"I don't...I don't know which are our clothes," Michelle managed between sobs.

"That's easy," the old lady stroked Michelle's hair, "very easy. I'm the only other person who put anything out here today. So you see," she continued brightly, "if I take down my things, everything else will be yours."

Michelle's sobs subsided and became small sniffles. She watched as the old lady unpegged a few items and put them in her wicker basket and smiled at

Michelle.

"Would you like me to help you with yours? I'm not in a hurry."

Michelle nodded and together they unpegged and folded the family washing.

"I'm Lola, by the way."

Michelle studied her face. "It was you at the shop. You helped me."

"Yes that's right. I know those boys. I know their family, and I'll tell you a secret." She put one finger to her lips and bent towards Michelle. "Those great big boys are afraid of little old me."

Michelle gasped.

Lola continued, "One day I'll tell you all about it, but for now, that's all you need to know. I live in the caravan in the far corner. That's right, the cream and black one. And you're Ed's granddaughter aren't you? I've seen you visiting over the years, since you were a baby in fact." She beamed at Michelle who nodded.

Lola continued, "You and your mum, you've come to help while Ed's in hospital. That's nice—families helping."

"It's not nice," Michelle's tears started again. She rocked on the chair and splayed her hands.

Lola noticed the tense spread fingers and the thumbs that started to beat against each other as Michelle wailed, "It's not nice at all. I hate it... hate it... hate it..."

"Oh dear. What's wrong?" Lola leaned forward. "Tell me what's so very hateful about being here?"

"I had my own room in Sydney. It was my room with my things. Now I share." Michelle started to sniff again. "And Dad and Gareth only get here on weekends."

"It's nearly the weekend now," Lola smiled encouragingly. "They'll be here tonight or tomorrow then?"

"Um, yes, tonight." Michelle brightened up. "And I'll get to see Poppy. Mum'll take me." She smiled at Lola. "I've made him a card. It has seashells. I glued them on." She paused and added, "Both legs broken. That's bad, isn't it?"

Lola agreed.

As the late afternoon sun sank in the sky Michelle told Lola of how she felt left out when everyone was so busy.

"And were they always so busy?" Lola asked.

"No. It's just here. No one has time for me anymore," she said sadly as she stared at her basket of washing.

"Well, I'm not busy most of the time," Lola patted her arm. "Now I've told you my caravan's the cream and black one, you can come whenever you want."

"Can I really?" Michelle's face lit up.

"Yes, of course, but for now I think you'd better take that washing back, don't you?"

Michelle looked around Lola's small neat caravan. She held out a bunch of wild flowers. "I came to say Thank You. The other day... You helped me."

Lola smiled at her. "What a lovely bunch of flowers. Thank you my dear." She burrowed under the sink looking for a vase. When her head popped up again she continued, "... and are you all right now? Is everything healing nicely?"

Michelle turned her leg so that Lola could see a sticky plaster on her calf.

"That looks very neat. I'm sure it's fine under there. "Now, about this time of day I generally have a cup of tea and a biscuit. Would you like one?"

"Yes please, the tea but no biscuits." Michelle shook her head. She didn't notice the look of surprise on Lola's face, but continued, "I get fat. Mum says only healthy food."

"I see." Lola nodded. "Well, come outside with me and I'll find something healthy." She moved towards the door.

Lola and Michelle walked around to the back of the caravan. There, in the north-facing light, was a rectangle of soil. Neat rows of fresh green feathery leaves sprouted. Michelle didn't recognise anything except for half a dozen tiny lettuces.

"I've got baby carrots under here, look." Lola grabbed a few fronds, and tugged.

Michelle watched in amazement as a small shaft of orange came into view. She clapped her hands, and Lola drew out a few more.

Lola washed the carrots and passed one to Michelle.

"I think your mum's quite right. These are much better than biscuits. I'll have a carrot too."

They sat on faded green plastic chairs outside Lola's caravan, the table between them holding mugs of tea and the bowl of carrots. When the carrots were finished Michelle turned to Lola. "I knew about lettuces but I've never seen carrots come out of the ground before."

"Oh plenty of other things come out of the ground," Lola grinned. She got up and went into the caravan, returning with a cardboard shoe box which she put on the table.

"Look in there. Those are the seed packets."

Michelle fingered the packets gingerly. "You grew all these?"

"Mm. that's right. Look at that radish packet. I haven't opened it yet. Radishes grow underground too. Would you like to grow some?"

"Oh, yes! Yes!" Michelle's face lit up.

Gareth arrived early on Friday evening. Michelle jumped up and down in the doorway.

"We've missed you. We've missed you. Mum's cooking. I'm helping." She hugged him.

Gareth hugged her back then disengaged himself. "So what's for tea, Princess?"

"Dinner!" she reprimanded, wagging a finger at her brother.

Stella appeared at the door. "Dad's not here yet, Michelle. We can call it whatever we like." She kissed her brother on both cheeks and offered him a drink.

"A beer would be good. Should I help Mum?"

"I'm sure she won't need it. Princess here has been a great little helper."

Michelle's face fell. She looked at the floor and bit her top lip. Gareth looked at Stella sharply. She stared defiantly back at him and he shook his head at her. Michelle went into the kitchen.

Later, when the dinner plates were cleared, the sound of Neville's car drifted through the windows. Michelle jumped up and ran outside. She started talking to him before he had even stopped he engine.

"Whoa, whoa there." He jumped out of the car and gathered her up in his arms and whirled her around. She squealed with delight.

He put her down and held her hand. "Come on Princess, let's get into the house."

Trish and Stella walked down the path to greet him.

The hospital was lighter and brighter than Trish thought it would be.

Michelle raised herself up and down on to her toes. "Can I give Poppy the flowers?"

Trish held out the cellophane wrapped bouquet, "Of course you can. Do you want to carry them now?"

"Um, no, later." Michelle clasped her hands tightly. It was enough that she could walk into the ward holding the flowers. She didn't want to hold them on the long walk out of the lift and up the corridor.

Just outside Ed's room, Trish handed her daughter the flowers. Michelle reached for the hard shiny plastic. It rustled as she closed her right hand round the bunch. With her left hand she stroked the satin bow.

"It's really pretty. Poppy'll be pleased, won't he?"

"For you, Poppy. I made the card and I chose the flowers. And the ribbon. Pink, my favourite colour. You like pink?"

Ed reached towards the card. "That's a great card. Did you get the seashells from the beach at Pelican Bay?"

Michelle nodded. "I glued them on carefully. I hope they don't fall off." She looked anxiously into his face. "You do like the flowers, the colour, don't you Poppy?"

"The flowers are lovely. I'm very happy with pink, Princess. Thank you for bringing them." He lay them on the bed as he tried to reach towards mother and daughter to give them a kiss. After trying to sit up he beckoned to them. "You have to come to me, girls. I can't get to you like this, you know."

Michelle looked at him earnestly. "Poppy, why did you have to break both legs?"

"I didn't have much choice Princess. If it had been up to me, I wouldn't have broken anything."

"Oh. Only Stella said..." Michelle looked uncertainly at Trish.

"I expect Stella said something like 'Trust Poppy to break both legs'. Is that what she said?"

Michelle broke into a huge smile. "Yes. How did you know, Poppy?"

"Oh, I'm a wily old thing. I know perfectly well that my oldest granddaughter doesn't think I ought to go fishing off the end of a rocky outcrop."

Trish laughed. "Not just the end of a rocky outcrop, but at night, and in a storm. Honestly Dad, how irresponsible can you get?" "Anyway I'm sorry we haven't got here earlier. How have the first few days been?"

"Ugh. Painful. Grim." Ed shook his head.

Michelle looked puzzled. "What's wrong Poppy?"

"There's nothing wrong Princess. I'm just being a miserable old man."

"You're not an old man, Poppy," She put her

arms round his shoulders. He smiled and patted her hands.

"A man should hear that more often," he laughed and waved to chairs near the bed. "Come, sit down, and let me look at you."

After they sat, Trish told Ed about the first few days at the caravan park. "It's been frantic. I know it's still the summer holidays, but I didn't realise you'd have so many people staying. Just tidying up and keeping on top of everything has been a full time job." She nodded towards her daughter, wanting to include her in the conversation. "And you've been helping too, haven't you?"

Michelle brightened again. "I helped Mum move some tables and chairs from the café. They're outside the office now."

Ed looked puzzled.

Trish reached out for his hand, "Dad it was the only sensible option. I couldn't run the café as well. There's an electric kettle in the office. I can just make coffee if anyone wants it. I know it's very makeshift at the moment, but we're doing our best. Neville and Gareth came last night. We'll get something sorted, don't you worry." She turned to her daughter, "Why don't you go and find a vase, and put the flowers in water for Poppy while I tell him what we've been doing?"

Michelle got up. "Where…?"

"On the way in we passed a small room. I saw vases and a sink. It's over there. You can find it, can't you?"

"Yes." Michelle's face brightened. "Yes, I can do that."

Ed watched her. "Will she be all right Trish? She

won't get lost or anything will she?"

"The flower room's just outside the door. She'll be okay. Anyway she'll enjoy arranging them. She likes doing things like that."

"She won't overfill the vase, will she?"

"No, really Dad, she'll be fine."

Ed relaxed and Trish talked about the things that Neville and Gareth were doing, back at the caravan park.

"They'll have to go back to Sydney during the week, but it's great they're up on weekends though."

"And Stella? Surely she won't want to leave Sydney?" Ed asked.

"Oh, you know, being freelance, it doesn't really matter where she is. It helps me a lot to have her around—although I have to say she and Michelle do argue a bit!" She wondered whether to tell him about the incident with the boys in the shop. She began,

"The day before yesterday…"

Michelle returned with a vase of flowers in each hand. She took over her mother's sentence, "Yesterday, Dad and Gareth came — " She set the flowers down on Ed's bedside table. "There were too many for one vase." She looked from the flowers to Ed, "There isn't much water in them. I didn't want it to flood, spill, I mean. I could get a jug and, and you know…" she mimed pouring.

Ed laughed, "You're priceless."

"I know. I'm a princess, aren't I?"

Chapter 2

Stella sat in the middle of the living room of the family's Sydney home. She was surrounded by CDs and DVDs.

Her brother walked in. "Most people take cases of clothes—not my sister. No, Stella has to take sacksful of music!"

"Yeah, well you know Michelle's idea of good music is still the stuff she grew up with. I need something to keep me sane."

"That's okay Sis. I've an evening in. Fliss is out with the girls. Is a barbie okay?"

"Mmm great. We've been spoilt with Dad haven't we? I used to wonder how other kids managed if their dad wasn't a chef," she laughed. "Left to our own devices we can never do anything more creative than a barbie."

They sat eating steak and salad and talking about their grandfather's caravan park.

"I guess Lady Fliss isn't too happy about you spending weekends up there, huh?"

"You bet, absolutely right! Fliss wants us to go to a wedding exhibition next weekend."

Stella leaned across the table. "Oh Gareth, she'll be so disappointed. She's been going on about it for a while."

He shrugged. "I tried explaining that we're all needed at Pelican Bay on weekends."

Stella put down her knife and fork. "Look, I've known Fliss a lot longer than you. We worked in that travel agency for two years remember? D'you want me to see if I can smooth her ruffled feathers, get you back in her good books?"

"That would be great, Sis." Gareth grinned.

Stella consulted her diary. "I'm due back at *Pelican Bay* tomorrow," she made a face. "Look, I'll try and catch her next time I'm down here. Okay?"

"You don't sound altogether too pleased about being up at *Pelican Bay*, Sis."

Stella shrugged. "I know Mum needs all the help she can get during the week. It's just that it's not good for me and Michelle to be so cooped up together."

Gareth nodded. "At least here you've got your own bedrooms."

"Um. Sharing that tiny room in that minute house drives me mad." Stella made movements, pretending to pull out her hair. "The other day I found her trying on my clothes—that's why practically everything's ripped. Still, Mum's got a place for her at the local Day Centre."

"She won't think she's being palmed off?"

"No, at least I don't think so. It's only one day a week—moving to two later if it's successful. I think

Michelle's looking forward to it."

"Maybe it'll help a bit. What's it like? Have you seen it?"

"Yeah I drove out and had a stickybeak for Mum. It's great. I have to say... better than anywhere we'd have found in Sydney. It's called Eden House, set in really pretty grounds, lots of trees and flowers and great activities going on."

"What sort of things?"

"The day I visited there was a little drama group, and there was dancing and a really good art room."

"She'll love that."

Trish discussed the idea of asking Stella to take Michelle to Eden House, but Stella refused.

"It's her first morning there Mum. She'll really think you're trying to get rid of her. Look, you can spare the time. I'll hold the fort. I know what I'm doing here, and anyway I'm not the best sister for her—think how much we row!"

"OK. You'll be able to manage here and I don't want to risk making her feel rejected. We'll meet the coordinator and have a look around, then I'm sure I can get back.

"Bye Mum," Michelle looked uncertainly at Trish. "Phone me at lunchtime?"

"Promise."

The coordinator was a large lady with a flamboyant dress. She took Michelle into the art room. She noticed Michelle's lightly fluttering fingers, and smiled at her.

"My name's Kessie. If you chose to do art, you'll be with me a lot of the time."

"That's good." Michelle's hands became still.

The art room was light and airy. About eight people sat or stood making different things. She walked around slowly. A short stout boy was tearing bits of newspaper into a bowl of water.

Michelle smiled at him. "Pap… pap…ier, that's it, pap…ier maché."

The boy nodded. "How d'you know that?"

"My mum. She showed me."

The boy smiled at Michelle, "It's fun. Wanna join me?"

"Maybe." Michelle grinned, "I want to see other things first."

"I'm Hal. I'll be your friend—even if you don't join me."

"Thanks Hal. I'm Michelle. Think I'll just paint. I like painting."

A voice at her elbow hissed, "Boring old paint. I bet you're boring too." Michelle looked up to see a pretty girl about her own age with smooth dark hair and mean green eyes, which she narrowed as she looked at Michelle.

"Now, now Josie," Kessie remonstrated. "It's Michelle's first day. Let's be welcoming, hey?"

Josie shuffled back to a box of ceramic tiles which she was sorting in a desultory way.

A tall boy with dark curly hair waved from the back of the room. He was printing with blocks of wood. "Hi Michelle. Most of us want to welcome you." He bent his body in a low bow as if he were performing in a play. Everyone, except Josie, clapped.

Josie glared at Michelle and stomped back to her seat.

There was a mid-morning break. Hal moved on

unsteady legs.

"D'you want coffee Michelle?"

"Um, oh. Is there tea?"

"Yeah. I can make you tea."

Michelle watched Hal move towards a kettle. She saw Josie dig her elbows into Hal's ribs. A small amount of tea spilled onto the counter.

Josie called out, "Clumsy Hal!"

The boy who had bowed to Michelle brought the tea over to her. "Don't mind Josie. Hal's okay." He nodded before wandering off.

During the second half of the morning everybody was encouraged to talk about what they had done. Michelle discovered the boy with dark curly hair was called Billy. He sat next to her.

"I've been doing printing for a few weeks. I've got to choose something else next week. Not sure what I'm going to do."

"Oh. Can't I just paint?"

Kessie joined them. "You can if you want Michelle. It's just that I think it's a good thing to try other things. Look, Josie's got to move on from the mosaics. She's been doing that for a long time. Why don't you try next week?"

Josie looked up from across the room. "I heard that." She held the box of tiles close to her chest, then suddenly dropped the box on the floor. "Stupid tiles. Who wants them anyway?" She stared from Kessie to Michelle and walked towards the door.

As she reached the door, Kessie called out, "If you leave the art room without picking up those tiles, you won't be doing art next week Josie." Josie slammed the door. Michelle walked over to the scattered tiles. She knelt down and started picking them up. Hal and Billy joined her.

Hal said, "You can try mosaics next time. Josie won't be here."

Michelle and Trish looked around Ed's new hospital room.

Trish nodded approval and Michelle said. "You've got a wheelchair. I like this place. I hated the lift..."

Trish added, "You've got a garden too."

"Yes, but I can't use the garden unless someone takes me. Here, Princess, how about you take me for a whirl, while your mum finds me a coffee? I could kill for a coffee."

Michelle's forehead creased.

Trish put her hand on Michelle's arm, "It's a way of talking, remember?"

"You wouldn't really kill, would you Poppy?" Michelle grinned.

"No Princess. Now, how about you take me for a spin?"

Michelle wheeled Ed to the small courtyard garden. Frangipani gave shade, colour and scent. Clivias grew under the canopy of the trees and bright brash geraniums splashed abundant colour to the small paved area.

"They're pretty aren't they, Poppy?" She picked a few dropped frangipani flowers. "They're perfect." She put some on his knee. "I'm growing things with Lola."

Ed looked up sharply. "Really? What are you growing?"

"Radishes. We planted them ..." Michelle stopped and counted on her fingers, "five days ago.

There are little tiny leaves already." She clapped her hands. "It's exciting." She stopped and looked at Ed's thoughtful face. "What is it, Poppy?"

"I was just thinking about Lola. I'm glad she's growing radishes with you —"

"Not just radishes. We're going to grow lots of things. Lola's my friend. It's nice having a friend."

Ed took her hand. "I'm glad you've got a friend at the caravan park. It can be a bit lonely ..."

"Lola said she knew me when I was a baby. She must have lived there a long time."

"Yes. She and Henry were living in that caravan when I bought the park."

"Who's Henry?"

"He was her husband. He died about ten years ago."

"Oh." Michelle said thoughtfully. She rearranged the flowers on Ed's knee. "Poppy... The new day centre. It's called Eden House. Mum took me yesterday. I did painting and next week I'm going to do mo ... mos ... mosaics. I met Kessie and Hal and ..." she clapped her hands, "... and Billy."

"Ah!" Ed looked at her mischievously. "Is Billy special?"

"Oh yes," Michelle breathed as Trish returned to the room with a tray of coffees.

Chapter 3

Billy and his dad stood at the counter in their kitchen.

"What do you want for lunch Billy?" Grant asked.

"Beans and sausages ... and tomatoes."

"Okay Billy-Boy. Your meal, you do it." Grant opened the fridge door and brought out sausages and tomatoes.

Billy opened a can of beans and put them in a saucepan.

"You check the tomatoes, Dad. Last time I burned them, remember?" he giggled.

"Yep. And they were the last tomatoes we had that day. You didn't laugh at the time."

"And you said something rude when the smoke alarm went off!" Billy chuckled.

Over lunch, Billy nodded towards a greetings card on the table. "Is that from Mum?"

Pelican Bay

"Yes. You can read it for yourself."

"Why did she send it? It's not my birthday. It's not Christmas." Billy reached for the card. There was a picture of a string of palm trees on a golden coastline. Billy looked at the picture and opened the card.

He read, 'I saw this and thought of you both. Hope you like the picture. Love from Mum.' Funny. Why palm trees? Why us?"

Grant shrugged. "Dunno. It's your birthday soon though. Maybe she just got muddled."

"No. No. No." Billy almost shouted. "When it's my birthday she buys one that says 'Happy Birthday'. Always—and she sends a present too."

"Yep. There'll be a present too."

Michelle sat at the centre table in the art room. She looked at the mosaic that she'd started the previous week, then dragged a box of small clay tiles over to where she was working. She selected some plain terracotta squares and then some more; glazed white, turquoise and bright cobalt blue. She selected a few at a time, holding them up to the light before putting them against her half-finished mosaic. She placed them around a dolphin that she had already made.

Billy sat opposite her. He pointed to her picture. "You've got good colours," he said.

Michelle blushed. "My favourite colours."

Josie was at the far end of the room. She held up her collage. "Look at mine Billy. Mine's nice too."

Billy looked quickly in her direction and nodded, then he turned back to Michelle.

Michelle smiled at him. "You're painting Ned Kelly."

"Yes," he grinned pointing to the helmet, "...easy to guess." After a moment he frowned. "But it doesn't look metal. I don't know how to make it look like metal."

Michelle left her own work and walked round to the other side of the table.

"White. You need white. A bit of white, about here." She moved her finger, then pointed to a spot about three quarters of the way up Ned's helmet.

"Won't that look funny?"

"No. Mum's an artist. She says it re... re," she paused, and took a breath, "re-flects the light."

Billy looked uncertain.

"Go on, try. You can black it out if you don't like it."

Josie got up and walked over to them. "Sounds silly to me." She stuck out her lower jaw and stared at Michelle, who hung her head.

Billy picked up his paintbrush and rinsed it in the jar. He dried it on a piece of paper towel, then slowly and deliberately put the tip into a small tub of white paint.

After he had added the white paint, Billy stood back and looked at his picture. "Yes, that's better. I like that."

Josie's eyes darted towards Michelle, but Michelle wasn't looking at her. She was looking at Billy who had turned around. He walked to a cabinet of large folders.

Josie looked at Billy's back then stamped very quickly on Michelle's foot before walking back to her table.

Michelle bent down and rubbed her foot.

Billy returned with a large folder. "I've got lots

of Ned Kelly pictures. Would you like to see them?" He talked to Michelle about the paintings as he showed her.

"This is the last one," he finally said. "It's where the judge tells him he's going to be hanged."

Michelle's hands started moving. Her thumbs struck each other. She shook her head.

Billy looked at her face and hands. Gently he put his hands round her beating fingers. He felt the fluttering come to a halt. "It's all right. It's a just a story… "

Michelle felt reassured by his hands around hers. "It's a story," she smiled at him. "That's okay."

Billy looked at her with his head tilted to one side. "I like you."

Michelle felt her heart beating fast. She wanted to move her hands over her heart to feel it, but she wanted to leave them where they were as well. It felt nice standing there with Billy's hands over her own. "I like you too Billy. I do," she said quietly.

The day came to an end. The art room was cleared and tidied. Michelle gathered her bag and hat, and sat waiting for her mum. She held a few strands of hair and twirled them. A few other people also waited to be collected. Some fiddled with things as Michelle did, some simply sat waiting patiently.

Michelle looked up as Billy walked towards her. She smiled.

Josie stood at the bus stop outside. "Come on Billy," she yelled.

Michelle noticed Billy frown.

"I'm saying goodbye to Michelle," he called out.

Michelle felt her heart lurch. She stared at Billy,

and felt her heart beats gathering speed.

Billy held out his hand. "I want to see you next week." He pumped Michelle's hand up and down.

"I want to see you too, Billy."

"Come on Billy," Josie's voice insisted in the background.

Michelle looked at Billy, then outside to the bus stop where Josie was hopping up and down.

Billy sat down next to Michelle. "I don't have to get that bus," he confided.

Michelle looked at her feet. "Josie's waiting."

"I don't have to get that bus," Billy repeated. "I know the buses. I can get any bus." Billy stuck out his chest. "I can wait with you, then get the bus."

"You're clever. I can't do buses."

" I can, and I don't have to get on the same bus as Josie."

Michelle asked the question that had been burning her all week. "Is Josie your girlfriend?"

"Ha!" Billy scoffed. "No. We live in the same street. We get the same bus."

Michelle smiled. "I'm glad."

Josie got on the bus, and Billy stayed with Michelle.

After a few minutes, Michelle saw another bus in the distance. "Is that your bus, Billy?"

Billy screwed up his eyes. "Yep, that's my bus. See you next week Michelle."

Michelle couldn't wait for Trish to arrive so she could tell her about Billy… But the car that drew up was driven by Stella. Michelle walked towards it just as Stella whipped out her phone. Stella nodded in her direction and signalled for her to get in the car.

Michelle's excitement evaporated. Stella finished her phone conversation, put the car into gear, selected a CD, put it on and turned the volume up, then drove off.

Once home, Michelle ran into the house. Trish sat with a pile of paperwork. She had glasses perched half way down her nose. Michelle knew Trish only wore glasses when she was very busy so she put down her bag and went outside to look for Gareth or Neville. Then she remembered it was Monday, and they were back in Sydney.

Michelle half skipped, half ran towards Lola's caravan. "Lola, Lola," she called out.

A muffled voice answered, "I'm out the back."

Michelle hurried around to the back of the caravan.

Lola was bending over the vegetable patch. "Hello. How nice to see you. I'm just doing a bit of weeding, so my veggies won't get strangled. I'll stop, and we can have a cup of tea."

"Yes please." Michelle made small jumping movements. "I want to tell you about Billy. You know, Billy, at Eden House. I told you about him. I thought Josie was his girlfriend. She isn't." Michelle clapped her hands.

The following month Michelle finished her mosaic. She'd brought stones and shells and added them each week.

Kessie looked at it thoughtfully. "That's really good Michelle." She thought for a moment, "I mean really, you understand? I don't just mean good for here, I mean good by any standards."

Kessie moved round the art room. "There's some lovely work today." She stopped at Billy's table. "Tell me about this painting."

Before Billy could answer, Kessie was called to the phone.

Michelle walked around to Billy's table. "Show me, Billy."

Billy put his paintbrush down. "It's my family." He pointed to two figures, "That's Mum and Dad. Mum used to live with us." His finger moved to a small figure. "That's me." After a slight hesitation he pointed to a shape that seemed to be in a sling, hanging beneath a tree, "and that's Grace."

Michelle peered at the shape. "Is Grace a baby?"

"Was," Billy corrected solemnly.

Michelle thought she understood. That was what people said when somebody had died.

"Accident. Swimming pool. She was drowned. I'm still here," Billy said.

"Oh. Oh, I'm sorry Billy." She put her hand on his.

"It was a long time ago." He looked at her hand on his. "That's nice. You're very nice Michelle."

When Trish collected Michelle that afternoon, she watched her daughter carry a wrapped object to the car. "This is very exciting Michelle. Do I get to see it now or when we get home?"

"Um, home. Too difficult to unwrap here." Trish opened the boot of the car and stowed the object. Michelle sang all the way home. When they arrived, she wrapped her arms around the mosaic protectively and carried it into the small house and unwrapped it carefully then held it up for Trish to see.

Trish clasped her hands, "That's really good Michelle."

Michelle smiled. "That's what Kessie said. Can it go up in here?" She looked around the small living room.

"I don't see why not—except, perhaps we should talk to the others first. After all, we share this space."

"Dad and Gareth are only here on weekends. There's only St... "

Stella walked into the room. "What..?" she stopped and stared at the mosaic.

"Michelle's brought it home from Eden House. Good, isn't it?" Trish said.

Stella swallowed. "Ah, well, yes, it's okay."

"You don't like it!" Michelle wailed.

Stella struggled to look at Michelle as she spoke. "Oh, I just don't like mosaics. It's not your particular mosaic. I just don't like them."

Trish's eyes blazed. "Stella!"

"Look, I did my best. I was honest. I wasn't rude. You always want me to pussy foot around her, Mum. I had to say it. She might have wanted to put it up in here for goodness sake!"

Trish took a small sharp intake of breath. Michelle looked at the floor, and moved towards her mother.

"Aha, I was right." Stella looked from Trish to Michelle, then left the room shaking her head.

Trish turned to Michelle and said, "You know Sweetie, Dad and I don't have any pictures in our bedroom. Would you give it to us? We would really like to have it."

"You would?" Michelle's face transformed.

"Oh yes, we both would." Trish hugged her

daughter.

Michelle greeted her grandfather with a kiss. She clutched a box of biscuits and held them out to Ed. "Mum had shopping to do. You okay with just me today Poppy?"

"Sure, Princess. Mmm, thanks for these." He peered in the box. "They look as if they're homemade. Are they?"

Michelle grinned. "Yes. Mum helped me make them. I said they were for you. We don't make biscuits normally. It was a treat."

"I'm so glad Mum helped you. It wouldn't do to have Dad help you."

Michelle stood still with her mouth half open. She saw her grandfather laughing.

"You're teasing me Poppy." She brought her hands together.

Ed waved her to a chair, and asked about the caravan park.

"It's very busy. Even when Dad and Gareth come. Dad wants to open the café on weekends. Mum says we should wait till you get back." Michelle wriggled in her chair. "I want to tell you about my mosaic. I made one. At Eden House. Kessie said it's good. Mum said it's good, but Stella doesn't like it. Look I've brought a photo."

She rummaged in her bag and brought out a photo. She passed it to Ed.

"And you made this Princess?"

"Yes. I like doing mosaics. But I have to do something different now."

"Why?"

"Kessie wants us all to do different things. Ex …

ex, something or other—different things."

"That's a bit of a pity, if you like doing the mosaics."

Michelle clapped her hands. "But Lola said she will do mosaics with me." She looked triumphantly at Ed, "So I can still do them!"

"That's great, Princess."

Chapter 4

Billy finished his cereal. "Today's the day, isn't it, Dad?"

"Day for what?" Grant looked up from his breakfast.

"The lawn mower. You're going to show me how to use it."

"Yes, I forgot Billy. That's fine. You want to do it after breakfast?"

"Too right!" Billy got up and moved his bowl to the sink. He went back to the breakfast table and started clearing other things.

"Steady on. I'm still eating." Grant snatched at the milk carton as Billy was about to remove it. "We will do the lawn, but not until after I've finished breakfast. Okay?"

Billy hovered, waiting for Grant to finish.

"Billy-Boy, I'm not ready yet. Go and clean your teeth, make your bed, or something. I promise, we will do it this morning. I'll let you know when I'm ready." As Billy left the kitchen, Grant called out, "You need to get changed. You've got old clothes. Wear them."

Billy cleaned his teeth, inspected them and rinsed the brush carefully before putting it away. He made his bed, tugging at the cover a few times till there were no creases. He looked around his room. He looked at his train collection and the shelves with CDs and books. He realigned the trains and tidied the shelves. Then he opened his wardrobe. There were shelves on one side. He selected an old tee shirt and shorts. He folded up the clothes he had worn to breakfast and hesitated, moving from the wardrobe to the bed and back again. After a few minutes he laid them down on the bed and returned to the kitchen.

Billy loved the garage. He liked the smells and all the strange things that his dad kept in there.

Grant pulled the lawnmower out and made Billy look at the way it had been put away.

"It should look like this when you put it away Billy—not covered in grass …"

"I know Dad. You've told me already. I've used it before, remember? I just haven't ever started it."

"Okay. So we've checked that nothing's leaking, spark plugs are okay and …"

"And there's petrol in it," Billy finished.

"Well done. You remembered."

Billy demonstrated the checks. "Now I want to start it. You always hand it to me when it's already going."

Grant talked him through holding down the safety bar, priming the engine and pulling the cord. At each step, Billy nodded and followed instructions. He mowed the lawn at the back of the house.

"Can I do the front now Dad?" Billy asked.

"No. I want you to switch off, clean up and put it away. Do the front late this afternoon. That way you get to do all the checking again."

"Good idea Dad," Billy grinned.

Back inside Billy stirred the coffee before taking it to Grant.

"That letter," he put the mug down carefully. "The one … this morning."

"Ah, you noticed."

"It's from Mum, isn't it?"

"Yep. No hiding anything from you, is there?"

Billy's eyes narrowed. His eyebrows crept towards each other. "What's it about?"

"Just wants to know what to get for your birthday. She got it wrong last year, remember?"

"She always gets it wrong. She thinks I'm a little boy."

"Yeah, well last year I wrote and told her. I said it was a waste—to either get you something you'd like, or forget it!"

"Oh. She didn't forget it, then?"

Grant put his mug down hard. "For goodness sake Billy. I've just told you. That's what the letter was about."

Billy flinched.

"Sorry, Billy. I haven't even thought what to get you, and now I have the responsibility of thinking for a grown woman who could perfectly well do her own thinking. I'm not mad at you Billy. Honest."

Billy sat quietly for a few moments, then he grinned. "I've got it. I've got it. I know what I want. I want you to take me to Oceanworld in Manly ..." He leaned forward, and said excitedly, "and Mum can send money so we can have popcorn and coke and fish and chips."

Ed looked at the thick cream envelope. He turned it over and examined the handwriting. The loops and curls reminded him of his handwriting lessons at school.

Trish sat in a visitor's chair watching him with a smile on her face. "Playing Inspector Clouseau, are you, Dad?"

"Just wondering …"

"Why don't you open it?"

Ed fumbled with the corner of the envelope, and pulled out a card decorated with pressed flowers.

"Ah," Trish leaned forward. "That's really beautiful. It's handmade. I wonder who went to the trouble …"

Ed opened the card. He read slowly, smiling. "Lola. How kind of her to send a card. I'd forgotten Henry broke a leg – only one… and of course he was a lot younger then."

"Who's Henry?"

"He was Lola's husband. Don't you remember him?"

Trish shook her head.

Ed ran his fingers through his sparse hair. "We used to play the occasional round of golf together."

"I didn't know you played golf. You dark horse."

"I don't anymore. That was a long time ago. Henry was a member of the Falconville club, up on the hill. After he died I somehow lost interest, took up fishing instead."

Trish picked up the card and moved it at different angles to catch the light. "She's quite a clever lady, isn't she, that Lola?"

Ed nodded. "Yes, and she seems to have befriended our Princess, doesn't she?"

"Mmm. You don't think that's a bit odd, do you?"

"Nah. Lola's always been like that. She and Henry couldn't have children. She's kept quite a few kids out of trouble, over the years, in her own quiet way. Then of course there have been the ones she's helped bring out of themselves. It's good that Michelle's taken a shine to her."

Trish nodded, "You're right. I'm glad Michelle has a friend."

Josie walked out the gate at Eden House. She turned and stared malevolently at Michelle, Hal and Billy as they sat talking at the end of the day. They didn't notice her, and she stood at the bus stop muttering.

A red sports car drove up.

"It's your mum Hal," Billy said

Hal got up unsteadily and walked unevenly towards the car. Michelle and Billy watched as he bent to get into the small space. They waved as Hal's mother drove off.

Billy's eyes shone as he looked on, "Nice car!"

Michelle smiled. "Stella—my sister—she'd like that." Then her face fell. "Last time … she came for me … instead of Mum. I don't like it when Stella comes."

Billy didn't know what to say. Two minutes earlier she'd been smiling.

"Cheer up," he said. "We could go to the

movies."

Michelle's face transformed again, "We could?"

"Why not? We could go Saturday arvo. Go to Falcon Court. There's five movies. You can choose. " He looked at her happy face, then watched it suddenly crumple.

"How will we get there?"

"Bus."

"I can't do buses," Michelle wailed.

Billy saw Michelle's hands start to flutter. He held them lightly. "It's all right. I'll come and get you. I can do buses. I know you live at Pelican Bay Caravan Park. I'll be there at one o'clock."

Lola was tying up tomato plants.

Michelle hopped on the grass at the edge of the vegie patch. "I'm going to the movies. I'm going with Billy." She crossed her hands in front of her chest.

Lola looked up. "That sounds very exciting. What are you going to see?"

Michelle stopped hopping. She took a deep breath, "I don't know." Her mouth started to quiver. "Billy said I could choose." She looked at Lola with wide eyes. "I don't know what to choose. How will I know?"

"We could look in the paper and see what's on. But have you told your mum?"

"Mum was busy. Stella was busy."

"Well maybe tonight. You could tell her when you have your evening meal. I'm sure your mum will want to know."

"Okay."

Michelle's excitement continued to bubble, but she waited until the meal was on the table.

Trish was serving vegetables.

Michelle announced, "I'm going to the movies with Billy." She beamed at her mother and sister, and bounced slightly in her chair.

Trish's spoon hovered over the vegetable dish. "Ah. The movies. Billy from Eden House. We haven't met Billy, have we?"

"You can meet him when we go to the movies. We're getting the bus."

Trish's eyebrows moved closer together. There was a trace of irritability in her voice. "You don't know how to use buses, Michelle."

"Billy does." Michelle stuck out her bottom lip.

Stella grabbed the serving spoon from her mother. "For Heaven's sake Mum, she's eighteen years old. Did you think she was never going to have a boyfriend?"

Michelle looked from mother to sister. "He just asked me to the movies."

Trish was still silent. Stella continued serving the food. "Well, we'll all get to meet him on Saturday, won't we?"

Michelle continued to chatter, while Trish ate quietly and Stella tried to talk normally. At the end of the meal Stella turned to her mother. "Why don't you phone Billy?"

"How can I? We don't even know his surname. I can't even begin to look him up in the book."

Michelle's voice was small. "Trent. It's Billy Trent. But please don't phone. I'd feel," she raised her shoulders and splayed her hands in front of her, "I don't know … small."

Trish looked at Stella whose eyes indicated Michelle, before shaking her head very slightly.

Trish saw Michelle's dejected form, hunched over the table. The girl's joyous babble had stopped and her humiliation infused the room.

"Okay Sweetie. I'll phone Dad, instead."

After dinner Trish phoned Neville. Michelle saw her mother nodding and shaking her head. Her dad seemed to be saying a lot.

When Trish put the phone down, Michelle looked at her expectantly.

Trish smiled at her daughter, "It's alright. Dad thought I might be overreacting. I think he's right."

Michelle counted the rest of the days of the week. The next day went very slowly. The following day she went to see Lola.

Lola sat outside under an awning. On the table in front of her was a sheet of newspaper with a large pile of peas, which she was shelling into an enamel bowl.

Lola smiled at Michelle, "Would you like to join me?"

"Yes, please. I'll…" she mimed washing her hands. "The radishes will be ready soon won't they?"

Lola nodded. "Another week, and I reckon we can start to pick them."

"What about the lettuces and tomatoes?"

"Come, see for yourself."

Lola and Michelle walked around to the back of the caravan.

Michelle clapped, then peered at the space where they had planted the lettuces the previous week. "They haven't come up yet."

"No, lettuces take a bit longer, but look, the little tomatoes we rescued from the compost heap, they're doing well."

Michelle peered at the small plants. "Dad said they'd take a while—the tomatoes."

"It's nice your dad takes an interest."

"Sometimes ... but they're very busy. They want to tidy everything, get it all nice for when Poppy gets out of hospital."

"And is he coming home soon?" Lola asked.

Michelle nodded, "I think so. The nurses, they want him to walk. There's a wall with a bar. Sometimes when I visit, I walk with him. I hold his hand. And he holds the bar." Michelle looked at Lola with trembling lips, "... but he says it's tiring."

Later that evening Michelle set the table. The phone rang. She started walking towards it when Stella snatched it up.

"Pelican Bay Caravan Park. Stella speaking. Can I help you?"

"Grant Trent here. May I speak to Michelle's mother please?"

Stella paused. She remembered the conversation of the previous evening. Hadn't Michelle said that Billy's surname was Trent? She called to Trish, then mouthed, "Billy's dad," to Trish.

Michelle put the cutlery down and looked from sister to mother. Her mother sounded happy. Michelle made herself listen to the end of the conversation.

Her mother was talking. "No, no. Not at all. Thank you for phoning ... Yes, it was nice of you to think of that ... No, that really won't be necessary ... Yes, we look forward to meeting Billy on Saturday."

Trish put the phone down and smiled at Michelle. "Well Sweetie, that was Billy's dad. He sounds very nice. He offered to drive you both if I was worried.

Wasn't that kind of him?"

Michelle widened her eyes and splayed her fingers. "But, Billy can…"

"I know, Sweetie. That's what his dad told me. He said Billy can use buses." She stroked Michelle's hair. "My little girl's growing up; going on a date."

Michelle's teeth covered her bottom lip and a huge grin spread over her face.

Chapter 5

Michelle and Billy blinked into the daylight after the dark of the cinema. Michelle looked around. They were in Falcon Court's central well. There were small cafes and bars around the outside.

Michelle smiled at Billy, "That was great!"

"Let's have a coffee." Billy grinned.

"Um, yes. Tea. I don't like coffee."

Billy struck his forehead with the heel of his palm. "Silly me. I know that. You always have tea at Eden House."

They found a small café full of alcoves and dark wooden tables. There was a sofa in a corner away from the door. "Look, we can have the sofa. You ..." he waved towards it, "while I order."

They talked about the film.

A girl with blond spiky hair brought coffee and a small tray with teapot, milk jug, cup and saucer for Michelle. She saw the movie tickets lying on the table. "It's good isn't it? I took my sister yesterday. She didn't stop laughing."

"Neither did we," Michelle grinned at the girl.

After the waitress had gone, Michelle started pouring the tea. The pot dribbled.

"Oh dear." She put the pot down, and wiped the wet patch on the table with a paper serviette and tried again. Once more the teapot dribbled. She started to rub her thumbs together.

The girl with spiky hair reappeared with a cloth. "I forgot to tell you, these are terrible tea pots. I don't know why the boss doesn't get rid of them and buy some that don't drip." She wiped the table. "Shall I?" She indicated the teapot.

Michelle nodded.

The girl continued, "There's a knack to them. I've worked here long enough to know how to do it." Michelle pushed the teapot towards her. The girl poured deftly.

Michelle smiled shyly. "Thank you."

Billy reached for Michelle's hands. "It wasn't your fault ... the teapot."

Michelle felt the warmth of Billy's hands around hers. She wanted the moment to stretch for ever.

Michelle listened to Gareth and Neville talking about the work they'd done on the caravan park. "I want to help, too." she said at last.

Neville smiled at his daughter. "Okay Princess. This morning we're going to smarten up the café. Those wooden tables need a coat of paint, but first they need to be sanded. I'll give you some sandpaper."

Gareth and Neville brought out the tables. Gareth

wrapped sandpaper around a small wooden block and showed Michelle how to use it. "You okay with that?"

Michelle rubbed at the surface happily while Gareth and Neville started to paint the walls of the café.

Michelle looked at the newly-painted walls. "That looks really nice. Poppy'll be really happy."

"I hope so, Princess. Didn't a little bird tell us that Poppy wanted to open the café again, when he comes home?"

Michelle stood with hands on hips. "No. That was me. I told you."

Gareth grabbed her hands and shook them gently. "Only joking. We know it was you. It's a way of talking. Remember?"

She broke into a small laugh. "Can we paint the tables now?"

"I don't see why not. It's more tricky than sanding, but let's see how we go…"

The afternoon tea things were cleared. Michelle emptied the teapot. "Can I visit Lola now?"

Neville winked at his daughter, "That's fine, Princess. There are only a few tables left to paint. We can do them."

Stella spooned coffee into a plunger. She looked up, "I can help. That'll give me a chance to see what you've done."

Neville, Gareth and Stella walked towards the café. Gareth's phone rang. He walked a little distance from the others. When he returned Stella looked at him questioningly.

Gareth met her gaze, "Yes, it was Fliss. She's

angry that I'm not in Sydney this weekend. One of her friends has an engagement party. I just can't be in two places at once." He pulled his fingers through his hair.

They arrived at the café and viewed the tables.

Stella laughed, "You can tell Michelle did them. There's far too much paint. They're dreadful. Surely, they'll have to be done again."

Gareth said absently, "It's not as bad as that. I'll let them dry, then just give them a quick sand before the second coat."

Stella flared, "What a waste of time! You should be able to just shove on a second coat. Now you've got to take ages sanding. Sometimes I don't think it's worth getting Michelle to do things."

There was a brief stunned silence.

Neville recovered first, "I'm sorry you feel like that Stella. I thought you understood that with Michelle it's not about her pulling her weight. She needs to feel valued, to feel she's being helpful, and to learn things along the way."

Stella's face reddened. She looked down for a moment. "I try to remember that … it's just that sometimes … Oh, sometimes things take ten times as long because she helps."

Gareth put an arm round her shoulder, "Well Sis, that's what having a special sister means. I remember us both feeling very conned when we worked that out as kids. But hey, we're adults now …"

Later that afternoon, the white walls of the café reflected the early evening sun. The wooden tables drying outside, hinted at a possible reopening. Michelle brought Lola to look at it. "I did the tables."

Lola admired the tables then looked at the white

walls. "It looks really Mediterranean."

"Med...What does that mean?"

"Mediterranean. It's a big sea in Europe. In some places the houses are painted white.

Lola's eyes were drawn to patches of bare sandy soil surrounding the café. "Some colour would be nice... You have a good eye for colour." Lola patted Michelle's arm. "What do you suggest?"

Michelle raised her shoulders and held her hands out in front of her, "Flowers..?"

"That's just what I was thinking. Geraniums. Red and green against that white."

Michelle clapped her hands. "There's a plant shop, a nurse-place thingy, near Eden House. We can get some. Surprise Poppy." She stopped, statue-like, hands open, spread out to the sides. "Do you think he'd like that?"

"I think he'd be very pleased. Why don't you ask your mum and dad what they think? Perhaps they'll take you to get some."

Michelle's face fell. "They're always too busy."

"Well, ask. Find out if they think it's a good idea. If they're too busy, we can go on the bus. How does that sound?"

"Great! I'll do that right now."

The following day, Michelle and Lola returned from the nursery with carrier bags full of bright red geraniums. They took them to the side of the café.

"You wait here. I'll pop home and get a couple of trowels so we can plant them."

"I'll come and help."

"We only need the trowels. You stay and decide where the flowers should go."

Michelle arranged the geraniums and sat on the grass to look at them. She heard voices from the beach. She shuddered as she recognised Darryl's laugh.

"Hey, look, here's the Dumbo sitting on the grass." He stopped and nudged his friend before addressing Michelle. "Hey Dumbo, aren't you going to say 'Hello' to us?"

Michelle looked at the ground.

Troy kicked her arm. "My friend just spoke to you."

Michelle rubbed her arm and continued to look at the ground. Her hands began to flutter.

"Dumbo doesn't have anything to say …" Darryl mocked. He turned to Troy. "Mate, gimme the can."

Troy passed an aerosol can to Darryl, who swiftly sprayed a red zigzag shape and a smiley face on the white café wall.

Michelle looked up in horror. She opened her mouth and Darryl moved as if he were going to spray inside her mouth. She quickly covered it and spoke from behind her hand, "You can't …"

"Can't what? We just did, Dumbo."

Troy bent down and leered, his face only a few inches from hers. "And don't even think of telling that little old lady, you hear me?"

The boys walked off laughing.

Lola arrived a few minutes later with trowels and a watering can. She saw the café wall and Michelle slumped on the grass. She hurried to Michelle and put her arms around her. "Are you all right?"

Michelle nodded. "They said not to tell you," she sniffed.

"You must tell your parents what happened,"

Lola said as she walked Michelle home.

Neville looked at Trish, "The same boys. D'you know which caravan they live in?"

"Yes. It's one of the permanents, about three or four along from Lola's. Luckily the lease is coming up for renewal. We'll tell them they have to go."

Michelle looked from parent to parent, "Will they … Will they go?"

"Yes, Sweetie. We wanted to talk to Poppy about not having permanent caravans anymore. I'm sure he'll agree, especially now ..."

Michelle's face fell. "What about Lola …"

Trish looked at Michelle's crumpled face. She opened her mouth to speak, but Neville put out a warning hand. "We'll discuss that with Poppy. It's his caravan park. It'll be his decision."

Chapter 6

"Welcome home, Poppy." Michelle jumped up and down as Trish helped Ed out from the car.

He stood holding tightly onto a walking frame. "I need to concentrate, Princess. See you inside." Ed nodded towards the front door.

Michelle plumped cushions and stood sentinel over Ed's arm chair.

Ed looked at the chair, "Too low. Can't sit there." He nodded towards a dining chair. "Get that out for me please, Princess."

Ed lowered himself into the chair.

Trish brought him a mug of coffee. After a while she said, "We need to talk to you about some of the permanent residents."

"Oh?" Ed's eyes were sharp. "Must be serious … I've just walked through the door …"

Trish told Ed about the boys and the graffiti. Michelle stood next to her grandfather and looked at the floor.

Ed reached for Michelle's hand. "And you saw this yourself?"

"Yes. The same boys that pushed me over in the shop."

Ed's eyebrows shot up. "When was this?"

Trish interrupted, "It was soon after we arrived. We didn't tell you because we didn't want to worry you."

"You should have told me," Ed looked accusingly at Trish. He put his other hand around Michelle's waist. "I didn't want you to come here and be bullied, Princess. We'll certainly make sure that doesn't happen again. I'll tell them to go when their lease is up."

After lunch Ed told Michelle, "I couldn't wait to get out of hospital. I'm going to open the café now I'm back. What do you think of that, eh Princess?"

Michelle's eyes widened. "I don't …"

Trish frowned, "I know everyone's been working flat out to get it ready for you, but you're not ready to run it on your own yet."

Ed glowered at his daughter.

Trish continued, "Now you're back I'll have less time for everything. I won't have time to help you with the café as well."

"Hrumph." Ed pursed his lips.

"Dad, I mean it. I've been working flat out, just keeping things going. You've seen all the things that Neville and Gareth have been doing to make the place look better. You even said how good it looked when I drove you in just now."

"Okay." Ed grumbled. "But I want to see what

they've done with the café."

He called across the room to Michelle. "Hey, Princess, I'm going to take a little walk to see the café. Will you come with me to make sure the old man doesn't stumble?"

"Yes Poppy!"

Michelle and Ed walked towards the café. Ed's progress was slow but he got into a rhythm. Michelle walked at his side. Soon she fell into his pace. Walk, walk, jump. She timed it so that her jump coincided with the movement of Ed's frame.

Ed smiled at her. "Are you being a cheeky little monkey?"

"Um, no. It keeps us at the same…" she used her hand to mime the step, step, jumping movements.

"Okay, but slow down." Ed puffed. "I can't keep up with you." Michelle slowed but after a few more steps, Ed stopped. "It's no good Princess. I'm not going to make it. We'll have to turn back."

Trish stood at the front door. She shook her head. "When will you ever learn? It's too far."

Ed bristled. "Won't be cooped up here all day."

"No, but …"

The doorbell rang. Trish looked through the screen to see Lola holding a plate covered with a tea towel.

"Welcome home Ed!" she beamed, "I've brought you these." She put the plate down on the table.

"Smells good." Ed lifted the corner of the tea towel to reveal chocolate muffins. "Thank you Lola. They look great! And thanks for the letters while I was in hospital; they brightened my days there."

Lola smiled. "I was wondering whether you've considered one of those battery operated scooters. My friend Dot Barker has one you can borrow."

Ed looked at her with his head to one side. "Dot Barker, do I know her?"

"Sure you do. She lives in that big house on the hill. Her dad had one. He moved into a nursing home a couple of years ago and she never got round to getting rid of it. She said you can borrow it, if you want to."

Ed rubbed his chin. "If you'd have asked me half an hour ago I would have said I didn't need it, but I think I might just take you up on the offer."

The scooter was to be picked up by Neville and Gareth the following weekend. Michelle made small hopping movements. She beat the heels of her hands together, "Can I come too?"

Gareth's phone rang as he shook his head in reply. He put his fingers to his lips and mouthed, "It's Fliss."

As Gareth moved out of earshot, Neville ruffled his daughter's hair. "No room, Princess. Needs both of us. We've got to lift it into the ute."

Michelle's face fell, and she dropped her hands to her sides.

Trish noticed her daughter's dejected air. "You could do something for me, Sweetie."

Michelle responded quickly. "Yes, what?"

"The mugs we've had in the office will need to go back to the café, now that Poppy's determined to open it. Could you help me?"

Michelle and Trish packed mugs into cardboard boxes. Trish wiped her forehead and looked at her watch. "D'you think you could take them for me, Sweetie?"

"You come too!"

Trish tidied a tendril of hair behind her ear, "Sweetie, I really am pushed for time this morning."

"Okay."

Trish looked at her watch again, "Sweetie, that would be great. I've so much to do. I'll just get you the key." She returned with a key on a lanyard. "I'll put this around your neck, then you won't have to carry it as well. Just put the boxes on the central table in the café."

Michelle nodded and picked up the first box. She remembered how much she had hated the caravan park at first. It didn't seem so bad anymore.

As Michelle approached the café, she heard running footsteps.

"Hey, wait for us. Wait for us, Dumbo."

Michelle froze. She clutched the box to her chest. She felt her body drenched with sweat as she recognised Troy's voice. "You didn't listen to us, did you Dumbo? We told you not to tell that little old lady. But you didn't fucking listen. And you told that useless old man you call your Poppy."

Michelle started to shake.

Troy grabbed her hair and jerked her head backwards, "You know he's given us notice to quit?"

Michelle squeaked. She wanted to grab his hands but she was holding the box.

Troy let her hair go with a sudden jerk.

As Michelle's neck was released her head snapped back to its normal position. Her mouth opened and closed.

Darryl reached towards the box and lifted the top flap. "Wot'cha got in there? Oh, mugs. Gonna make us a nice cup of coffee then, Dumbo?"

"Aa… aa… aa," Michelle's mouth was dry. Her tongue protruded over her bottom lip

Troy's voice came urgently, "Didn't you hear my friend?" He darted towards the open box and ran his fingers along the first row before picking a mug out at random. He held it high up. "I'll have mine in this mug, Dumbo."

Darryl joined his friend, and picked another mug. "And I'll have this one."

Michelle's breaths came in small gasps. She clutched the box tightly. "Give them back …"

Troy turned to his friend. "Oh, listen to that, the Dumbo doesn't want to make us coffee."

Darryl looked at Troy. "I think it's the least she could do, after arranging for us to get chucked out …"

Michelle's heart was beating fast. She swallowed then started, "I didn't …"

Troy strode in front of her. He leaned over the box so that his face was inches from hers.

Sour breath invaded Michelle's nostrils.

Troy's top lip curled, "You didn't! Don't give us that, Dumbo."

Michelle tried to back away, but Darryl stepped behind her to block her exit.

Michelle was sandwiched between the two boys. She could feel Darryl's hot damp breath on the back of her neck. She clutched the box even more tightly.

"Maybe she doesn't know how to make coffee," he sneered.

"We'd better show her, eh?" Troy whipped out a knife. "You gonna make us that coffee, or what?"

Michelle wanted to run, to scream, but no sound came and her limbs wouldn't move. Darryl grabbed the box and wrenched it from her. He hurled it to the ground, and laughed at the sound of breaking crockery. Michelle saw the knife in his hand.

"Gimme the key." Troy twirled the knife, making it glint in the morning sun.

Michelle stood, a terrified statue.

"I said, gimme the key." He walked towards Michelle and inserted the blade under the lanyard and pulled. The lanyard pulled tight and jerked Michelle's head forward, but the knife didn't cut through it.

"Fucking useless knife," Troy withdrew it. "Let's see if it'll do anything else then..." He pulled at her blouse. "Let's have all those cutsie little buttons off!"

He held her blouse taut and the knife swept up towards Michelle's face. Pink heart shaped buttons scattered to the ground. When Troy withdrew his knife, Michelle grabbed at her blouse and pulled it to cover herself.

"Huh. Don't flatter yourself. We don't fancy you," he mocked giving her a shove. He took a step and swung the mug he was holding high into the air. Michelle watched it arc before it smashed in the small area reserved for tents.

A young woman came out of a bell tent and shouted at Troy. Darryl sent his mug flying too. The woman's eyes narrowed as the mug just missed her head. The boys ambled away from the tents, each turning to put one finger in the air. The woman caught sight of Michelle and hurried over.

Michelle shook as tears cascaded down her face. The woman put her arms around her shoulders. She fumbled in her pocket for a tissue, "Here. You'll be all right."

Michelle took the tissue and dabbed at her eyes. Soon her tears subsided. The woman looked at her closely. "Which is your ..."

"I live over there," Michelle pointed. "Next to the office."

"Ah," the woman brought her hands down from Michelle's shoulders to her arms. Her eyes were drawn to the gaping blouse.

Michelle grabbed her blouse and pulled it across her. "They ..." She pointed to the buttons lying on the ground. The woman bent down and picked up the small pink buttons. Michelle sniffed, "Thank you."

"Come on. I'll take you home."

Michelle nodded.

Trish thanked the woman and led Michelle into the house. She washed her daughter's face and hands and helped her change into a clean blouse.

Neville looked at Trish helplessly. "They didn't ...?"

Trish shook her head. "She's just very frightened. They had a knife and used it to cut the buttons off her blouse. "

Neville shook with anger. He clenched his fists. "How could they? What sort of monsters are they?" He watched Stella come through the door and open her mouth. He put his hand up to stop her from talking. "Michelle's been attacked ... those louts, the Frampton boys. They've been given notice to quit, but this time they've gone too far. I'm not waiting that long. I'm going to call the police."

Michelle burst into tears. "I don't like it here."

Trish held her close, "Hush, hush, Sweetie. That's why Dad's calling the police, to stop it from happening again."

The police car arrived. Michelle looked from the middle-aged sergeant to the young woman constable with sandy hair.

The sergeant spoke first, "My name's Bruce, and this is Ella. We'd like you to tell us what happened."

Michelle looked uncertainly at them both. Her eyes rested on Ella, who stepped forward. "May I sit down?"

Michelle nodded.

Trish held her daughter's hand while Michelle stammered out her account of the morning's assault. She also told of the time when the boys graffitied the café, and the morning when they pushed her into spilled marmalade at the shop.

The police listened and, made notes and sympathetic noises. Bruce spoke to Michelle's parents. "We'll go and talk to the Framptons next."

The Framptons weren't in.

Ella returned and gave Trish a business card. "We'll call back later. In the meantime, please give me a call if you see either of those boys." Trish took the card and nodded.

Michelle looked from Bruce to Ella, "The boys …"

"There's nobody at home at the moment. We'll look around the caravan park and check the beach too. We've got the description you've given us. We'll let you know when we find them."

Michelle fretted. "My blouse … my favourite buttons … "

Stella looked from Trish to Michelle. "Hey, why don't I take you shopping? We could get some new clothes."

Michelle's face transformed. "Oh, yes!" Then she looked uncertainly at Trish. "Is that all right?"

Trish smiled from daughter to daughter. "It's more than all right. It's a great idea." She looked at both girls framed in the doorway and took in Stella's fashionable attire, carelessly flung together, stylish and confident. A small flicker of shame burned within her at the sudden realization that her younger daughter was dressed in clothes not unlike her own. She turned to Stella, "I'll give you my card. Why don't you get Michelle a whole new wardrobe."

Michelle's eyes opened wide.

Stella smiled at her mother, then said, "C'mon, Baby Sister. Let's hit the shops!" She reached for her keys.

Michelle looked at her mother. "Thank you Mum. Thank you," then bounded out of the door, after Stella.

Chapter 7

As they walked to the car Michelle laughed. "You don't call me Baby Sister anymore. You used to ... all the time."

"And you used to call me Star Sister ... remember that?"

"Yes. That's what Stella means."

Michelle trotted happily beside her sister. They entered the cool shopping centre and Michelle exclaimed at the first chain store she recognised.

"Nup," Stella steered her away. "I know Mum buys you clothes from there, but you don't need to wear the same sort of clothes as her. You're only eighteen, Michelle."

Michelle smiled shyly. "Can we go in there?" She pointed to a shop with rows of glittery tops.

"You're not going to a night club. Let's just get you some nice clothes for every day." Stella steered her towards a shop with swimwear and surfboards in the window.

Michelle looked around. Clothes were everywhere, stacked on shelves and hung from rails, spilling out of plastic bins on the floor; a bright array of colour and texture. She looked at Stella in awe. "I don't know …"

"Don't you like the clothes in here?" Stella selected a few tops and held them in front of herself. She propelled her sister to a mirror and held them in front of her. Michelle stared at herself.

Michelle blinked, "They look like your clothes."

"Mm." Stella put the tops back. Suddenly she put her arms around Michelle. "You're right. You don't want to look just like me …and you know what, Baby Sister, I'm proud of you." She looked at Michelle's puzzled face. "That you don't want to be a clone of me."

"What's that?"

"It's when someone wants to be exactly like someone else."

Michelle giggled, "I'm me."

Stella held one hand high, fingers outstretched. Michelle clapped it.

Stella continued, "We'll have to think of a whole style for you. Let's try to find a shop that has clothes you like—but not any of the shops Mum goes to."

At the end of the afternoon, the sisters walked towards the car armed with carrier bags bearing Eastern sounding names. Michelle skipped.

"I'm going to wear the flower dress next time I go out with Billy."

"Oh. Where are you and Billy going to next week?"

"Um, we're going bowling, up at Pelican Nest."

"Bowling eh? Best not to wear a dress."

Michelle's smile faded.

Stella continued, "Believe me Baby Sister, a dress is no good in a bowling alley."

Michelle's face continued to droop. Stella put a hand under her sister's chin. "Don't worry. You've got heaps of choice now. I'll help you put something together."

Michelle and Stella arrived back at the caravan park just as the police car with Bruce and Ella was pulling out.

Michelle said in a very small voice, "I'd forgotten … You know, about …"

Stella said briskly, "Well they looked pretty happy to me, so I don't suppose it's bad news."

"Oh." Michelle struggled to make sense of Stella's statement.

Trish fussed over Michelle's new attire. Michelle jumped up and down, pointing to a pair of small silver dangly earrings that she was wearing. "And these. Stella gave me these … a present ... She paid from her purse. They're pretty."

Michelle went to her room to unpack her parcels. On her way back to the living room, she saw Ella's card. She looked nervously at Trish. "The police. Did they …?

"The Framptons have gone. Bruce and Ella looked through the windows. They said that the caravan's been stripped bare. The car's gone too."

Michelle's eyes widened. "Poppy told them to go. I'm glad they've gone."

Michelle sat on the bed, swinging her legs and deciding what to wear for her outing with Billy.

She emerged in a long paisley dress. Stella glanced at her and shook her head.

"Remember what I said about dresses and bowling?"

"Yes, but …"

"No buts. You'll get tangled up and fall over, besides …" Stella waited for Michelle to notice the unfinished sentence.

After a while Michelle said, "Besides, what?"

"It's just not cool, Baby Sister—right?"

"Right," Michelle said uncertainly.

"You don't sound convinced."

"Bowling's next week. We're going to a disco. At Eden House."

"Ah … in that case, your dress is stunning. You're sure to be the belle of the ball."

"It's not a ball. It's a disco."

Stella drove Michelle to the disco. Michelle hummed Billy's favourite song as she sat in the car looking forward to seeing him.

Stella smiled.

Trish and Ed sat in the office. They were checking the bookings sheets for the coming week.

Trish looked up with a her glasses perched on the end of her nose. "There won't be many bookings, now that summer's ended, will there Dad?"

"No." Ed shook his head. "We don't have any except the permanents right now. I think your Gareth might have a point. It could be a good time to spruce up the place up a bit."

Trish picked her words carefully, "I think, he means a bit more than 'spruce up'."

Ed looked at her sharply. "I don't have the money to do the fancy things he wants to do."

Trish didn't answer. Her eyes opened wide as a heavy, black clad motorcyclist roared past the security barrier and into the caravan park. He raised his arm. The streetlight glinted on studded leather as he hurled a bottle. That too, caught the light as it smashed into a nearby bin. Flames erupted, then hissed, spluttered and died. The sinister figure turned to face into the office window.

Trish felt him staring at her. She wanted to see into the smoky rectangle that hid his eyes. Seconds later he squeezed the handlebars, and brought his weight to the back of the motorcycle. The front sprang up like a wild animal about to attack. Trish froze. She was sure the bike and its rider was going to charge into the office. She held her breath, staring at the dark grey eye shield.

Ed tried to pull Trish away from the window.

She stood rooted to the floor, her breath coming in short sharp bursts.

Ed tugged harder.

Trish's knees crumpled and she landed on the floor. She heard the motorcyclist grinding gears and screaming away.

Another motorcyclist followed. He hurled a can at the office window. Trish screamed and covered her face. The glass shattered. Bright red paint poured over the office photocopier and furniture. Small shards of paint and glass landed on her tee-shirt and in her hair. Paint dripped down the backs of her hands.

Ed dragged Trish under a table. She put her arms

over her head and tucked herself into a small round ball.

The rider roared off deeper into the park.

A third villain joined him, thundering past the other two. He paint bombed the caravans. Then he produced small fuel laden bottles stuffed with rags. He stopped, flicked a cigarette lighter and threw the bottles into the amenities block. Flames shot up.

Ed yelled into the phone over the noise. "Come. Come quickly. They're like madmen. We're not safe." He held a lever-arch file up over his head as a shield.

The intruders circled around, shouting, whooping and revving their bikes. When they ran out of paint cans and home-made fire bombs, they revved up and left amid a cloud of dust. The smell of burning invaded the air. The sudden silence seemed eerie.

"It's okay Trish, they've gone," Ed said.

"Are you alright Dad?"

Trish crawled out from under the table. She helped Ed up, then with trembling fingers, picked pieces of paint laden glass from her tee shirt and hair. "Thank God there's hardly anybody here."

The attack took just minutes.

"I'll check the permanents." Trish reached for torches by the office door. She handed one to Ed and took one herself. You check the temporary caravans—but don't go into the amenities block. We don't want anyone in there, till we know what's happened."

They opened the door as the police pulled up. Both Trish and Ed were accompanied by a policeman while they checked out the damage. They tied a roll of red and white stripy plastic ribbon firmly round the amenities block. A note was pinned to the doors,

'Closed. Sorry for inconvenience. Use toilets in café.'

Ed muttered as Trish put up the sign. "Now every vandal in town can get into the café."

Trish threw her hands in the air. "For Heaven's sakes Dad! There's nothing in there yet, except the toilets. What do we expect people to do, pee in the bushes?"

Ed grunted and called the glaziers. Blue overalled men worked with gas lanterns, methodically fixing up broken windows.

Meanwhile, the disco at Eden House had ended. People were waiting to be collected. Michelle and Billy stood holding hands.

Billy squeezed Michelle's hand and looked into her eyes, "That was really awesome. I like dancing with you. I wish we could go home together."

Michelle smiled dreamily. "So do I, but Stella's coming—"

As if on cue, Stella drove up. She pressed the horn.

As Michelle was about to say 'Goodbye' to Billy, he pulled her to him and kissed her hard, enveloping her in his arms. Michelle's universe exploded with fireworks. She forgot about Stella and flung her arms around him.

The car horn sounded again. Reluctantly Michelle pulled herself away from Billy. "I'm sorry I have to go. Bye," she breathed softly.

Stella stuck her head out of the car window, and spoke to Billy.

"Look, I hate to disturb love's young dream, but I need to get my sister home."

Billy frowned. He kicked the pavement, "We

were just saying 'Goodbye'."

Michelle smiled sheepishly, and got into the car.

Stella drove slowly. She glanced at Michelle furtively. "I'm sorry I was sharp, but something's happened. Mum's just phoned me. We need to get back quickly."

Michelle's thumbs sought each other. "What's wrong?"

"Some hooligans threw things around, all over the caravan park. They lit some fires too."

Michelle shook her head. She took small shallow breaths.

Stella pulled over. She turned to her sister, then took her shaking hands. "It'll be all right. Nobody's hurt. Mum and Poppy were in the office. The place is just a bit of a mess, that's all. They've called the police."

Michelle swallowed. "Lola?"

"Lola's okay. I told you, nobody's hurt."

"Mum's okay. Poppy's okay. Nobody's hurt." Michelle's voice had a sing-song quality to it.

Stella smiled and nodded. She put the car into gear and drove off slowly.

Michelle repeated, "Mum's okay. Poppy's okay. Nobody's hurt," like a mantra all the way home. She didn't notice Stella grit her teeth after the first few repetitions.

When they arrived at the caravan park Stella drew a deep breath. Michelle screamed and ran to her mother.

"It's only the park. No people were hurt." Trish put her arm round Michelle.

Michelle began her chant. "Mum's okay. Poppy's okay. Nobody's hurt."

Stella frowned. She looked at Trish, "She's been saying that non-stop."

Trish glanced at Michelle. "Well, it's important," she said.

"Yes, but she won't stop saying it!" Stella snorted.

Stella brought hot chocolate and cake to the kitchen table. "It'll take a while to fix all the broken glass, let alone make good. It's so unfair. Dad and Gareth have worked all hours to try to improve the place, and now we're back where we started… only worse."

Trish looked thoughtful. "Gareth's been saying that some of the caravans need to be replaced."

Ed frowned. "Depends if there's any insurance. That would cost a fortune, you know."

"Well, he'll be here in the morning. I phoned him a while ago."

Ed spoke gruffly, "Gareth's ideas always cost money."

Michelle looked from her mother to her grandfather. Her fingers were spread wide and taut. She was slowly rubbing her thumbs.

Trish reached out to Michelle's hands, stilled them, then bit her lip, and passed the cake around.

Michelle accepted her plate. "This is good. You don't let me have cake very often."

Stella rolled her eyes. "It's not very often that the caravan park gets wrecked."

Michelle bent her head over her plate.

Ed reached out for her hand. "It's okay, Princess. Stella didn't mean to snap. She's just tired. She spent a lot of time this afternoon cleaning up."

Michelle turned to her grandfather. "I want to help clean up too."

Ed smiled at Michelle. "Tomorrow will be soon enough. And yes, I'm sure you can help."

The following day, Michelle dragged bags of rubbish to the garbage area.

Ed gestured towards heavy duty gardening gloves. "Hey, that was smart, Princess. Where did you get those?"

"Lola. I went to see her. None of the permanent caravans got…" she rolled her hands in the air… "dam…" She winced, "I know, damaged. Lola gave them to me, so I don't get sp, spl… bits of things in my hands."

"Well, you've done really well. I reckon you've earned a break. Gareth's here now and we're going to do all the boring talking bits. Why don't you go and return those gloves. And say 'Hello' from me?"

Michelle arrived at Lola's caravan just as Lola was arriving home with two large carrier bags. Michelle's face lit up. She waved the gloves in front of Lola.
"Thank you. Poppy said to bring them back. He says 'Hello' as well."

"And did you get all the clearing up done?"

"Mmm. Poppy said I'd done enough. They're all talking now. Lucky your caravan didn't get d… damaged."

"Yes, I was lucky. Now do you want to see what I've got in these bags?"

Michelle hopped about. "Yes, please."

"I got these for you." Lola gestured to Michelle

to look inside one of the bags.

Michelle rubbed the palms of her hands together. She grinned broadly and bounced up and down. Her fingers trembled as she opened bag.

She looked puzzled. "It's just a lot of broken things."

"What do you think we might do with them?"

"I don't know. Stick them together again, maybe?"

"Now that didn't occur to me, though I suppose we could make some pretty weird and wonderful things if we did that. No, I was thinking about making mo…"

"Mosaics!" Michelle screeched. Can we make them now?"

"I don't see why not. I just need to find some hardboard. I've got a couple of pieces, somewhere."

Michelle arrived home late for lunch. Gareth, Ed and Stella had already eaten and gone back to their business discussions. Neville had arrived and was also in the meeting.

Michelle asked, "Why aren't you in the meeting, Mum?"

"I'm happy to go along with whatever they decide. Anyway, someone had to be here to give you your lunch."

"Thanks Mum." Michelle began to eat. "Dad made this didn't he?"

Trish laughed. "You can always tell can't you? Yes, he said it would be quicker if he did it, and luckily it stayed hot. Anyway, what were you doing that was so engrossing?"

"I've had a great time Mum. Lola went to a shop.

The lady gave her a bag of broken plates. I've been making a mosaic. Lola's making one too."

By evening, Michelle's mosaic was well underway. She skipped into the house to find the other family members full of talk and ideas. "Nobody's listening. I want to tell you about my mo…"

Stella gritted her teeth, "For Heaven's sake Michelle, it isn't always about you. The bloody park's been practically razed to the ground. What d'you think we've been … "

Gareth put a hand on Stella's arm. "Steady on Sis."

Neville drew Michelle close. "It's like this Princess: while you've been with Lola, we've been talking about what's going to happen to the park. We're going to sell our house in Sydney and do this place up properly."

Michelle knitted her fingers, and pumped her palms together. The family had already been at the caravan park for months. Whenever things went wrong, Michelle wanted to be back home, but lately hadn't thought of Sydney at all.

Gareth grinned at her, "And here is where Lover Boy is."

Michelle blushed. She unclasped her hands and looked at Trish shyly. "I can see Billy lots."

Trish tried to smile at Michelle, but Gareth's words had worried her. She knew 'Lover Boy' was only an expression. She made a mental note to talk to Neville about Michelle and Billy.

Chapter 8

Stella arrived at the Sydney family home in the early evening. "Got time for a drink before you head out, Gareth?"

"Yeah. Vodka, if there's any in the cupboard. It'll relax me nicely."

"Not looking forward to seeing Fliss the Fair?"

"Of course I am, but not to telling her all about the plans for Pelican Bay."

Stella glanced at the ceiling. "Could be tricky."

"Yeah, I know, but I think it'll be exciting. I want to involve her. It'll be better if I'm relaxed." He winked as he raised his glass. "So, here's to you my Star Sister. How's it been up there?"

"I think it's going really well most of the time, but they're all making such a fuss of Michelle's ghastly mosaics."

"That's a bit harsh!" Gareth put his glass down

and leaned back, "I mean, isn't it great that she's doing them?"

"Yes—I mean, no. Seriously, yes, it's good that she's doing them, but they're awful. Have you seen any of them?"

He scratched his head, "I think I saw the first one she brought home. A dolphin or something, wasn't it? Seemed okay to me. Actually, I think I was quite proud of my baby sister for making it."

"She's not a baby, Gareth!" Stella fought the habitual irritation she felt at any mention of Michelle being a baby. She stared moodily into her wine.

"I think you're a bit two faced about that Stella. If you're still happy to be called Star Sister, I don't see why Michelle can't still be Baby Sister!"

"Okay," Stella admitted grudgingly, "but aren't you being a bit insulting? You only say the mosaics are good because she has Down Syndrome. You wouldn't say they were good if anybody else had made them!"

Gareth pulled his chair back up and looked at his sister's sullen face. Very softly he asked, "Is that the green eyed monster showing, Sis?"

Stella met his gaze, "Maybe. I'm just fed up with everything being about Michelle. It's always been about Michelle. I think those hideous mosaics are about the limit, that's all."

"C'mon Sis, I know it was tough when you were seven or eight, but hell, you're adult now. Let them make a fuss. Let her be special for something; other than having Down Syndrome, hey?"

Stella gathered the glasses and forced a thin smile. "You're right, as usual. Go on with you. You'll be late, and Fliss will think you've stood her up. Give her my love, won't you."

The restaurant was lit with a soft glow from red paper lantern shades.

Gareth looked across the table at Fliss. "What would you like to drink?"

"I think I'd like a mint julep."

"Are you sure?" he frowned.

"I know it's only Thursday night Babe, but you'll be away at the weekend. Don't I deserve a cocktail?" she simpered.

Gareth winced slightly as he heard the word Babe, but ignored it. "It's okay, but you hate bourbon."

"I didn't know it had bourbon in it." Her voice quivered, "I liked the sound of it. I guess I'll have a Margarita then."

The cocktail ordered, they picked up their menus.

Gareth looked at her over the small vase of roses in the centre of the table. "Shall we order different things and share?"

"I know your family goes in for that sort of thing, but you always order things that have far too many calories," she sighed.

"Sharing seems to be the best way to enjoy Chinese food, but we don't have to."

They made their choices and sipped their cocktails. Gareth found himself looking along the walls of the restaurant which had been opulent in its day, but had since become somewhat faded.

Fliss followed his gaze. "It's a bit of a dump. I'm surprised that Joel and Tamsin recommended it."

"Perhaps the food is good ..." Gareth's tone was light.

She looked around as if she hadn't heard him. "It would make a good project for a reno though," she murmured. Suddenly her face was transformed with a wide smile and she tilted her head in the other direction. "So that's why you brought me here!" Her eyes danced. "Is this your next big project?"

"No way. I'll be far too busy with the family business for that."

Fliss put her drink down with a bang. "What?"

"You heard me Fliss. I've promised Mum and Dad I'll give them however long it takes to completely…"

"But you can't do that, Babe! You'll lose too much business. There's far more money to be made here in Sydney."

"It isn't all about money," Gareth murmured.

"Oh, isn't it? Aren't we supposed to be getting married next year? Haven't we waited all this time, simply because we don't have enough money yet?"

"Fliss, fair and fabulous Fliss," Gareth reached across the table for her hand. "We can still get married. It just doesn't have to be such a posh do. I can get back to the Sydney constructions once the caravan park is sorted."

She shuddered, "Don't even use that word. You know I have a caravan phobia."

"Don't be absurd Fliss. People don't have phobias about caravans. Spiders, blood, open spaces, enclosed spaces … all sorts of things, but not caravans."

"Well I have!" she shouted, pulling her hand free.

Diners at other tables looked up. Once again Gareth tried to reach across the table for her hand. She snatched it away and got up, shouting angrily.

" I have!" Tears were brimming at edges of her eyes. "Every time I even think of those…" she shut her eyes, then opened them wide and stared at Gareth, "those nasty feral places, I come up in hives. I do! I really do."

The room fell silent. Fliss sat down abruptly and looked into her lap. Gareth pushed a paper serviette across the table. She accepted it, and dabbed her eyes. "Oh Gareth, I'm sorry for such an outburst, but I can't stand caravans or anything to do with them. They remind me of… " Fliss snapped her mouth shut.

" I know, I know, Fliss. Way back some of your family were what Americans rather rudely call Trailer-trash. But that's in the past. We're moving the place up market. There won't be any permanent residents at all."

"It'll still be a caravan park … " Fliss sniffed.

"No it won't. We're not even going to have caravans. They're all going to be …" Gareth tried to outline the plans, but he sensed Fliss's ears and mind were shut. His hopes for the evening lay in tatters as he tried to explain.

Gareth returned to Pelican Bay without Fliss. He brought his workers from Sydney and together they started to clear the site.

On Friday evening, he drew a bottle of beer from the fridge. He put his arm round Trish's shoulder. "A fine birthday you're going to have this year, Mum!"

Stella stared across the kitchen. "C'mon Gareth, we never said it would be easy. The fire and paint thrown everywhere. We're on course. That's not so bad is it?"

Trish said, "It isn't so bad, but it is my birthday. I

would like to do something special."

Michelle stood in the doorway. She smiled and twisted her hair. "Let's have a picnic on the beach. We wanted … in Sydney … Now we're here."

Stella didn't wait for a reply. She glared at her sister. "Stop being so selfish Michelle. Just because you want to, and you love the beach, doesn't mean everyone has to have sand with their food. Anyway, it's Mum's birthday. She should choose."

Gareth took a swig of his beer then turned to Michelle. He smiled, a lopsided smile. "That's not such a bad idea, Princess."

Stella stared at Gareth. "Oh, it's a good idea, because Princess here has thought of it! And come to think of it," her eyes darted towards Michelle. "Isn't she a bit old to still be called, 'Princess'?"

Michelle looked from her brother to sister, "I still like pink. Princesses wear pink."

"Quite right." Gareth nodded at Michelle again, before locking eyes with Stella.

Trish thought that whatever she said would offend somebody. "Why don't we see what Dad would like to do?" her voice was light. "He's coming up tomorrow."

Gareth winked at Trish, "Excellent idea. It'll be the same food, it's just a question of where we have it. We'll let him decide."

Neville was weary from his week in Sydney, but he jumped out of the car and hugged both his daughters. "So, how are my favourite girls?" he asked as he headed for the house with an arm around each of them.

Stella looked up and smiled at him, "All the

better for seeing you. You have to be settle a family disagreement."

"Oh? What's that?" he asked.

"You'll see."

Michelle looked at her feet.

The matter of Trish's birthday lunch took a back seat, while Gareth told the family how upset Fliss had been, about his decision to work full time on the family venture.

Trish leant across the dinner table, "But Gareth, it's not going to be forever. Once you've done what needs to be done here, you'll be free."

"I know, I know… but try telling Fliss! She thinks it's a backward step. She's worried about the big contracts in Sydney that I'll be missing out on."

Trish bit her bottom lip and got up to make coffee.

Gareth told Neville about the proposal that he should decide whether Trish's birthday lunch would be at the beach or somewhere else.

"Oh ho, I've been set up." Neville put his hands in the air in mock surrender. "I'll be somebody's favourite father and somebody's ogre won't I?" He rummaged in his pocket, "Tell you what, we'll toss a coin … " He turned to Michelle, "Princess?"

"Heads," Michelle was quick.

Neville looked at Stella. She nodded.

Neville tossed the coin. "Heads it is. Beach picnic, here we come."

The day was bright and clear. The disagreements from earlier in the week were forgotten as the family set up beach umbrellas and carried folding tables and chairs.

Neville insisted he be left alone to bring the food, grumbling that the others would only bring things in the wrong order. He made sure that Trish sat down with a glass of champagne.

Stella and Gareth went for a swim.

Michelle smoothed tablecloths and arranged cutlery. Her face was serious as she concentrated, pushing her tongue to the corner of her mouth.

Trish said, "I can do that if you like Michelle. Don't you want to go in the water with the others?"

"I'm happy doing this. I can swim later."

After their swim, Stella and Gareth ran up the beach and Michelle solemnly handed them towels. As Gareth dried himself, his phone rang. He grabbed it, and with an apologetic shrug to the family, moved away a little.

Trish watched her son's relaxed frame tense up. She could see his shoulders hunch and watched his jaw tighten.

He returned to the family with a small forced smile. "Fliss. She, um …"

Michelle looked up from laying the table, "She misses you."

"That's right, Princess." Gareth seemed relieved not to have to explain what Fliss had actually said.

Just then, Neville arrived with trays of exotic canapés. There were gasps of delight from the female members of the family, but Gareth's eyes remained dull and he was obviously distracted.

Michelle watched Gareth walk up and down. Her hands started to get agitated. She rubbed her thumbs together.

Neville put his hand under Michelle's chin, "Hey Princess, I forgot the mayo. How crazy is that? Would you get it? It's on the top shelf of the fridge."

Michelle walked towards the cabin.

Trish mouthed, "Thank you," to Neville.

Stella looked questioningly at her brother, who refused to answer her gaze.

The phone rang as Michelle walked towards the fridge. She was still agitated from Gareth's phone call. She stood still. Her hands flapped. She stared at the phone. Her thumbs beat.

The phone stopped ringing. Michelle stood with pounding heart. She let her hands drop to her sides, before putting one hand over her chest. She gulped a few breaths and opened the fridge door.

The phone started ringing again. Michelle took a deep breath, then picked up the receiver.

"Hello," she said in a timid voice.

"Michelle, Michelle." Billy shouted into the phone excitedly.

"Oh Billy!" She burst into tears, "I thought you were Fliss."

"No. I'm Billy. How can I be Fliss?" his voice was perplexed.

Michelle was sobbing. "No, I mean Fliss phoned. Gareth's upset. It was horrid." Michelle wiped her eyes with the back of her hand. "Oh Billy, I'm glad it's you. I really miss you."

"Me too. I miss you."

Michelle heard a muffled voice in the background, then Billy spoke again. "Michelle, I want to go to the RSL next week. It's a big music night. Will you come?"

"Yes. Can we dance?"

"Too right!"

Chapter 9

Trish and Michelle walked to the car with Neville who had to return to Sydney.

"Bye Darl. Bye Princess." Neville kissed his wife, and scooped Michelle into his arms. "With any luck I'll have good news next week. I'm going to tell Donald Swanson that I'll be working here full time. Keep your fingers crossed for me, eh?"

There were only four permanent caravans left on the caravan park. Even that area was not left undisturbed. Sewage pipes were laid, and small bathrooms fitted onto the end of each caravan. Michelle watched the remains of the temporary caravans being taken away. She laughed and clapped, as the ugly old amenities block was broken up and removed.

The family disagreed about the café. Gareth argued for pulling everything down. "It'll be easier to start again with a clean slate."

Ed shook his head, "But while this is going on, there is no income from the park. Let's keep the café going."

"Oh, Poppy," Michelle laughed. "There's nobody now to come to the café."

They reached a compromise and decided that the café would be razed and replaced with a mobile coffee-caravan.

Even though it was autumn, Ed was convinced there would be enough trade to make it worthwhile. He looked at Michelle, "Hey Princess, would you like to help me on the days you don't go to Eden House?"

Gareth saw Trish nod. He smiled at Ed and Michelle, "I think a van will work well. Can I leave you to arrange it, Ed? I don't want to have to stop and get involved in researching coffee vans. Is that okay?"

Ed phoned some fishing mates who turned up to help. He looked at his friend Joe, "We'll use the Framptons' caravan. None of the permanents got damaged and the Framptons just upped and left. It's on its last legs anyway, but we can hitch up running water and electricity. We'll be in business."

Joe shaded his eyes to look at the van. "Framptons' van eh? Aren't they the boys that terrorized your granddaughter?"

"Yeah. They went too far. Their lease was up anyway, so we gave them notice to quit."

"How come they didn't take the van?"

"The bastards attacked her again … used a knife."

"Was she hurt, bad?"

"No, but she was terrified. We got the police in, but the whole family vanished …just before the fire, too."

"Well, I guess you can do what you want with the van, then." Joe scratched his head. "It's a bit rough and ready, though. I thought you were bringing the place up-market."

Ed chuckled. "This is only temporary. We can give it a lick of paint, something fun and wacky. It'll do for the moment."

Other mates and favours were called in. The men hitched the van and moved it to the site of the old café.

Joe stood with arms crossed in front of his chest. "It's a good spot. You'll get beach walkers too."

"Yeah. It's right where the old café was." Ed clapped each man on the shoulder. "Thanks. I owe you each a slab, and, once she's up and running, the first coffee's on me."

The phone rang. Michelle knew it would be her father. She chattered happily for a while then passed the receiver to her mother.

Trish took the phone from her daughter and settled on the sofa. "Hi Darling. How's it going?"

Michelle stood with her hands on the back of a chair. She watched her mother's eyes grow large. She saw Trish sit bolt upright. "What...?"

Trish waved Michelle away and directed her conversation into the phone again. "Oh," she groaned, "How awful for you. What did she say? Oh no! That makes it worse, so much worse. Poor you."

Michelle sat down quietly. She could hear her dad's voice muffled by the receiver, but the only words she could hear were her mother's.

"You had spoken to Donald first? ... Oh, that's a

relief! ... No, no, he isn't vindictive. If he said he'd give it to you, he will. This car thing is between you and Isabelle ... I know, I know, Darling."

Eventually Trish put the receiver down.

"What's wrong?" Michelle moved from the chair to the sofa. She flung her arms around her mother's neck. "Is Dad all right?"

"Yes. He's okay. He just scraped Isabelle's new car."

"Isabelle Swanson? That doesn't matter. She's got lots of money."

"That's not the point—but in some ways you're right, it wouldn't normally matter too much." Trish sighed. "Her new famous footballer-boyfriend bought it for her. It's been in all those stupid magazines."

"I like those magazines." Michelle smiled.

Trish hugged her daughter. "I know you do, Sweetie. I'm sorry"

"And I saw a picture of Isabelle's car. It was in my magazine. It's a nice car. Pink. I'd like a pink car."

"Well, now Dad's scraped Isabelle's beautiful pink car."

"I bet she's angry."

"I bet she is too. I bet she's very angry... Anyway, the good news is, that Donald's given Dad a very generous redundancy package. I don't think damaging Isabelle's car will affect that."

"What's that, re—redun thing?"

"That's when someone isn't needed in a job. They get paid a lot of money not to do it anymore."

"But Dad is needed. He's a chef in Swanson's Hotel."

"The hotel's changing though. It's going all fast

food. You know how much Dad hates fast food."

Michelle nodded, but her brow was furrowed.

Trish continued, "Oh, it's complicated." She wiped the back of her hand across her forehead, "You know Dad wants to come up here and work on Poppy's caravan park full time. He can't do that though, not unless Donald pays him the redundancy money. Remember I just said, it's what people are given—if they're lucky—when they're no longer needed."

"I think I understand." Michelle's face was serious. "Dad still gets money even though he scraped Isabelle's car."

"We hope so." Trish smiled at her daughter.

"Bad journey?" Trish stood at the front door.

Neville put his bag down and rolled his shoulders. "Not too awful. A few hold-ups getting out of Sydney, then fairly plain sailing."

Trish walked into the living area. "Here, sit down. I'll massage your shoulders."

His body relaxed as she pummelled at knotted muscles. "Umm, thanks Darl. Traffic might not have been so bad, but it's been a hell of a week."

"You said on the phone ... about Isabelle's car. "

"Oh Trish," Neville moaned. "It wouldn't have mattered so much if that damned car hadn't have been bought for her by her new boyfriend. She was really out of control. She lunged at me. Those nails," he shuddered, "were that close. Luckily those bouncers of hers pulled her off. She's a real nutcase. I don't know what Donald did to deserve such a daughter. She screamed that she'd have me fired." Neville broke off and gave a small laugh before continuing,

"It was just after I'd been to see Donald about my severance pay, and he'd been so generous. I felt so awful ..."

Trish laughed too. "I suppose there is a sort of irony to it. She threatens to get you sacked just after you've got Donald to give you a good redundancy package."

The following day Ed and his mates cut a hole in the Framptons' van. A roll-up awning and push-out counter were installed.

"Looks the business, doesn't it?" Ed smiled at Michelle.

Michelle looked at the van's tired grey exterior. "It doesn't look very nice."

"You're right, Princess. We'll paint it. Bright red – that would stand out, wouldn't it?"

"Blue. Make it blue Poppy, please." Michelle's voice was urgent. She pointed to a thin stripe in her blouse, "This blue, Poppy."

Ed was about to agree, when Michelle started jumping up and down. "No, not all blue. Blue at the top and blue at the bottom. Yellow in the middle. Like this." She drew wavy lines in the air.

"I don't quite understand, Princess." Ed frowned. "Tell you what, I'll find paper and pencil. You can draw it for me."

That afternoon, Ed and Joe painted the top part of the caravan a brilliant turquoise. The blue ended in a wavy line. The middle third was painted bright buttercup-yellow, and the bottom portion, again delineated by a wavy line, was a deep sapphire.

While Joe and Ed were painting, Michelle and

Billy walked along the beach collecting shells. They arrived back at the coffee van just as Joe and Ed had finished painting one side.

Billy put out his hand, "Hello, Mr Farmer. We've been collecting shells for ..." he gestured towards the coffee van.

Ed looked from Michelle to Billy. "Very nice, but I don't quite …"

Michelle jumped up and down on the spot with small quick movements. She tried to clap her hands. The bag she was holding was in her way. "Poppy, Poppy, they're going on the van."

Joe started to laugh. "Hey, we've just spent this arvo painting it, getting it to look good. You can't go sticking seashells on it."

Michelle opened her mouth, but no sound came out. Her nostrils widened and her bottom lip began to quiver. She looked at Billy.

Billy took her hand and held it firmly. He glared at Joe.

Ed turned to Joe, "Michelle makes mosaics. They're good. She'll make this van something special. You'll see."

That evening after supper, Ed told Trish about Michelle's plans for the coffee van. He laughed as he told Trish how put-out Joe had seemed when Michelle announced she was going to stick seashells on it.

Trish asked, "Do you really believe that she can make something special?"

"Yes, I do." Ed rubbed his chin, "Not that long ago, I wouldn't have thought she had the talent or the sticking power." He stopped rubbing his chin and rested it on his knuckles. "But now, I know her a bit better. Yeah, I reckon she'll do it."

For the next few weeks, Gareth supervised the arrival and construction of new cedar-wood cabins.

Trish looked at the plans with uncertainty. "I don't want to live in a cabin on a permanent basis. I know we have so for the last five months, but…"

"I know, but we can replace the family home. These are modular. We can join them together—like lego. We can have five bedrooms, just as we did in Sydney." Gareth held out a catalogue, "C'mon, we agreed at the meeting. You and Dad chose this one. It's huge. Please don't get cold feet on me now, Mum."

Gareth's phone rang. He mouthed, "Sorry Mum," and walked away kicking at pebbles in the dust.

Trish watched him hugging his phone to his ear and heard his voice, "Yes, I'm afraid it is. No, no, I'm sorry …" There was a long pause while he listened. When he spoke next, his voice had a weary quality. "Yeah. Me too. Always remember, it was your choice." He snapped his phone shut and walked back towards his mother.

She gave him a quick glance, forcing herself not to search his face. "Fliss?"

He nodded, biting his bottom lip. "Mum, d'you mind if I don't talk about it? She's not coming up for the weekend, after all." He hurried out, and started unpacking a crate of wooden panels.

Neville prepared to work out his notice at Swanson's Hotel. He began to cross off the days until he was free to join the family enterprise. He circled his wife's waist in his arms and nuzzled her neck.

"Why don't you come up and join me for the last few weeks in Sydney, Darl?"

Trish shook her head, "I hate not being with you in the week but I can't leave Michelle on her own, and I really don't want to move her again. Not right now. She's beginning to settle a bit after the fire. I couldn't do that to her."

The Sydney house was put on the market. While Neville worked, Stella coordinated estate agents, possible buyers and removalists. She wrapped up the Sydney end of her freelance work.

Michelle took her seashells to Lola. "I want to put these on the coffee van. Will you help me?"

"Mmm." Lola picked up one of the shells and turned it upside down. "I think we'll need to fill this in, or it won't stick. We'll get some plaster-of-Paris and experiment."

Michelle nodded.

Lola continued. "It'll take a long time. Is that all right?"

"Yes. Mum's going to Falcon Court this arvo. We can get the plaster."

"You'll need sandpaper too, and a big tub of really strong glue. I don't think I have enough... D'you want me to write it down?"

"I can try, if you help me."

Lola produced paper and spelled out the words. Michelle's tongue protruded from the corner of her mouth as she formed the letters on the page.

Trish listened as Michelle repeated the items she needed. She looked at her own grocery list. "Michelle, I don't have time today. I'm sorry Sweetie, not with Dad and Stella returning tomorrow."

Michelle's face dropped. "But then everybody'll be too busy, won't they?"

Trish said thoughtfully, "I suppose you could ask Lola if she'll go to Falcon Court with you."

"Good idea," Michelle's face brightened.

Lola had an appointment that Saturday morning. "I'm sorry Michelle. I really would have been happy to come with you. Why don't you ask Billy?"

"Oh yes! I'll phone him right now."

The next morning Neville gave Michelle money for shopping. "Oh, and here's some for lunch too. Shout that boyfriend of yours. He usually treats you, doesn't he?"

"Yes ... thanks Dad." Michelle put her arms around her father.

Neville felt the familiar bear hug, her cheek against his chest and her arms only half circling his broad back: but he noticed the hug was shorter than usual and smiled at Michelle's enthusiasm to get away and meet Billy.

Around midday, the family stopped work for lunch.

Stella pushed pieces of chicken around her plate. She wrinkled her nose, "You cooked this Mum, didn't you?" She showed no signs of beginning to eat.

"Yes. Sorry, it was more important for Dad to help Gareth this morning."

Gareth grinned at his plate, "Actually Mum, I reckon this looks pretty good."

Neville nodded and grinned at Trish across the table, "This looks great. I wonder what Michelle and Billy are having. D'you think they'll have got any further than the food court?"

Gareth put his fork down. "Depends on how adventurous Billy is. Our Princess wouldn't think of going further afield on her own. I bet Billy has the imagination to go somewhere different. What d'you reckon, Sis?"

Stella stared at him across the table. "Don't be so awful. This is our sister you're talking about. We're not having bets on where she has lunch with that creepy boy."

Gareth looked puzzled, "I didn't know you found him creepy. I don't. Does anyone else?"

Ed waved his fork in the air, "He's very polite ... always shakes my hand. Is that what you find creepy Stella?"

Stella shrugged. "Dunno. He's never polite to me. Doesn't seem to like me at all."

Gareth laughed, "Oh ho, so that's what makes a bloke creepy, is it? Someone who doesn't like Stella!"

"It's my fault Michelle went shopping with Billy," Trish said to Neville as they cleared the dishes. "I was too busy to take her yesterday. I suggested she go with Lola. Silly of me really."

"Nothing silly about that. Lola's her friend."

"She needs friends her own age, not someone her grandfather's age."

"Well, Billy's her age isn't he?"

"That raises a different question. D'you think she's ready? I mean, she's never had a boyfriend before. D'you think she can handle it?"

Neville put the tea towel down. He turned to face Trish, encircling her in his arms. "Don't you remember being young?" He kissed her forehead lightly. "Try to think back ... the shock of it all, and the delight ... nobody's really ready for it."

Chapter 10

Billy and Michelle returned from Falcon Court. They took their bags of plaster, sandpaper and glue to Lola's caravan.

Lola beamed at Billy. "I could have gone shopping with Michelle, but I think she had more fun shopping with you. Did you have a nice lunch?"

Billy puffed out his chest. "Yes. There's an Italian café outside Falcon Court. I've been there before. We had risotto with lots of garlic." He grinned, opened his mouth and breathed out hard.

Lola laughed. "The thing about garlic is that it's okay if you both have it. I haven't had garlic today, Billy. It's a bit strong for me."

"Sorry," Billy put his hand over his mouth.

Michelle looked at Lola. "We bought some Italian biscuits for you. I'm not usually allowed …"

"That was very kind of you, dear."

"It was Billy's idea."

"Thank you, Billy. Now let's start work."

Gareth took time from erecting the cedar wood cabins to help Michelle sand the parts of the van where she wanted to glue seashells.

Stella grumbled, "I thought we were going to spend all our energy getting the cabins built. What's with pandering to Michelle's little whims?"

Gareth shook his head. "I know you don't like mosaics, but even you might think of it this way: a little time spent now, and Princess is as happy as a sand boy. She'll be out of your hair too."

Michelle stayed focussed with her project for the coffee van. She and Lola set up a small table with shells and glue. For weeks they glued shells on to the line which delineated sea from sand. Some days Billy arrived and helped too.

On the days that Michelle went to Eden House, she spent her time designing. She drew pictures of the coffee van and the wavy lines. She experimented, placing smaller pictures of fish, seahorses and seaweed on the turquoise parts of the picture. She consulted Kessie, who found reference books for her.

When Michelle returned to the caravan park she drew a fish for the van. "D'you think this is the right size for the van, Mum?"

"Let's go and see. I'll hold it up against the van and you can walk away and look at it."

At the coffee van, Trish held the fish up and Michelle walked away. Michelle stood with her head tilted to one side. She screwed up her face, "It's too small."

"Do you want all your fish the same size? Would be all right for your smallest fish?"

"No. It's too small." She pursed her lips, and pushed her toes into the sand.

Michelle drew another fish. When she was happy with it, she cut it out and took it to the van, pencilled around the edges and sanded the space inside it. She gathered glue and small pieces of orange, black and white broken pottery, and put them on a small table by the van. Slowly and methodically she filled in the shape. She took Lola and Ed to see her fish.

Ed was the first to speak. "That's lovely Princess. It's a clown-fish, isn't it?"

"It's Nemo."

Ed looked baffled.

Lola put a hand on his sleeve. "I think you'll find that Nemo is the name of a particular clown-fish. There was a film …"

"Yes, my favourite!" Michelle exclaimed. "But the other fish will be different."

A few days later, although Billy came to help, he and Michelle walked along the beach collecting seashells. Billy found a discarded child's bucket. They made sandcastles. Billy dug a hole and buried Michelle's feet. They fell about laughing and giggling.

Michelle lay on the sand. She moved her arms up and down, and her legs out and in.

"What are you doing?" Billy laughed.

Michelle jumped up. "Look. It's a sand angel."

Billy put his head to one side. He looked at the indentation in the sand. "Oh yes, I see. I'm going to do it."

He lay down and moved his arms and legs.

Michelle stood grinning at him.

Suddenly Billy sat up and pulled her down onto

the sand. She landed next to him. Sand sprayed up and over both of them. Michelle reached to brush the sand off him. He put his arms around her, pulling her towards him. He held her face, brushed the sand from her hair, then kissed her slowly and gently. Michelle's whole being melted. She returned his kiss, slowly at first, then hungrily, pressing herself close to him.

Later that afternoon, Trish looked at Michelle sideways, "However did it take you so long to collect just a few seashells?"

"We didn't find many. Just a bucket. We made sandcastles. D'you think we could have buckets and spades on the coffee van?"

That night as Neville drifted off to sleep, Trish propped herself up on one elbow. She shook him lightly, "I'm worried about Michelle."

"Uh, uh."

Trish shook his shoulder a bit harder, "I think Michelle and Billy are ... you know."

"Sorry Darl," Neville blinked. "You know … I know … What am I supposed to know?"

Trish pushed him. "Sex, you idiot. I don't know why I'm being so coy. I just can't quite grasp Michelle and sex in the same sentence."

Neville sat up, rubbing his eyes, "Why not?"

"Am I hearing right?" Trish's voice rose half an octave.

"Ssh," Neville put his finger to his lips. He took both of Trish's hands in his own, and tried to find her eyes through the darkness, "Look, why don't we talk to Billy's dad? We could check that Billy knows about condoms."

Trish pulled her hands away and tugged at her

hair, "Are we really having this conversation? I'm hoping things haven't got that far."

"Well, they're teenagers aren't they? Don't you remember what it was like?" Neville rolled over with his back to her.

Trish lay back on her side of the bed, remembering rampaging hormones and unbearable longing. She tapped Neville on the shoulder. "Sorry."

The next day, Trish phoned Grant and invited him and Billy to a meal. "Just a barbie, nothing fancy. We thought it would be good to meet you."

"That's great. I'd love to meet you all."

Chapter 11

Michelle was distraught. She phoned Billy. Together they commiserated, grumbling about the unfairness of parents.

Billy's voice was full of rage. "It's like we're little children."

"I know," Michelle's voice was meek, "I don't want ..." She held the phone against her shoulder and wrung her hands. Tears started trickling on to the receiver.

Billy could hear small sobbing sounds. "Don't be sad. It'll be all right."

"Oh Billy, I miss you," Michelle sighed into the phone. "Come and help me with the van."

"This arvo. I can come this arvo."

"Come and see what I've done," Michelle pulled Billy towards the coffee van. "I've done lots since ..."

"Since I was here."

Michelle smiled and nodded. The van was on the edge of the caravan park, right next to the beach.

Billy admired the work Michelle had done since he'd last seen it. They walked along the sand. Billy picked up a few shells.

"We don't need any … at the moment."

"Oh. Why are we ..?"

"'Cos it's nice … walking. Nice just being …" she squeezed Billy's hand.

They walked together happily.

Billy put an arm around Michelle's shoulders. After a while, they reached the southernmost part of the caravan site. Billy pointed to a derelict boatshed, half hidden by Norfolk Island pines.

"What's that?"

"It's Poppy's boatshed."

"I didn't know he had a boat."

"Don't think he does anymore."

" Let's check it out!"

Michelle tried to push the door open. It was stuck. She raised herself up on tiptoes to peer in the windows. Newspaper covered the inside of the glass.

"I can't see." Michelle stood on her toes, shifting her weight from one foot to the other. "You try the door, Billy."

Billy pushed. The door shuddered. He tried again, lifting it slightly. This time it moved.

Michelle clasped her hands. Her shoulders danced in anticipation.

Billy grinned, "Come on, Michelle," he said urgently as he pulled her into the boatshed.

Michelle shivered. "It's cold in here."

"I'll warm you up," Billy rubbed her arms.

Michelle wriggled towards him. "That's nice."

Billy put his arms around her and drew her close.

They could feel each other's heartbeats and hear one another's breathing. They tasted the warmth of each other's skin.

Although it was winter, the occasional passer-by stopped and asked about the coffee van. Ed put up a notice which said, 'café—opening soon'.

Regular beach walkers began to ask, "When?"

Ed put up another sign, 'Café open 10am – noon.'

Trish asked, "Are you sure you want to commit yourself to two hours every day, Dad?"

Ed installed himself in the van. "Might as well. That's when most people come by. I can take the newspaper, do the crossword. Michelle's there a lot of the time too, working on her mosaic."

Michelle drew large buckets and spades on the side of the van. She started to fill in the shapes.

A middle-aged couple stopped their morning walk to admire her work.

"We've seen you working away every day. We think it's going to be very good," the woman said.

Michelle grinned. "I like doing mo … mosaics."

"It's a very big project," the man said.

"My biggest," Michelle squinted into the morning sun and smiled at them both.

The man continued, "I'm sure it will make people notice the café when it opens."

"It's open now. Today. Poppy's in there. Do you want coffee?" Michelle asked eagerly.

The man looked at his companion, "Why not? We haven't lived here long. What better way, to get to know people?"

Michelle looked at them anxiously, "Is that 'Yes'?"

Ed had never enjoyed making a cup of coffee as much as he did that day.

"My very first customers. You get a free biscotti." He chatted to the couple as he made their coffee.

They wanted to know what had happened to the caravan park. Ed told them briefly, explaining that the coffee van was temporary. In turn, they told him where they lived, "Up on the hill. Right next to the big house. I gather it's something of a landmark around here," the man said.

"Yes, it's so high up you can see it from miles away. The big house, that's Dot Barker's house. Nice lady, Dot. She lent me a little scooter thing when I came out of hospital—broke my legs, you see. Give her my regards when you see her."

The couple assured him they would. They finished their coffee and continued their walk.

The day of the barbecue dawned.
Billy looked resentfully at his father. "Don't know why this fuss. They know me. You know Michelle. Why do you all have to meet?"

Grant shrugged, "They thought it would be nice, that's all."

"Well, it makes me feel like a little kid." He kicked the table leg. "Don't like feeling like that."

"Right now you're behaving like one. We're going in half an hour. Have a shave and a shower, and put on some decent clothes."

"We don't need to go yet."

"Yes, we do. I want to stop and get some wine …

and flowers for Michelle's mum."

"Flowers!" Billy's face brightened. "Can I get flowers for Michelle?"

"Don't see why not, Billy-Boy."

Billy smiled for the first time that day. "Thanks, Dad."

Grant nodded.

Billy's smile faded, "But—"

"But what?"

"You won't call me Billy-Boy when we're there, will you?"

Grant forced himself to keep his face blank. He even managed to look puzzled. "Don't you like being called Billy-Boy?"

"Yeah, I do Dad, but …"

Grant burst out laughing. He looked at Billy's concerned face, "Of course I know what you mean. I'll try hard to treat you like a grown-up."

"Thanks Dad." Billy went off to get changed.

During a lull in the conversation at the barbecue, Michelle met Billy's eyes. She smiled shyly.

Billy winked at her across the table, then looked around furtively to see if anyone had noticed.

Stella had noticed. She stared at him, trying to work out if she really did think he was creepy or not.

Billy reddened. He picked up a corn cob and started chewing at the end. He saw Stella staring at him. He felt uncomfortable. He tried to reach Michelle's foot under the table.

Gareth felt Billy's foot. "Hey wrong foot, Mate," he laughed.

Michelle saw Billy's red face. She sensed his

discomfort. She looked at his almost empty plate. Michelle knew there would be a desert next, a big oozing Pavlova. She'd seen it in the kitchen. She liked Pavlova, but she wanted to be with Billy all on her own, more than she wanted Pavlova.

She sat with the desert in front of her. Her appetite suddenly disappeared. She stared at it, wondering why she couldn't wolf it down as Billy was doing.

Neville saw her plate, "Lost your appetite, have you Princess?"

Michelle nodded.

Gareth took her plate. With a clean fork he divided the Pavlova. He put half on Billy's plate and the other half on his own. "Michelle's loss is our gain, eh?"

Billy grinned at Gareth, "Right. Thanks." He started to eat.

Ed was explaining to Grant why the best places to fish were also the most dangerous. Grant tried to look interested. Everybody except Ed realised he wasn't.

Michelle sensed it would be a good time to slip away with Billy. "We're going for a walk. See you later." They left the family and wandered towards the beach.

Grant looked at Neville and Trish. He leant forward in his chair, "I'm guessing you might be a bit worried about your daughter with Billy."

Neville was quick to answer, "Well, yes. We really like Billy, but—"

Trish broke in, "But Michelle's been very sheltered. She's never even had a boyfriend before."

"Well, for what it's worth, Michelle's a first for

Billy too. If it's any comfort, I don't think they're ..."

Trish's back stiffened. "I certainly hope not!"

Gareth looked at her questioningly, "Why not, Mum?"

Neville took Trish's hand, "I think Gareth has a point. Michelle's eighteen, and Billy's ... what ... the same age?" he looked at Grant for confirmation.

"Nineteen."

Gareth looked at Trish. "Mum, it is the twenty-first century. People do have sex. You wouldn't want to police her all the time, make it something forbidden. Isn't that the point? We want her safe ... and not pregnant."

Grant said, "When Billy was at school, he had a whole term of learning about contraception. His school took the subject very seriously. They sent leaflets home. We were all told to get them to practise putting condoms on cucumbers. The village shop ran out of cucumbers that week!"

Everybody laughed.

Grant wrote to Billy's mother, Natasha, about the barbecue. He was surprised when she replied immediately, saying she was coming to stay.

Billy looked at Grant over a cereal box on the breakfast table. "Why does she want to stay? She sends presents. Isn't that enough?"

"Don't you want to see your mum, Billy-Boy?"

Billy moved his shoulders backwards and forwards, "No. She left. We don't need her."

"Ah, well I'm sorry, but I've written back saying she's welcome. She'll be arriving the day after tomorrow." Grant started buttering some toast.

Billy looked up between spoonfuls of cereal. "Is

she going to sleep in your bedroom?"

Grant's knife clattered to his plate. He looked at Billy indignantly, "Of course not ... We haven't been married for fifteen years. She'll have the spare room."

"Okay," Billy said as he left the table.

Grant sat for a while wondering about his son's vehemence. He washed up the dishes, remembering Billy asking if Natasha could send money for a birthday treat. He wondered if that had precipitated Natasha's desire to see the son to whom she had been sending childish presents for so long.

Later that morning at Eden House, Michelle sat with Hal and Billy. Despite the cool winter air, they sat outside on benches. They stirred hot tea and Hal talked about a group house where he wanted to live.

Michelle was puzzled, "Don't you want to live with your mum and dad?"

"I haven't got a dad. Mum always has new boyfriends."

Billy said, "I want to live in a group house too. Dad wrote, and we've been there."

Hal smiled at Billy. "We might live in the same house." He continued to talk of his mother's boyfriends. Sometimes they were unkind to him.

Michelle's eyes opened wide. I, um ... my mum and dad." She shook her head.

Billy frowned, "You have two parents. It's different."

Michelle persisted, "But wouldn't you miss your mum, Hal?"

"She doesn't want me." Hal shook his head and his lips quivered, "Not when she has boyfriends." His lips started to tremble and he pushed his knuckles into his eye sockets.

Michelle's nostrils flared and her mouth turned down at the corners. Tentatively, she put her hand on Hal's arm. "I'm sorry Hal. I didn't mean to upset you."

Hal patted her hand, "It's all right Michelle," he sniffed, "I know you didn't mean …"

Billy shook his head slowly, "You don't understand, Michelle."

Michelle had spent much of her life being told she didn't understand, but she hadn't thought Billy would ever say that to her. She bit her bottom lip and walked slowly away.

Hal hurried after her, "It's all right Michelle. Don't be upset."

Billy followed them both and said to Michelle, "Why does Hal think you're upset?"

"'Cos you said I didn't understand. People always used to say that to me … before I came here … Makes me feel stupid."

Billy put his hand over his mouth, "You thought … you thought I said you were stupid?" He looked incredulous.

Michelle nodded.

"But how can you understand? You live with two parents. Hal only lives with one. I only live with one." Billy shook his head vigorously, "No one with two parents can understand."

At the end of the morning tea break, Michelle and Billy washed up.

Billy took a dripping mug. He carefully dried the outside. He thought of Hal, frequently sharing his mum with new boyfriends. "I like it best with just

Dad." He scrunched the tea towel up and dried the inside of the mug, "but Mum's coming to stay."

"Don't you want to see your mum?"

Billy stood on one leg, pawing the ground with his left foot, "No—I—don't." In his agitation he dropped the mug. Tears sprung to the corners of his eyes. He stared at the broken crockery on the floor.

Michelle bent down and collected the broken pieces, "It's all right Billy." She put her arms around him, "It's only a mug."

When Billy got home that evening Grant said to him, "There's a letter for you. It's from Quality Living Foundation."

Billy frowned, "Quality Living Foundation. What's that?"

"The house. The shared house you wanted to go to, remember?"

"Oooh," Billy put his hands to the side of his face. He swayed his upper body backwards and forwards.

Grant handed him the letter, and Billy began to read slowly. He passed it back. "You read it."

Grant read the letter. "You've got a place, Billy-Boy. The house will be ready next month. It's called Yoorooga. We can go visit, to get to know everybody."

Billy tapped his foot on the floor, "Can't wait."

Grant was still reading. He said, "The letter says there will be four of you sharing and two carers. The carers are called Coral and Si. One of them will be there all the time."

Work in the caravan park continued. Most of the cabins were up. Plumbers fixed bathrooms and kitchenettes. Electricians were scheduled, and the time for the reopening seemed to be in sight.

Gareth phoned Fliss. "We're nearly there … You know I said I might be able to get away to Sydney for a day or so …but now our schedule's so tight, I don't think that will be possible at the moment … No, no … I'm really sorry Fliss … Fliss?" His phone went dead.

Stella put a hand on his shoulder, "She's not buying any of it, is she?"

"Nup. She doesn't understand that I can't get away. She thinks I just won't. I'm losing her."

"Wouldn't she come up here for a weekend? At least she could see you, and have some idea of what you're actually doing."

"No go, Sis. I've tried that, but thanks." He shook his head.

Ed continued his daily two-hour stints in the coffee van. A few morning walkers became regulars. Shirl and Dave, the walkers who had recently relocated, asked Michelle about the progress of the mural on the outside of the van. Michelle showed them sketches and talked of the different materials with which she was experimenting.

One morning when they stopped for coffee, Shirl gave Michelle a large plastic bag.

Michelle took the heavy bag. "For me?" She made small jumping movements and opened her mouth wide, taking in numerous small breaths before remembering to breathe out. She opened the bag to find a tangle of broken necklaces, earrings and broaches.

"Oh, thank you!" She hugged Shirl, then called out, "Poppy, Poppy, look what Shirl's brought."

When Ed appeared, Michelle dipped her fingers into the bag and drew some of her shining treasures out into the morning sun. She twirled her fingers, letting the light catch at the cut edges of glass and stone.

"They're like the ocean," she waved towards the bay.

Ed looked at her with his head to one side. "I don't quite …"

Michelle's face shone. "The sea … it sparkles." She put the bag on a table and fetched her sketch book and opened it. She pointed, "I want the jewels here … on these fish."

When the family was gathered for lunch Michelle bubbled about the new trinkets. Trish half listened; she was thinking about the suppliers she would phone for the linen order. Gareth was worrying about a conversation he had with Fliss. Neville was wondering whether his plans for the restaurant would ever come to fruition.

Michelle continued to talk about the jewels.

Stella interrupted, "Shut up, Michelle! Can't you think of anything else? Not everybody is interested in your wretched mosaics. Everyone's been working flat out on the new park this morning. What've you been doing? Your hideous mosaics, that's what." She threw her cutlery down.

Michelle stopped talking. She looked at Stella's beetroot-stained fork. Small drops were seeping into the tablecloth. Michelle stared at the tiny spots of deep red.

The rambling thoughts of other family members

came to an abrupt halt. Nobody else had taken in what Michelle had been talking about, but everyone was aware of Stella's words.

Gareth opened his mouth.

Stella stared at him belligerently and put a hand in the air, "I know, I know. Don't even think of giving me a lecture." She stood up, pushed her chair away noisily, and stormed off.

Trish glanced at Michelle then looked at Neville, who started to get up.

Gareth shook his head and mouthed, "I'll go," then left the room.

Trish collected plates and cutlery and took them into the kitchen.

Michelle looked down. She rubbed at the tablecloth, smearing the small red stain left by Stella's fork.

Trish returned to the table and gathered her daughter in her arms. They could hear Stella and Gareth arguing outside the room.

Michelle shook her head rhythmically and clung to her mother.

Neville looked anxiously at Trish, who shrugged. Sounds from outside became louder.

Just then Gareth's phone started to ring.

That night when Michelle went to bed, she lay listening to the rest of the family. She knew that Gareth's phone call from Fliss had stopped the family argument. The last words she heard were her mother's, "Oh Gareth, I'm so sorry. I'll always feel that it's our fault she broke the engagement."

Chapter 12

Billy was impatient to visit the new group home. He counted the days, and crossed them off on a calendar. When the day came, he and Grant arrived at the house bright and early.

Yoorooga was at the end of a cul-de-sac, only a few kilometres from Eden House.

Grant got out of the car. He noted spacious, well-cared-for houses, neat front gardens, and clean cars. "Nice neighbourhood," he said, "I hope you have nice neighbours."

Coral, one of the carers, met them at the door. A halo of light grey curls surrounded a soft gentle face. "I'm Coral," she smiled … "I couldn't help overhearing you. Yes, the neighbours are nice," she gestured towards a well-built man in his thirties. "This is Si, the other carer. We've both visited the neighbours and introduced ourselves."

Billy and Grant assured Coral that they

remembered both her and Si.

Si pushed light brown hair from his eyes and said to Grant, "You are welcome to stay and look around. You can stay for our chat, or leave and come back later. The morning's really for the boys, but it's up to you whether you stay or not."

Billy hopped impatiently and waved Grant away, "Go Dad! Come back later."

When Billy was properly inside the house, he saw his friend Hal. Billy greeted him exuberantly.

Hal plodded towards Billy, "I'm glad you're going to be here Billy. Is Michelle here?"

Billy looked puzzled, "Michelle. Why would she be here?"

"I thought …"

Coral intercepted. She said gently, "We just have boys in this house. It's too complicated having boys and girls together."

"Oh …" Hal said, "Who else is there?"

Just then the doorbell rang. Si brought in a tall gangly young man. He walked with fast jerky movements.

"Tom!" cried Billy and Hal in unison.

Tom greeted Hal and Billy, then stuck his neck out and peered at the two carers through thick pebbly glasses. He squinted behind blurred lenses.

Billy said, "Hey Tom, your glasses are all smeared. Give them to me. I'll clean them."

Tom took off his glasses and handed them to Billy who wiped them carefully with the bottom of his tee shirt.

"Thanks Billy. Will you be my special friend?"

"I'm everybody's friend," Billy smiled.

Billy checked the calendar on his bedroom wall. There were only two months more living at home, then he would move to Yoorooga. He went downstairs and found Grant clearing away the breakfast things.

Billy fidgeted for a while, then picked up a pile of newspapers and put them down again. "What are you doing today, Dad?"

"Tidying the garage, Billy-Boy. D'you want to help me?"

Billy shook his head, "I'll clean the car."

Billy stood at the side of the house with the hose. He had just rinsed the car and was about to start polishing. A little blue car draw up in front of the house. He glanced at the car, then reached for his polishing cloth.

A tall blonde lady got out of the car and opened the boot. She hauled out a large red suitcase on wheels and a matching bag. Her heels click-clacked up the pathway towards his house.

Billy stopped polishing. His forehead wrinkled. He wanted to tell the lady that she had the wrong house … that he lived there with his dad, and they weren't expecting any visitors until the next day. He stared at her, and tried to formulate his sentence.

The lady put her cases down when she saw him. Her voice trembled, "You must be Billy." She walked slowly towards him with arms outstretched.

Billy backed away. "I don't know you." The words he had been taught to say as a child came out automatically. He stood flattened against the fence, one hand holding the polishing cloth and the other held rigidly out in front for protection.

The lady put her hand to her mouth. "Oh dear, such a bad start. I'm sorry." She shook her head, "Where's Grant?"

Billy stood against the fence, unable to move.

"Your dad! Where is he?" The lady seemed to be getting impatient.

Billy felt the blood return to his feet and legs. He ran along the side of the house to the garage, banging the metal fence and shouting, "Dad, Dad! Someone to see you."

Grant heard the panic in Billy's voice before he registered the words. He hurried out of the garage, blinking into the strong sunlight. He had chisels and a hammer in his hands.

He stopped and stared at Billy and the lady. He chuckled, "Oh my! You never could get the day right, could you?"

She looked affronted. "I'm here, aren't I?" She glanced with irritation from Grant to Billy and back again.

Grant moved towards Billy. Still holding a chisel, he put an arm around Billy's shoulder. "Billy-Boy, this is your mum."

Billy shook his head. "Mum's got brown hair." He stared at the unfamiliar lady in front of him, "… and she isn't coming till tomorrow."

To Billy's surprise both his dad and the lady started giggling. Small amused laughs became guffaws which rose and rolled into large uncontrollable roars. The lady held on to one of the decking posts for support, and tears rolled down her cheeks. Grant tried to clutch at his belly and dropped the hammer and chisels in the process. The sound of metal meeting concrete was drowned by laughter.

Billy walked back to the car and started polishing it.

After a few minutes the laughter subsided. Grant and Billy's mother walked around to the side of the house where they found Billy furiously polishing the bonnet.

"Come on son. I'm sorry we got carried away. It's just that ... your mum always got mixed up with days and dates. It seemed so funny that nothing had changed." He took the polishing cloth from Billy. "Let's go inside."

Grant turned to his ex-wife, "Come on Natasha, let's get you settled." He followed her into the house, with Billy holding back behind her.

"Coffee?" he asked as he walked towards the spare bedroom. Without waiting for an answer, he called over his shoulder, "Put the kettle on, will you Billy?"

Natasha watched Billy fill the jug. She noticed his teeth covering his bottom right lip as he reached for the coffee jar.

Billy didn't look at her as he spooned coffee into the plunger. His lips moved as he counted the spoonfuls. When the jug clicked off, he picked it up with slow measured movements, began to fill the coffee plunger, then abruptly stopped. He looked at it, chewed his bottom lip and frowned. He called out, "Dad!"

Natasha wondered what had suddenly worried him. She was about to ask when Grant came back into the room.

"Dad," Billy's voice quivered, "I know where the water goes up to for two people. Where does it go up to for three people?"

"Darned if I know," Grant reached for a mug and filled it with boiling water then tipped it into the plunger. He grinned at Billy. "I've no idea either. That's enough."

Billy relaxed. "Good idea Dad. I'll remember that."

Billy finished his coffee and put the mug down with a thump. He looked at his watch, "Time for me to go."

Natasha looked quickly from Billy to Grant.

Grant clapped Billy on the shoulder, "That's a bit rude. Your mum's only just arrived."

"But I'm going to meet Michelle. We're going to—"

"Billy-Boy, you see Michelle a lot. You can see her tomorrow. At least give this day to your mum."

Billy continued looking at his watch. "The ferry. I don't want to miss the ferry. It's the Eden House picnic. We're going to Bangalore Island."

Grant slapped his forehead, "Sorry Billy I'm sorry. I forgot it was the Eden House picnic." He turned to Natasha, "Sorry Tash. It's Billy's day centre. This is something that's been planned for weeks." He gave a small chuckle, "and after all you have arrived a whole day early!"

At the end of the day Billy returned home frowning. He kicked the gate and jabbed his key into the front door lock. As he opened the door, he heard conversation coming from the back of the house.

Natasha and Grant were sitting on the back veranda with drinks in their hands. The evening was chilly and an outdoor heater warmed the air. Grant wore a sweat shirt.

Billy noticed that Natasha wore one of Grant's jumpers. He stared at it, then looked at his father accusingly.

Grant met Billy's truculent stare. "Your mum came down from Queensland and forgot to bring anything warm. Come and tell us about your picnic."

Billy sat down heavily. "Not a good day." He stared at the scuffed toes of his trainers. "Couldn't be on our own. Tom and Hal came too."

"It was a picnic for everyone, wasn't it?

"Yes, but afterwards. I wanted to be with Michelle … just us. Tom and Hal followed us."

Natasha giggled and Grant burst out laughing. Billy kept his head lowered but looked up with his mouth still pursed. "Not funny. Tom doesn't like Michelle. He kept saying things."

Natasha knelt down so that she was in Billy's line of sight. "Let's open some presents. I went shopping before I left home." She delved into a big bag by her feet, "Here, this is for you."

Billy held the parcel and looked suspiciously at the shiny wrapping. He picked at the sticky tape. When he had pulled off all the tape, he slowly pushed the paper back. A neatly folded maroon polo shirt and a pair of grey trousers, pleated at the waist, lay in front of him.

Billy felt anger well inside himself. "I don't wear clothes like that."

Grant's face contorted as he tried not to laugh.

Natasha's face was stony. She could hear Grant's stifled laugh and see Billy's angry face. She put her wineglass down. "I can't get it right, can I? Your dad told me the things I bought were too childish, so I tried to buy proper grown-up clothes for you."

Billy thrust the clothes onto a table, "But they're old. Michelle's poppy wears things like that." He folded his arms and turned away from Natasha.

Later, when Billy went to bed, he could hear the muffled voices of his parents talking and laughing. He felt a small stab of jealousy. He turned over and grabbed his phone. He looked at the photo of Michelle on the screen, stroked her hair and kissed her image before turning out the light.

The following morning, Natasha appeared at the breakfast table with a small diary and pencil in her hand.

Billy was running around the kitchen waving a letter. He whooped, "Yoorooga ... I can move next month."

Natasha looked quizzical, "Yoorooga?"

Grant grinned. "It's a group home for young people with learning disabilities. Billy wants to have a go at living more independently."

"Ah."

Grant looked at Natasha. "We applied ages ago. It's is a new house. We've been to have a look at it."

"And I've got a place," Billy puffed out his chest.

"Can I see the letter please, Billy?" Grant held his out hand.

Billy passed the letter to him.

"We've got another meeting with the carers, Coral Smiley and Si Fielding," Grant said. "Ten o'clock on Tuesday at Yoorooga. Tom and Hal will be there too."

"Aren't they the boys you didn't want with you yesterday?" Natasha asked.

"Yes. We'll all be in the house. That's all right ... I just don't want them around when I want to be with

Michelle!"

Natasha shrugged, "Well, I guess that it's good news then." she raised her glass of orange juice, "Here's to you, Billy."

Billy grabbed his glass and clinked it against Natasha's and Grant's glasses.

Natasha pointed to her open diary. "I've just had a call from my friend Lizzy," she turned to Grant, "You remember Lizzy, don't you?"

Grant shook his head.

Natasha put her diary on the table. "We used to work together. She's opening a new salon at Falcon Court. That's near here, isn't it?"

Grant nodded.

Natasha poured coffee and continued, "She's having a grand opening at the end of the month—that's another two weeks. If it's not too much to ask, could I ..?"

Billy jabbed his knife into the marmalade. He looked from parent to parent.

Grant took Billy's knife out of the marmalade jar and put it down quietly on Billy's plate. "What d'you think Billy-Boy? Can we bear to have your mum around for another two weeks?"

Billy shrugged, "Dunno." He got up and stumbled out of the room.

Grant stretched his legs under the kitchen table. He leaned back and folded his arms behind his head. His eyes danced as he looked at Natasha. "You didn't think getting to know Billy would be plain sailing, did you?"

"He doesn't seem to ... like me." Natasha stirred her coffee. "Everything I do is wrong."

"He's a teenager! He wants to do the things that

teenagers want to do. Just because he's brain-damaged doesn't mean—"

Natasha pushed her coffee away. "It seems to mean I can't get it right!"

Grant grabbed her wrist, "No!" He shook it gently and looked into her eyes, "It only means you haven't got it right, yet."

The next time Billy went to Eden House, Natasha looked around his bedroom. She looked in his wardrobe, and saw neatly folded tee shirts emblazoned with popular brand names. Even socks and underwear seemed to have been chosen with teenage fashion in mind. She bit her lip, remembering the clothes she had brought with her. She wondered why she had thought it appropriate to buy him clothes from an old-fashioned gents outfitters.

Natasha came out of Billy's bedroom and looked sheepishly at Grant. "You're right. He's just a teenager. I've got to go into town to extend my car hire. I'll try and get him something more … appropriate."

Grant winked at her, "Go for it, Girl."

When Natasha returned with armfuls of shopping, Grant was at work and Billy was at Eden House.

She went to the kitchen and opened the fridge and cupboards, wondering if there was anything she could cook.

Grant returned to find Natasha beating eggs. "What're you doing?"

"I thought I'd cook. If I'm going to be here for another two weeks, the least I can do is cook the occasional meal."

"That's a nice idea. What are you cooking?"

"A frittata. I found these in the fridge."

Grant inspected the chopping board. He saw broccoli, chopped potatoes, tomatoes, peas and mushrooms. "Not sure Billy-Boy will eat that. Why didn't you ask me? I could have given you a list of forbidden foods."

Natasha put her hands on her hips, "Okay, so what doesn't he like?"

"Broccoli…" Grant picked all the little florets off the chopping board. "He'd be very cross. It would undo all the good you're trying to do. The rest are all right."

"So, how come you've got it in the fridge, if Billy doesn't like it?"

"Billy doesn't like it, I do. Lighten up Tash. I can tell you're doing your best, but you just have to accept him the way he is."

Natasha put the frittata in the oven. "Can I show you some things I bought today? I'm sick of getting it wrong."

Grant reached out and rumpled her hair, "You are a funny old thing. Anyone would think he was some sort of monster. He's just … Billy."

"Nevertheless," Natasha pulled her head away from Grant, "I want another opinion. On the way to Falcon Court, I passed a car boot sale up on the hill. I love poking around in those things. Look, I got this." She showed him an old computer game. "D'you remember this?"

"My goodness, yes. I had it when I was a kid. That'll be a sure hit. There's only one problem," Grant looked at the clunky box. He turned it over thoughtfully, "I don't think our computer will handle this."

"Ah, I picked up an old laptop too. One of the early versions. It'll take the game. I made the woman demonstrate." She turned around and burrowed under other shopping. "D'you want to have a look at the game?"

When Billy returned home he found his parents in the sitting room intent on a laptop. He felt excluded, but he also felt curious. He didn't like seeing his dad sitting quite so close to his mum, but he wanted to see what was on the screen. He stood in the doorway deciding what to do.

"Hi ya, Billy. Good day at Eden House?"

Billy thrust his fists forward with the thumbs pointing downwards. "No. Josie and Tom … unkind to Michelle."

Grant looked up in surprise, "I thought Tom was your friend."

"Yes, but he shouldn't be nasty," Billy shook his head, "not to Michelle."

Billy wanted to see what was on the screen. He edged towards them. "What're you two doing?"

Grant grinned, "I thought you'd never ask!" He gestured towards Natasha, "Ask your mum."

Billy forced himself to look at Natasha. "What're you doing?"

Natasha smiled and beckoned to him. "I bought this for you, the game and the laptop. It's a game I remember from when I was—" Natasha was about to say 'a child', but then stopped in case Billy felt diminished.

"A game!" Billy's eyes danced. "Thank you. Thank you."

Billy spent most of the evening playing the game.

Eventually he got up to go to bed. He stretched and yawned, "I want to play this with Michelle. She'd like it."

Natasha looked up from her conversation with Grant, "When am I going to meet Michelle, Billy?"

Billy gave a quick shrug "Dunno. When you want to?"

"How about tomorrow?" she replied, with a wink at Grant.

When Billy announced he was going to see Michelle the following day, Natasha spoke quickly, "I'll drive you Billy. I've never been to Pelican Bay Caravan Park."

"Okay. Michelle's poppy can make you coffee at the coffee van."

"I'll look forward to that. G'night Billy."

Chapter 13

Natasha stopped outside Pelican Bay Caravan Park. As she and Billy began to walk through it, she noticed generously-spaced cedar cabins. Eye catching strelitzia, brightly coloured hibiscus, and other plants sat in pots on bare earth, waiting to adorn each chalet.

Natasha turned to Billy, "It's going to be wonderful when it's finished."

"Yeah," Billy said. He couldn't see what was so special about a few cabins with pots of plants outside. "Wait till you see the coffee van."

They walked past a large bare concrete rectangle.

"What's that, Billy?"

"Dunno. Ask Michelle, or her poppy."

Billy glimpsed the bright colours of the coffee van through eucalypts. "We're nearly there," he called out rhythmically. "I can see the coffee van." He stopped, suddenly putting a finger on his chin, "I can't see Michelle yet." He raised himself up on his toes and peered between the trees. "We can surprise her!"

"I thought she was expecting us." Natasha sounded irritated.

"Yeah," Billy grinned. He ran behind Natasha and put his hands over her eyes. "Surprise her. Like this."

Natasha laughed. "Oh, I see what you mean …"

Billy didn't hear her. He ran off towards the coffee van, and veered off around the back, expecting to see Michelle gluing pieces of pottery or seashells onto it. He saw the table set up with shells and glue, but not Michelle. He ran around to the front.

Michelle was wiping one of the tables. She had heard Billy before he came into sight. As she turned, her shoulders rose and a huge grin spread over her face "Billy?"

Billy laughed. His moment of frustration was over. "I wanted to surprise you." He wrapped his arms around her. After a long hug, Billy let go of her.

Michelle saw Natasha waiting at a discreet distance. "Is this …?"

"Yes, this is my mum."

"Hello, Billy's mum. Would you like coffee?" Michelle pulled a chair out.

"Please … call me Natasha. I'm pleased to meet you at last, Michelle."

Michelle's face remained solemn. "Okay, Natasha. Poppy'll make the coffee. I don't like the machines … too noisy."

Natasha sat, and Ed busied himself making the coffee. He chatted to her through the hatch.

Michelle shifted from one foot to the other, trying to catch Ed's eye. "We'll go and get some more shells, Poppy. See you later."

Billy stood close to Michelle. "Yeah. You enjoy your coffee, Mum."

Ed brought the coffee out to Natasha and sat at the table with her. He grinned, "They always say that when they go off together."

"Sounds like you know Billy better than I do." Natasha's voice was sad. "Tell me about the shells. The mosaics …"

Ed laughed, "I remember the first one … I was in hospital at the time. She made it at that day centre, Eden House. She brought me a photo. I was quite impressed. Although she's my granddaughter, I didn't really know her too well at the time. Then she just started making more … they got better and they just kept coming. They've caused some family tension, I can tell you."

"Really! How?"

"Oh, my older granddaughter can't stand mosaics," he laughed. "She also thinks we all make too much fuss of Michelle."

"Do you?" Natasha stirred her coffee.

"I guess so," Ed chuckled. "She brings us so much pleasure."

Natasha searched Ed's face.

His eyes met hers briefly. He looked out over the ocean, cradling his coffee in both hands. "It wasn't always like that. When she was born … the diagnosis … that was a bleak time."

Natasha's voice was almost a whisper, "But at least you always knew …"

"Yes, but I didn't always appreciate her properly … not until they came to stay here a few months ago."

"They haven't always lived here?"

"Oh no. They lived in Sydney. They came up to help when I broke my legs, and then after the fire they decided to make it permanent."

Natasha nodded slowly, "But Michelle. You said …"

Ed leaned forward, "To be honest, I underestimated her. Now I know her a bit better, I'm beginning to see how much she can do."

Natasha looked down at her lap. "I don't know Billy at all. I keep buying him the wrong presents. I don't think he even likes me." Natasha's mouth twitched into something that resembled a smile.

Ed saw the brave attempt to look cheerful. He nodded slowly, "And Billy?"

"He was four years old. We were just a normal happy family with two kids … then that dreadful day hit us." Natasha's lips trembled. "There was a barbecue at a friend's house. The gate to the swimming pool wasn't shut properly. We heard shouts. We ran, but by the time we got there, both of them were lying still in the water. Our friends … they're lifesavers … they tried CPR. The ambos came …" she shook her head. "Grace was pronounced dead on arrival at hospital. Billy was in intensive care for a while." Her lips contorted, "You know the rest."

The tendons in her neck stood out as she tried not to cry. She blinked back tears, and looked up at Ed again. "I'm sorry. I don't think I've talked about it for … oh, so many years."

"It's not good to keep these things to yourself." Ed was surprised at himself. He shook his head quickly. "I'm sorry. I shouldn't have …"

Natasha reached for his hand, "No. I'm glad you did. I haven't ever really talked about it. I couldn't cope. My beautiful baby was dead, and my lovely son damaged forever. I never came to terms with that. It's very shameful I know, but I just ran away."

Ed clasped her hands. He looked directly at her. "It's time you stopped beating yourself up ... get to know him."

Billy and Michelle returned with a meagre bag of shells.

Ed laughed, "That won't last you very long, Princess."

Billy grinned, "No. We'll have to go and get some more when we run out." He put an arm around Michelle. She rested her head on his shoulder.

Before she left the coffee van, Natasha asked Michelle to lunch the following day. "I really want to cook a Sunday roast but Grant says it isn't worth it for three people. Could I tempt you?"

Michelle looked puzzled.

"I meant, would you like to come to lunch, at our place, tomorrow?"

Michelle took a quick breath in. She looked at Billy.

Billy nodded and squeezed her hand.

"Yes, I'd like that," she said to Natasha.

Ed cut in, "Hey, Princess ... don't you think you'd better check that it's okay with your mum and dad?"

Chapter 14

Grant cleared the dinner plates from the dining table after lunch. Natasha washed up. Billy and Michelle dried.

Natasha handed Billy a wet plate. "What are you two planning for this afternoon?" She looked expectantly at Billy.

"Um, dunno. Haven't thought, have we Michelle?"

"Maybe go for a walk. Could go to the beach," Michelle offered.

Grant came back to the dining table and looked out the window. "I think it's going to rain. Might be an idea to plan something indoors."

Billy looked disappointed.

A look of excitement crossed Michelle's face. She grabbed both Billy's hands, "Show me your new game on the computer. Doesn't matter about the rain."

Billy grinned and whistled through his teeth, "Wow—ee." He pumped both of Michelle's hands up and down. "We can both play ..."

Natasha smiled at Michelle. "It's not really a new game. It's one I used to play when I was younger. You have to find things. You go on a hunt."

Michelle smiled. "That's nice. Like an Easter egg hunt. I do that at Easter. Do you do that, Billy?"

Billy shook his head. "No." Suddenly his face lit up, "Mum sends an Easter egg though."

Natasha looked questioningly at Grant, who put a finger to his lips and stared at her intently. She said brightly, "So you two are going to spend the afternoon playing the quest game?"

Without waiting for an answer, Grant said, "Before you guys start, I'd better tell you I've been called out to work. I'll be back around four. You've got my number if you need anything." He turned to Billy, "And I think your mum's off to see her friend Lizzy. Will you be okay?"

"Sure. Fine." Billy turned to Michelle. "Let's go."

The computer was in a small alcove in the main living area. Michelle looked surprised as, hands swinging, she and Billy walked past it. "I thought ..."

"No. Not on this one ... game's too old. Mum bought an old laptop with the game. She got it just for me. It's in my bedroom."

Natasha smiled at Grant. He grinned and nodded.

Michelle looked around Billy's room. "It's very tidy. My room doesn't look like this." She walked to the bed and stroked the doona, then she saw the small table with a heavy old laptop.

Billy drew up a chair for Michelle.

"Where are you going to sit?" Michelle looked round the room.

"Oh, I'll get a chair from the living room. Wait. I'll just switch it on. It takes a while." Billy flicked a switch and left the room.

Michelle swung her legs and looked at the little blinking light.

Billy returned with a heavy dining chair. He placed it next to Michelle and put his arms around her shoulders.

"Um. Nice, but I want to play the game." She looked at the blank screen.

"Okay. You put the game in here, and press this to begin." Billy pressed the spacebar.

The screen jumped to life. A naked couple stared out at them. They were entwined on a large bed with white satin sheets. Michelle stared, mesmerised by their golden suntans and perfect shiny bodies. A well-known brand of olive oil was displayed prominently in front of them.

"Oops. I didn't know that was there." Billy turned his head sideways. "How do you think they do that?"

"I think that's how people fit. It's what we nearly do." Michelle was solemn. She too turned her head sideways. After a few moments of studying the couple on the screen she said excitedly, "Maybe that's what we need ... olive oil."

Billy looked intrigued too, "We could fit like that, with olive oil. We need to wait a few minutes, till Mum's gone out. I'll go and get some then."

They continued to look at the screen.

After a while Michelle said, "D'you think there

are anymore pictures?"

"Dunno." For a moment Billy looked apprehensive, "Shall I?" Gingerly he pressed the spacebar.

The same golden couple flashed up on the screen in a different position.

Michelle giggled, "We could do that too."

"Mm," Billy nuzzled her neck, "when we've got the olive oil."

There were twelve pictures. Billy and Michelle studied each one carefully. Eventually Billy said, "I reckon Mum's gone now. I'll go and get the olive oil."

A few hours later, Natasha arrived home laden with carrier bags. "Did you enjoy the game?"

"Ahh …Oh …"

Michelle looked directly at Natasha. "We didn't play the game. We looked at the …"

"Shh," Billy giggled.

Natasha shrugged, "I picked up the game and laptop at a market the other day. I thought you'd like to play, that's all. It really doesn't matter if you found something else to do this afternoon."

Natasha's visit came to an end. She promised to write more regularly and to visit again.

After breakfast the next morning, Billy frowned at the dirty plates in the sink.

Grant asked, "Will you miss your mum, now she's gone back to Queensland?"

"No. We were okay before she came. But I liked the presents, when she got it right … and I liked her doing the washing up."

Grant let out a mock sigh and shook his head. "Nineteen years of training destroyed in an instant."

Billy laughed, "I don't mind really. It's what grown-ups do, isn't it?"

Grant looked at him quizzically.

"The washing up I mean," Billy explained, "You always said grown-ups have to wash up. I'm not a kid anymore. That's what I mean." Billy thought of other things that grown-ups did. He puffed out his chest at the memory of himself, Michelle and the bottle of olive oil.

"I'm glad you like washing up so much that you smile." Grant laughed.

"Yes, it's good to be grown-up." Billy plunged the dishes in a sink of hot soapy water.

Grant dried the dishes, "What plans have you got for today?"

"We're going on a bush walk. It was Michelle's idea. Lola's given her a map. She said it'll take us about three hours."

"Sounds like a good day. Enjoy yourselves … and make sure you've got your phone."

"I'm not stupid," Billy retorted to Grant's back as he left the room.

Trish greeted Billy at the door. "Hi Billy, off to Squiggly Gums, I hear. I've seen Lola's map. It's good. We used to do that walk a lot when we just came up to visit. We haven't had time since we've been living here though. Michelle's just getting ready."

Stella looked up from her newspaper, "She's getting changed for about the millionth time. She knows it's a bush walk but she put on a dress and her good sandals."

Trish looked at her daughter crossly. "Come on Stella, be a bit more … "

"I bet she looked nice in the dress," Billy interrupted.

Trish laughed, "Yes she did Billy, but look, you've got sensible clothes for a bush walk. The dress wasn't right … She can wear the dress on your next date."

They strolled along cool dark protected paths. The silence was broken by the occasional bird squawk. Michelle shielded her eyes with a map when a cockatiel flew past noisily.

"Lola says we follow the coast till we come to a big twisted an, ang … ang …"

"Ang-o-phora" Billy finished helpfully. "Yes, I know the one. I used to try to climb it when I was little. Dad has photos of me sitting on the bottom bit … you know, the bit that grows along the ground."

Michelle clapped her hands. "Me too. When we visited Poppy, he put me on that bit. He called it my throne." She looked at Billy with admiration. "I never learned to say it though … it's a hard word."

They walked on slowly, swinging their clasped hands. Billy let go of her hand and put an arm around her shoulder. "Doesn't matter. Saying it, I mean. Knowing what it is, that's what matters. We can have our sandwiches there."

He stopped and looked at Michelle anxiously, "You did bring sandwiches, didn't you?"

"I did better than sandwiches. Dad helped me make something special."

"Oh, good. What?"

"It's a surprise," Michelle smiled. Her eyes danced. "You'll have to wait."

"I'm going to have a stickybeak," Billy moved to open the flap at the top of Michelle's backpack.

"No," she squealed, and broke into a run.

Billy pursued and they reached the angophora, hot, sweaty and giggling.

Billy rubbed his abdomen, "Let's have lunch now. I've got a picnic rug and fruit and drink. I can't wait to see what you've brought."

Billy laid the rug on the ground next to the tree whilst Michelle unpacked small plastic containers. He reached towards one and she swatted his hand.

"You have to wait. I must lay it out right. Dad says it makes all the difference."

Billy watched as Michelle took lids off and arranged and rearranged small quiches, dips and sticks of vegetables. "Gosh. That is better than sandwiches. My dad wouldn't think of anything like that."

"Dad made the quiches. I made the dips," she waved at the neat sticks of carrot, celery and cucumber, "and I grew some of the veggies with Lola."

They sat with their backs to the tree. Soon, all the food was finished. Billy put an arm around Michelle's shoulder. "That was good. I'm too full to move. Let's just sit."

She snuggled in to him. His hand moved over her shoulder, and tentatively down towards the top of her tee shirt.

"No Billy. Not here!" She pushed his hand away and wriggled away from him.

"I want to, don't you?" He held both her

shoulders.

"People could come." Michelle's brow was furrowed. She started to rub her thumbs together.

Billy reached for her hands. He wanted to reassure her, but his desire was rising too. "No one will come." He held her hands firmly.

"No Billy. No!" She wrenched her hands away, snatched up the small plastic containers and threw them in her backpack.

Billy looked on with dismay as Michelle prepared to leave. For a few moments he sat leaning against the tree. As she moved onto the footpath, he folded his arms and stared angrily ahead.

Michelle didn't look back. She walked off with a heavy thumping step. Her lips were clamped together and she took short, shallow breaths.

The main pathway veered sharply to the left and there was a smaller trail straight ahead. It was marked in pencil on her map. 'Turn here.'

Michelle didn't check her map or notice the relative size of the different tracks. She went straight ahead with stomping clomping movements onto the smaller track. After about twenty minutes the path she was on became smaller and smaller and disappeared altogether. She stopped suddenly when she realised she didn't recognise anything from the previous walks with her family. The trees were too close, and too prickly. There were many more banksias with their strange and weird seed heads. She remembered her childhood fear of the gnarled and twisted trees, and Stella telling her that the silhouetted shapes were goblins' houses. Her sister had woven the most fearful tale of Old Man Banksia who was really an evil magician. She knew it wasn't true. She knew that a tree was just a tree, but alone and frightened, her earlier terror returned.

"Billy," she breathed. Her voice was barely audible. "Billy, where are you?" A tear rolled down her cheek. She turned around and saw a small brown snake slither across the path in front of her.

"Billy. Oh Billy," she sobbed. The snake glided into the bush. Michelle wanted to sit down, but the path was littered with banksia seed heads and she was afraid that the snake might return. She put her hand in the side pocket of her trousers and brought out her phone. "Come on Billy," she urged.

Billy had left their picnic spot. He'd passed the small turning that Michelle had taken, and was nearing a lookout over a river.

"Billy," Michelle's voice came in short sharp bursts, "I'm lost."

Billy shook his phone.

"Can't hear you very well, Michelle. Where are you?"

"I don't know. Oh Billy, I don't know where I am," Michelle wailed.

As the phones crackled and hissed, and went in and out of range, Billy realised what had happened to Michelle.

"A dead end? Just turn round and come back the other way. Don't stop till you come to the big path. I'll come back. I'll wait where the paths meet. See you soon Michelle."

"Stay on the phone Billy. I'm frightened."

Billy assured her he would, and Michelle started walking and talking as she went. Suddenly Billy's voice cut in.

"Michelle, turn it off. My battery's low. We might need it. Stop talking now. Just keep walking, right." The phone went dead.

Michelle looked at the silent phone. Her thumbs started banging each other and the phone slipped to the ground. With trembling hands, she bent and picked it up. As she straightened she saw a kookaburra staring solemnly at her. She wanted the kookaburra to laugh. There would have been some comfort in a laugh, but for once it was silent. It watched her. She stared at it, willing it to laugh. Eventually it turned away. Michelle put her phone away and forced her hands to her sides. She poked her tongue out at the kookaburra, set her mouth, and walked on.

The return journey took less time than the outward one. Michelle was looking up and walking purposefully this time. It wasn't long before she could see small slivers of Billy's red jumper through the branches.

"Billy ..." she called out.

"I can see you Michelle. I can see you." Billy raised himself up onto his toes, peering into the bush.

Michelle ran for the final few metres. She could see Billy standing with arms out-stretched. She arrived sobbing and panting and threw herself at Billy's chest and clung to him.

Chapter 15

That night Michelle refused to talk about the outing. For the first time since her daughter was born, Trish felt completely excluded from her. She was hurt, confused, and suspicious.

When Michelle had gone to bed, Trish said to Neville, "Michelle's getting very secretive."

"Lighten up, Trish. That happened to Gareth and Stella too. They were younger, that's all. Look at it this way: because of Michelle's Down syndrome we've had her as a child for longer."

"Hmm. It was the first girlfriend / boyfriend thing, wasn't it?"

"Well, that is what happens … generally," Neville grinned at Trish.

Trish's mouth formed a thin line on her face. She nibbled her lips. "But—"

"But nothing, Darl. If you're so worried, take her to Dr Grey. Get her on the pill."

In Dr Grey's consulting room, Michelle pulled at her fingers.

Trish sat next to her. She reached an arm across Michelle's lap. She intended to hold her hand, to still the incessant wringing.

Michelle brushed her mother's hand away.

Dr Grey looked directly at Michelle. "What can I do for you today?"

Michelle looked in her lap. "Mum wants me here."

Trish began, "We've come because—"

"We've come because you made me," Michelle's hot face stared accusingly at her mother.

Dr Grey nodded. She had seen Michelle occasionally as a child, but not since they'd moved to Pelican Bay. She looked at Michelle's red face and noticed Trish's fierce possessiveness.

Trish spoke fast. "Michelle has a boyfriend. It's sexual. She needs to be on the pill." Her words jabbed the air.

Michelle looked at her with an open mouth.

Dr. Grey looked steadily at Trish, "And you're here because …?"

"Because she needs to be on the pill, or an injection."

"Nooo," wailed Michelle. The word reverberated around the room. She started rubbing her arm and shaking her head.

Dr Grey leaned towards Michelle, "We're not going to make you do anything you don't want to do. D'you understand me?"

Michelle looked into Dr Grey's eyes and nodded.

"Tell me about your boyfriend," Dr Grey said to Michelle.

"I don't want Mum here."

"But, I'm her ..." Trish left the sentence hanging in mid air.

"Exactly. Think how you would feel Mrs Grafton. You wouldn't have wanted your mum in on the conversation about you and your boyfriend, would you?" Dr Grey's eyes were kindly but firm.

"But I'm her legal ..."

Dr Grey sat back. She looked at Trish's seething face and felt Michelle's wounded pride. She decided on a compromise. She turned to Michelle, "If I see you on your own, would it be all right if I talked to your mum afterwards?"

Michelle nodded.

When Michelle and Trish left the surgery, Michelle had a prescription tucked in her bag. They walked into a nearby chemist.

Ahead of them was a mother and her young son. The toddler held a child's cutlery set in his hands. Trish watched as the mother bent over and gave the boy a ten dollar note. He reached up on tip-toe and handed the cutlery set and the note over the counter. The assistant beamed at the toddler and chatted happily as she gave him change. Trish had been about to ask Michelle for the prescription to hand over. She looked at the toddler and remembered the conversation with Dr Grey. She bit her bottom lip and smiled at Michelle when it was their turn. She handed Michelle a fifty dollar note.

For the next few weeks, Trish stood over Michelle every morning before breakfast, ensuring she popped the little pill out of its casing and put it in her mouth.

The disused boatshed, half-hidden by trees at the southern end of the caravan park, became the regular secret meeting place for Michelle and Billy, who slowly squirreled domestic items with which to furnish it.

Whereas once Michelle would have asked to take things to the shed, her daily enforced pill-popping had taught her the rudiments of the art of subterfuge.

Chapter 16

Ed took a deep breath. He loved crisp winter mornings when the sun shone and the sea glittered. He opened the coffee van as Michelle waved to Dave and Shirl who walked along the beach towards them.

Michelle shouted against the breeze, "Hello. We're late this morning. Poppy overslept!"

"Don't tell tales, Princess," Ed wagged a finger at Michelle, but the smile in his eyes gave away his amusement.

"I'm glad your poppy woke up in time to be here for us. We'd have been seriously put out, if we had to miss our coffee … wouldn't we, Dave?"

Shirl and Dave sat and talked. The smell of fresh coffee soon rose in the air. "I've been looking forward to this for the last half hour," Dave said inhaling the aroma.

Michelle watched her grandfather. She wanted to

carry the coffee to Shirl and Dave just as soon as it was ready.

Ed tamped the coffee. Suddenly an excruciating stab of pain shot across his chest. The filter holder clattered to the ground.

Michelle rushed towards the hatch. "Poppy?"

Ed staggered backwards. Gasping for breath, he reached for a small stool.

Michelle's eyes widened. She made small distressed sounds, "a .., a .., a …" Her thumbs started beating furiously.

Shirl jumped up and ran towards Michelle, but then saw Ed gasping for breath at the back of the coffee van. His face was drained of colour and his forehead wet with perspiration.

"Quick, Dave! Call triple zero. He's having a heart attack."

Shirl loosened Ed's collar and moved him from the stool to a chair. "Maybe you could take Michelle to the office, while we wait for the ambulance," she told Dave.

"I don't want to leave Poppy," Michelle protested.

"Okay, then … just sit here quietly with him. We're going to keep him comfortable. It'll be all right. The hospital will look after him."

Shirl looked at Ed's face. She thought she discerned a slight nod and a 'yes' in his eyes.

Michelle took one of Ed's hands in her own and put the other hand on top. She stroked his hand rhythmically, "It'll be all right Poppy. The hospital will look after you."

Dave waited until Ed seemed settled, then said to Shirl, "I'd better go … see if I can find someone …

let them know what's happened."

Minutes later Dave reappeared with Stella.

"Thanks for looking after him. I couldn't find Mum. I think she went shopping this morning. I've left messages for everyone. I'll come with him."

Stella saw Michelle sitting next to Ed. She heard Michelle repeating words and phrases in her soft sing-song voice. Stella opened her mouth, then snapped it shut when she realised that Ed didn't appear to mind.

Shirl noticed Stella's sudden pursed mouth. She gestured towards Michelle, "Does she often do that?"

Stella let go of her breath with a small laugh, "Yes. Under pressure she just repeats things. I generally get cross, but I looked at Poppy. He doesn't mind. He even looks soothed, so why should I get cross with her?"

Ed spent the next few days in Falconville Hospital.

When Trish was told how soon he would have to be moved, she was shocked. She tried to argue with the hospital staff.

"This is an acute ward, Mrs Grafton. He's stable now. We can move him to Heron Gardens again."

"That's where he went when he broke his legs …"

"Yes," the nurse nodded. "We're lucky there's a place, and it's the nearest option."

"I'm glad Poppy's in there again." Michelle raised herself up on her tiptoes, "I liked the little garden there."

Trish smiled wanly at Michelle, "I'm not sure Poppy's well enough to be taken into the garden yet."

The next time the family visited Ed, he was semi-lying in bed, staring morosely out the window. Although he had his back turned to the door, he recognised Michelle's footsteps. He turned, his face transformed, and feebly stretched his arms outwards.

Michelle ran, then she stopped just before the bed. "Mum said to be careful ... hugging you."

"That's all right, Princess. I'm sure an old man could do with a very gentle hug."

Michelle held herself in Ed's enveloping arms. She was careful not to put any weight on him. After a few moments she disengaged herself, "It's hard ..."

Ed looked puzzled.

"Not cuddling properly."

Ed nodded.

Trish said, "Work on the caravan park is taking up all my time again. We've finished the cabins and landscaping and we're working on the building for the new restaurant ... We're so busy nobody has time to open the coffee van."

Michelle jumped up and down excitedly, "But Lola said she'd do it ... just while you're in here. Gareth showed her how to do the machines ..." At the thought of the noisy machines, Michelle put her hands over her ears.

Ed smiled, "That's great. I've been building up a regular clientele. It would be a pity to lose people so soon after the start." He looked from daughter to granddaughter, "But I'll miss your visits."

"I'm going to ask Billy."

Again, Ed looked puzzled, "Ask Billy what?"

"Billy can do buses. Billy can bring me."

Trish was about to interrupt, to say that she wasn't sure it was a good idea, but she saw the look of pleasure on Ed's face and forced herself to be silent.

Ed reached for Michelle's hand, "That's really great. I'll look forward to seeing both of you."

Although she was a tea drinker, Lola discovered an unexpected satisfaction in the coffee making process. Scooping the soft aromatic coffee from the bottom of the grinder and tamping it into the holder, held a rhythm which culminated in contentment, as she produced each hand crafted coffee.

Regulars at the coffee van felt her easy paced movements, sensing her pleasure which enhanced their enjoyment.

Michelle began to be less afraid of the espresso machine, and most importantly for Ed, Michelle and Billy visited him after they had spent the day at Eden House.

As they were leaving Eden House, Billy puffed his chest out, "We're going to the hospital." He held Michelle's hand firmly, ignoring Josie's hostile stare. "We're going by bus."

Hal clapped Billy on the shoulder, "Good on ya, Billy. I wish I had a girlfriend."

Billy and Michelle started visiting Ed every day. On the days they didn't go to Eden House, Billy collected her from the caravan park.

Trish confided to Neville. "It's a bit selfish of me I know, but I was really worried about not getting to see Dad, but I feel less guilty, now that Michelle is visiting him every day."

"Don't give yourself a hard time, Darl. Let's be pleased for both of them. After all Michelle's learned a new skill, so they've all three gained."

Chapter 17

Billy and Michelle sat under shade sails at Eden House. They had clasped hands. Billy moved so that he was at an angle, almost facing Michelle.

"Michelle, the hospital … it's going to be different today."

"I know. I think Poppy's getting a bit better." She swung her legs happily.

"No, I didn't mean that. Today you have to notice where we stop."

"What do you mean?"

"Today you have to watch the stops. Count them, so we get off at the right stop."

"But you know about that Billy. You're good at that." Michelle's smile was wide and carefree.

"Yes, but I want you to know, too."

"Oh, all right." Michelle paused, then tilted her head. "Why?"

Billy put his hands on Michelle's shoulders. "I

can't come with you next week."

Michelle shuddered. Her thumbs sought each other. Billy was quick. He covered her hands with his own. "It's all right Michelle. It's not till next week. Look, we'll count the stops today, and tomorrow from the caravan park. We've got the rest of the week. By Monday you'll know how to do it."

"Too soon. Too soon. I can't learn by Monday." Michelle was shaking. Billy was still holding her hands. She laid her head on his chest and sobbed. Billy let go of her hands and put his arms around her. She clung to him.

Josie walked past. She couldn't see Michelle's face which was still buried in Billy's shirt. She looked at the back of Michelle's head malevolently. "You two shouldn't do that here. Not the right place." She wagged a finger.

Billy spoke without looking at her, "Go away, Josie."

"Why?" Josie stared at Billy.

"Michelle's upset."

"Ahhh, poor little Michelle." Josie shook with mocking laughter, then walked off repeating her last words.

After a while Michelle's sobbing subsided. She burrowed in her pocket for a tissue and dabbed her face. "But why can't you come on Monday?" she wailed.

Billy stuck his chest out. "It's about the grass. Rolf's coming to see me on Monday."

"Who's Rolf?"

"Um," Billy put a finger under his chin. "He's from the sports ground. Dad said he's coming to see me cut the grass."

"But your dad cuts the grass."

"Dad cuts the grass at the bowls club. Rolf's from the sports oval. I might help Rolf there." Billy paused, "if he thinks I'm good enough."

"Oh, you are! You are! Billy you can cut grass really well." Michelle momentarily forgot her worry. "That would be good, like a real job."

"Yes, that's why…"

"That's why I've got to learn the stops!" Michelle opened her mouth and spread her hands wide. After a few moments however, her brow furrowed. "Billy, what if I forget?"

"You won't forget. We'll count the stops together …" Billy fumbled in his pocket, "and I've drawn this for you." He produced a folded piece of paper.

Michelle unfolded it. There were six little drawings and above each picture, Billy had written a word or phrase. She studied them all.

"That's clever Billy. The first stop's here. It says Eden House. It really looks like Eden House. Next, the school. I like that … all the children really little."

Billy pointed to the next picture. "I took a lot of time on that one. It's—"

I know. I know. It's the big house on the hill … Dot Barker's place." Michelle bounced up and down on the bench. "It's got a green roof."

They continued to talk about the pictures. Finally Michelle refolded the paper and put it in her bag.

"Thanks Billy," she squeezed his hand.

Billy looked at their interlocked hands, then brought hers quickly to his lips. "We'll count the stops together," he reassured her.

Michelle and Billy sat in the middle of the bus

which had just pulled away from the third stop of their journey.

"We've just stopped here." Her finger was pointing to a picture of traffic lights.

"That's right," Billy beamed at her. "Next one's …"

"Don't tell me!" Michelle bounced on the seat. She put her finger on the picture below the traffic lights. "It's the chemist." She turned to him, "You're so clever Billy."

He beamed. As the journey continued, Michelle checked off every stop against Billy's drawing.

"The park. Billy, the park." Michelle's finger was under the word 'park' and directly on top of a picture of a green open space with trees and flowers. She brought her finger down to the final picture. "Next, the hospital. Billy, the next stop!"

Ed sat up in bed. His glasses lay on the table in front of him. He squinted at an old fishing magazine. Michelle and Billy had almost reached his bed by the time he saw them. He put the magazine down and held out his arms for Michelle. "Hello, Princess," he said

"Hi Poppy. How are you?"

"All the better for seeing you," he smiled.

She giggled at the familiar family expression.

After a few moments, Ed released his granddaughter and held a hand out for Billy, who pumped it solemnly.

While Billy went to get another chair, Michelle told Ed about her day … and most importantly, about the journey. "Billy's drawn me pictures of all the stops. I can count them."

"And how many stops are there from Eden House to the hospital?" Ed asked.

"Six. Billy's drawn me all the stops. I can check them off. We'll do it again tomorrow … and the next day."

"So I'll get to see you every day this week? That's great."

After a while, Ed asked Billy, "What've you been up to, young man?"

Billy puffed out his chest. "Well, I might be getting a job … cutting grass at the sports oval."

Ed offered his hand. "That's very good."

Billy grinned and pumped it hard.

Michelle climbed on the bus with her precious drawing. She counted all the stops until she arrived at the hospital.

Ed's grey face shone when she walked in, "My my, Princess … and all on your own. You smart girl. Come and sit here …" He waved to a chair next to the bed. "I want to hear all the news."

"Mum said to give you this …" Michelle delved in her bag and pulled out a hastily scrawled letter from Trish. "… and Lola says to tell you she's kept all your customers. Yesterday I helped her. I did a bit more of my mosaic too."

"And how's that mammoth mosaic going, Princess?"

"Good … I'm doing buckets and spades in the middle bit …"

Neville took a break from overseeing the new restaurant block. He wandered over to the coffee van, arriving first at the back where Michelle was busily working on the middle section of her project. Tiles, shells and jewels caught the morning sun.

"Did you come to see my mosaic, Dad?" Michelle beamed.

"Not really, Princess. But since I'm here, I'll admire it. It's coming on well, isn't it?"

"Yes ... nearly finished."

He walked around to the front of the coffee van. "How's it going, Lola?"

"Good. I think I've kept all of Ed's regulars. People are beginning to ask when the caravan park will be reopened. What should I tell them?"

"No problem. Leaflets are on the way."

"Neville, I've been meaning to ask you about food for Ed. I'd like to take him something, but well ... after a heart attack ... I'm a bit nervous. I thought, you being a chef ..."

"You eat pretty healthy food, don't you, Lola?"

"Yes, but Ed wouldn't eat the food I eat. I want to find something that'll be tempting, but won't clog his arteries."

" I'll see if I can find some recipes for you."

"That would be great. Thanks Neville."

Billy called in to tell Michelle he'd got the job. Bursting with admiration she squeezed him tight. "You're so clever Billy," she hugged him.

Billy felt the warmth of her body through his tee-shirt. He felt a stirring desire. "Let's go to the boathouse after hospital ..."

Michelle smiled, "Mmm." She closed her eyes.

They visited Ed together. Billy talked earnestly of lawnmowers, grass and the correct height of blades.

Ed nodded solemnly, sensing that they wanted to

be away together on their own. "This old man's feeling tired today," he said. "I'm pleased about your news Billy, but for now be off with you both."

"Okay, let's go, Billy," Michelle answered quickly.

Ed smiled as he watched them leave hand in hand.

The weeks rolled by. Michelle became used to the bus journey. After a while, she no longer needed to clutch her paper instructions, but she kept them in her bag just in case.

Ed asked about the mosaics on the side of the coffee van.

"Nearly finished … but I can't reach the top..." Michelle told him.

"It's been a big project, Princess. You'll miss it when it's done."

"Stella wants it finished."

"Oh? I thought Stella …"

"She says she's fed up … the fuss."

"Ah. I'll have a word with that young lady when I …"

"No." Michelle shook her head. "We have to … ourselves."

"As you wish, Princess," Ed winked at her.

Chapter 18

Trish rushed around the living room tidying up. "You haven't forgotten that Dad and I are going to the furniture showroom, have you Michelle?"

Michelle looked at her mother, "Do you have to go as well?"

Neville interjected, "I need your mum, Princess. She has wonderful taste, and I need the restaurant to look perfect."

Michelle nodded.

"It's just that when you get home from Eden House, there won't be anybody here," Trish said, "and I don't want you to worry."

"Stella's here. Gareth's here."

"Yes, of course. It's just that ..."

"Stop fussing Trish," Neville's voice cut in. "D'you know where my car keys are?"

"Oh Neville!" Trish jerked her arm so that her watch was in full view, "We said we'd leave the house five minutes ago."

Neville found his keys.

Trish slammed the car door and fastened her seatbelt in silence.

As Neville backed out, he said, "What's the problem now?"

Trish pushed hair from her eyes. "I'm just really worried about Michelle," she sniffed.

"We've sorted that out." Neville gritted his teeth. "We had Billy and his dad over for a barbie. You've even taken Michelle to Dr Grey. What else is there?" His shoulders were hunched. He kept his eyes on the road ahead.

"… and then there's Lola …" Trish continued sniffing. She opened her handbag and fumbled for a tissue.

"Lola's doing a great job! We should be really grateful. She got us out of a hole there …" Neville looked swiftly at Trish then focused back on the road.

"I don't mean the café. I mean her friendship with Michelle. I think it's really odd."

"We've been through that too! Look, Lola just is odd. She's always been eccentric. Sometimes, Trish, you sound as if you're jealous." Neville stabbed at the horn as a P-plater wove in front of him and then out again into the fast lane. "Sure, we're finding Michelle a bit difficult at the moment. She's a teenager …"

They arrived at the furniture warehouse later than they had intended. They tried to put their family worries aside and applied themselves to the matter of choosing furniture for the soon-to-be-finished restaurant.

Trish ran her hand along the surface of a dining table.

Neville glanced at it, "Don't worry too much about the tables. They'll be covered in cloths anyway. We just need to make sure they are durable, won't warp or anything when the first person spills wine all over them!"

"Umm, it's a shame though. This is nice wood. Couldn't you leave off the cloths? It would save on the laundry."

"It doesn't work that way, Darl. A real restaurant, serving real food has to have white linen. You know that."

Trish still looked sceptical.

Neville frowned, "Trish, how many top restaurants have you been to, where the tables have been wooden?"

"Well … "

"Precisely. Nice bistro style, yes. Cafés, yes. I'm opening a proper restaurant. I'm a chef, remember?"

Eventually they stopped bickering, and chose and ordered furniture.

On the homeward journey the car suddenly lurched and pulled to the centre of the road.

"What the ..?" Neville rasped. "Hazard lights, Trish. Put them on. Quick! We've done a tyre ..." Sweat glistened on his forehead as he opened the car window and hand signalled. His teeth were clenched. He kept his hand fixed on the wheel, and slowly pulled the car to the side of the road, while he kept an eye on traffic in the mirror. The goodwill they'd eventually felt towards each another in the showroom, evaporated as Neville knelt by the side of the road changing the tyre.

Trish fretted about Michelle. She phoned. "I'm so sorry Sweetie, we're going to be late."

"That's okay, Mum."

Trish didn't hear what Neville muttered as he climbed back into the car, but his intent was clear. The remainder of the journey home was frosty.

Two hours later than intended, Trish and Neville arrived home. They could smell that dinner was underway. Stella poured wine for Gareth, herself and her parents.

Michelle was grating cheese. When she looked up and saw her mother's tired angry face, she put the grater down and went to Trish. She put her arms around her. "It's all right Mum. Stella's put potatoes in the oven. I'm grating cheese."

"Thanks Sweetie."

Michelle pushed coins across to the bus driver, "The hospital please."

The driver grunted as Michelle took her ticket.

Michelle found a seat on the left and sat, looking out of the window, watching for the landmarks that she remembered from her precious piece of paper. She bounced slightly, humming Billy's favourite tune. Every now and again her thumbs rubbed together, but she sucked in her lips and forced her hands apart.

A middle aged woman with a gaunt face and a sprinkling of grey hair, turned around in her seat, "You all right, Love?"

Michelle nodded, "Just checking. That's the chemist. Next stop's the park." The paper was just inside her bag. If she thought hard, she wouldn't need to look at it. She continued bouncing.

"That's my stop," the woman said chattily. "Is that where you're getting off?"

"No. The hospital. I'm going to visit my poppy." Michelle's bouncing had stopped, and she rocked slightly, "I need to concentrate."

When Michelle arrived in Ed's ward, he was bowed over a newspaper. His glasses had fallen down his nose and he snored softly. She tiptoed up to him and planted a kiss on his cheek.

Ed stirred. He looked at her with bleary eyes, "Oh, Princess, it's you." He rubbed his eyes, "Where's Billy?"

"Billy's working. We told you."

"So you did! And you came all the way on your own again, Princess? Good on ya."

Michelle looked at the newspaper. She saw a pencil rolling around in the curve that it made on his lap. "Are you doing ..?" she pointed to the crossword.

"Yes. Do you want to help me?"

"I can't do them."

"Oh, there are some easy ones. Here, let me find you an easy one." Ed looked at his newspaper. He pretended to read, "glides on the water. Has a long neck and webbed feet."

Michelle raised her shoulders and dropped them quickly, "I don't know."

"Hmm," Ed scratched his chin. "Four letters. It begins with sss." He drew out the sound.

"I know. It's a swan." Michelle clapped her hands, "I did it. I did it."

"And so you did, Princess."

After a while Trish walked in. She'd dabbed makeup over tired puffy eyes and carried with her, a general air of unhappiness.

"Hello Dad," she pecked his cheek, absently. "I'm sorry I have been so busy this week, but it looks as if Michelle's been keeping you good company."

Michelle grinned at her mother, "We've been doing the cross thingy," she thrust the paper towards Trish. "I got a word."

Trish smiled wanly. "That's great, Sweetie. Look, I've been to Falcon Court, the car's full of shopping. I thought I'd pop in and see Dad, and then drive you home."

"Aren't I ..?"

"No Sweetie. I'm here now. You might as well come home with me in the car."

Michelle sat swinging her legs. Usually she did this when she was happy, but Gareth noticed that every now and again she kicked the wall behind her. He said, "Hey, Princess, why are you looking so down?"

"I'm bored."

"Not going out with Billy, today?"

"He's working."

"Ahh, I forgot," Gareth said. "Tell you what Princess, I'm going to give blood. You can come along for the ride. Hold my hand, and talk to me while I sit there squeezing the stress-ball."

"What's that?"

"Just a little squishy soft ball. Come and see."

"Okay."

Michelle jumped from the chair, "Where do we go?"

"There's a mobile van parked outside Falcon Court. It'll be there for a while, before it moves on."

"Mum and Dad give blood, don't they?"

"That's right, all of us ... but everyone's up to

their eyes in work at the moment. I've got time because I'm waiting for some things to arrive. I thought I'd do something useful with my day."

As they drove along Michelle said, "I don't want a needle in my arm."

"It's not going in yours. It's going in mine," Gareth chuckled. "Anyway, why not?"

Michelle looked out the window. "I don't know," she smiled at Gareth. "Does it hurt?"

"No, but they prick your thumb for just a drop first. That always gives me a shock and makes me jump."

Michelle grinned, "I want to watch you jump!"

Gareth glanced at her, and said in a conspiratorial tone, "I'll tell you a secret. I always look away when the needle goes in."

Michelle watched when Gareth gave an involuntary start, as he got his pinprick. She laughed, "I bet, I wouldn't be a scaredy cat!"

"I'm sure you wouldn't, Princess."

Michelle sat next to Gareth and watched as the blood travelled from the tube into the little bag attached to the pole. She thought about the blood going into the bag. She remembered Trish telling her about its journey to be processed before being given to someone. She said, "I'd like to give blood."

"Let's think about it, hey?"

"Where's Gareth?" Neville stood in front of the dining table with a platter of roast lamb.

"He's just washing his hands. He'll be here in a minute," Trish put roast potatoes on the table. She turned towards Michelle, "Now the holiday park is open again, we're thinking about the restaurant. Would you like to make a mosaic for the restaurant foyer?"

"Boats and seagulls." Michelle sat tall and clapped her hands.

Stella flashed her eyes at her parents. "No one consulted me. I thought we were all supposed to be in this together."

Neville stared hard at his older daughter, "Yes, exactly. All. That includes Michelle."

"Well, you know I think mosaics look tacky. We're trying to bring the place up-market." Stella pushed herself back in her chair.

"What about Barcelona?" Trish put a serving of vegetables on a plate.

"What about it?" Stella rearranged her cutlery.

Trish left the room and returned with a large hardback art book. She stood behind Stella's chair and passed it to her. The book was opened at a page showing the *Sagrada Familia*.

Stella turned the pages slowly. Eventually she said, "These are different. They're real works of art … even if some of them are weird. Michelle's mosaics aren't in this league." She swept out of the room.

Gareth came through the door. "Sorry I'm late. What've I missed?"

"Stella's angry." Michelle wriggled in her seat.

"Why?" Gareth looked from Michelle to his parents.

"Mum said I could make a mosaic for the restaurant." Michelle started tracing patterns on the tablecloth.

"And she threw a wobbly about that?" Gareth

shook his head and murmured, "Get a life, Stella."

After lunch, Gareth told Trish about Michelle's reactions when he went to give blood. "… and at the end, she said she'd like to give blood."

"What did you say to her?"

"Oh, I fudged it. Have you seen those forms, Mum? Even if she had a reader …"

"Mm. I'm going to Falcon Court to do some shopping this afternoon. I'll drop by and talk to the Blood Service people. I'll explain about Michelle wanting to give blood. Let's see what they say."

Later that afternoon, Trish visited the Red Cross van. She lugged her trolley across the car park and explained that she was enquiring about her nineteen-year old daughter, who happened to have Down syndrome.

The attendant shuffled some papers, "Well, she would have to be able to read the form on her own, and understand it. Can she do that?"

Trish took a copy of the form and scanned it. "I reckon she could understand it, and answer the questions, but I'm not sure whether she could read it all."

"I'm afraid …" the attendant turned away.

"Wait a minute," Trish's voice rose half an octave. "Are you seriously telling me that being able to read, is a pre-requisite for giving blood?"

The attendant turned back to Trish, "Well, it all depends on how bad the autism is …"

Trish's eyes widened, "My daughter has Down syndrome. She is not autistic."

"Yes, well …" There was a small shrug, "It would depend on how badly she's affected by her syndrome. Even if she did all the paperwork, would she be able to sit down for ten minutes with a needle in her arm?"

Trish gasped. "How ..." She had wanted to say 'how dare you?' Instead she yanked her trolley around and stormed back to her car. She chewed her bottom lip as she put the groceries in the boot. She found herself muttering, "Nineteen years of misunderstandings and prejudices. I won't let Michelle suffer the ignominy of being talked to like that."

Once home, Trish slammed groceries into cupboards.

Neville came into the kitchen, "Hey Darl, what's up?" He tried to put his arms around her shoulders.

Trish shook his hands off, "I went to see if Michelle could give blood, and they were so ..." Her chest heaved and she shook her head furiously, "... condescending." She sat down amid the half unpacked bags.

Neville drew out a chair. "I take it they said, it isn't on."

"More or less, but the thing that really got me angry was that they didn't listen. They started by talking about her autism. I very clearly said she had Down syndrome, and then ..."

"I know, I know. Then they started being condescending?"

"You guessed it. I could have throttled the attendant." Small tears sprang from the corner of Trish's eyes. "We've tried so hard to bring her up normally – oh, I know I've been a bit over protective, but on the whole we've managed, haven't we?"

"Apart from the buses. It was Billy that showed

her …"

Trish swatted at Neville, and smiled ruefully, "Yes, but buses here aren't quite the same as in Sydney. And, anyway we might have got round to it, if we hadn't been so busy."

Trish brought her hands to her forehead and looked down, "It's my fault really. I've been too occupied to make the time to show her. At least Billy's done that."

Neville left the kitchen, and Trish let her elbows slide outwards, until her forearms lay on the table in front of her. She lay her head on her arms and cried softly.

Chapter 19

Billy's alarm clock buzzed. He slapped the button. His normally sleepy morning body, was wide awake. He leapt out of bed and ran around his bedroom with knees raised high, weaving in and out of suitcases and boxes piled on the floor.

"I'm going to Yoorooga today." He ran into Grant's bedroom. "Dad. Get up. Today's the day." He shook his father's shoulder.

Grant pulled the sheet over his head and groaned.

Billy continued shaking him, "Come on, Dad."

Grant pushed the sheet back. "Okay, Billy-Boy. You win." He sat up. "Have a shower and get dressed. I'll start breakfast."

Billy arrived downstairs to find fruit juice and cereal on the table. He could smell bacon. "Thanks Dad! I'll miss your cooking."

"I thought I'd better give you a good send off. I guess, from now on, if you don't cook it, you won't get to eat it."

Billy pushed his chest out. "I know how to make breakfast."

"You do indeed, Billy-Boy."

Coral and Si, the carers at the new group home, waited in the large living area. Si stirred coffee. "I wonder who'll be the first to arrive."

Coral grinned, "I reckon it'll be Billy. He's so keen about everything he does."

"It's good that he, Tom and Hal all know each other from Eden House. It should ease settling in."

"I'm glad we've only got Billy and Tom coming this morning. It'll be better for Hal if he finds them already here.

Billy was the first person to arrive. Grant followed, cheerfully carrying Billy's cases.

Coral told Billy that she'd guessed that he would be the first person to get there.

Grant asked, "Does that mean he gets to choose his bedroom?"

"Yes." She turned to Billy, "You can have any bedroom except mine. That's the staff bedroom. Si'll use it too, if he's the person staying over." She laughed, "You can't miss it. My things are on the bed. You wouldn't want that room anyway. I've chosen the smallest one. It's not much more than a broom cupboard."

Billy considered each room. He didn't choose the largest, but instead, one that overlooked the garden. "It's got the best view." He put his belongings on the floor. "Can I unpack?"

As Billy spoke, the second new resident arrived. Billy waved from the top of the stairs with generous arm movements, almost bumping the ceiling light. "Hello, Tom. I've got my room." Billy started to walk downstairs.

Tom peered up through heavy glasses. "Hiya, Billy." He dropped his case in the middle of the living area, groaned, then slowly bent to pick it up in the other hand.

Billy bounded down the stairs. "I'll help you, Tom."

Tom's mother hovered uncertainly, near the door.

Coral introduced her to Grant. "We'll wait till they've unpacked, then have some morning tea. I guess you'll both want to go then."

Si said, "That generally seems to work best."

After the parents had gone, Tom and Billy re-familiarized themselves with every room in the house.

Tom brought down a book of word search puzzles. He sat upright at the dining table and started circling words.

Si said, "That's not very sociable, Tom."

Tom put his pencil down and stared at Si, "Why?"

Si said, "You could talk to Billy."

"I see Billy at Eden House."

Billy looked from Tom to Si, "That's all right." He walked around the kitchen again, opening and closing cupboard doors.

Coral smiled at him, "Would you like to help me make lunch, Billy?"

"Yes, I like cooking."

"That's good. From now on you're all going to be doing a lot of that."

Soon after lunch was finished, the third member of the new household arrived.

Billy greeted Hal enthusiastically. His words shot through the air in a quick burst, "We've just had lunch … I helped Coral make it … Tom's washing up 'cos he didn't help cook … I can help you unpack."

Si laughed, "Steady on, Billy. Hal's just walked in the house. Give him some breathing space."

Hal grinned, "Billy's my friend." He reached out and patted Billy's arm.

Billy carried Hal's case upstairs.

The new household spent the afternoon playing board games. As time for the evening meal approached, Si asked for volunteers to peel potatoes.

Hal stood up and plodded into the kitchen area. He stood at the sink.

Si was near the work counter, "Are you going to help me, Hal?"

Hal nodded.

"Here, you'll need this," Si passed him a potato peeler. Hal looked at it, turned it over, then back again.

Si passed him a handful of potatoes.

Hal put down the peeler and picked up a potato and turned it over as he had done with the peeler. He transferred it to his left hand. After a few moments he picked up the peeler again and made sharp brushing movements away from his body. This didn't remove any peel. Hal looked puzzled, but carried on pushing away from his body.

"It doesn't work that way, Hal. You need to pull it towards you," Si took the peeler and demonstrated. His movements were sure and rhythmic.

Hal started to tremble. He shook his head and

plodded back towards the living area.

Billy got up. "I can peel potatoes. I'll show you, Hal." He took the peeler from Si. Billy concentrated hard. His tongue was just beginning to show at the corner of his mouth. Slowly, he pulled the peeler towards himself.

Hal plodded back towards the kitchen. He stood watching Billy. After a while he reached out his hand.

Billy passed him a half-peeled potato and the peeler. He nodded at Hal.

Hal took the peeler and pulled it towards himself. He watched a thin strip of potato skin snake off, and onto the chopping board.

Billy clapped.

Hal picked up the thin strip of peel and held it up to the light, twirling and admiring it.

When everybody was seated for dinner, Coral said, "You three already know each other, which is great ... and you also know that there will be one more person coming tomorrow. We wanted all of you to be settled before Ryan comes."

"Who's Ryan?" Tom peered at Coral through smudged lenses.

"Ryan's the fourth person. He's a little bit older than you three. You met him last month when we all came to visit."

Hal startled everyone, "He's got blue eyes, bright blue."

"Mm. I think you're right," Si nodded at Hal. He looked at Tom and Billy, "Do either of you remember Ryan?"

Billy shook his head. Tom stared at Si.

After the new residents cleared up, Si said, "I'm off now, but Coral will stay here tonight."

Billy, Tom and Hal waved to Si as he left the house.

The residents were finishing breakfast when Ryan arrived. He was followed by a woman with iron-grey hair in tight curls.

Hal was the first to speak. He stared at Ryan, "Blue. I said he had blue eyes."

Ryan laughed. His stocky body shook as his shoulders rose and fell. Coral stood up. "Welcome Ryan. As you can see, the others are already here. We're just finishing breakfast. Do you remember Tom, Billy and Hal?"

"Uh," Ryan's large chin projected forward.

The middle-aged lady behind him came forward. She shook Coral's hand. "I'm Ryan's social worker, Maggie. We've talked on the phone. Ryan's parents went into the nursing home this morning. He's still a bit unsure of everything."

Coral introduced everybody then asked, "Would you like to see your room, Ryan?"

"Uh, yeah," Ryan's chin relaxed for a moment when he spoke, then resumed it's uncomfortable prominent position.

When Ryan had taken his bags to his bedroom, he clumped heavily down the stairs. He stood a few steps from the bottom and looked out over the living area, where the others were sitting. "You three. Wocha do all day?"

Billy and Hal looked at each other. Tom looked at the floor.

Hal nudged Billy. Billy said, "We all go to Eden House sometimes."

Ryan trod heavily on the bottom two steps, "I

gotta job." He stood, looming over their chairs. His heavy frame dwarfed them. "You?" he prodded his finger in Tom's direction.

Tom looked at the floor, "I fold pamphlets."

"You get paid?"

Tom shook his head.

"Huh!" Ryan showed his contempt with curled lips and yellow teeth. He walked across the room towards Hal, "You! You gotta job?"

Hal met his gaze. His small frame seemed to grow inches. "Coles. I get the trolleys."

"You get paid?"

Hal met his eyes briefly and nodded.

"Uh." Ryan swivelled around to Billy. "You?"

Billy said, "I cut grass."

"You get paid?" Ryan's face was inches from Billy's.

Billy stood up. Although Ryan was thickset, Billy was taller. He looked down at Ryan's sneering face. "I get paid."

Ryan pulled a dining chair out and sat down, "Well I …"

The others got up and drifted off, leaving Ryan to tell the empty room about his job washing up in a local café.

Chapter 20

Michelle arrived at the hospital and saw Ed's bed and chair were empty. She anxiously looked around the small room. Her mouth drooped at the corners, her nostrils flared slightly and her forehead disappeared into her hair.

"Where's Poppy?"

The man in the bed next to Ed's was asleep. Someone across the room called out, "He's having physio. He'll be back soon. You just wait, Darlin'."

Michelle started to sit down.

Another voice broke in, "Nah, your poppy's gone for a walk. Don't you believe him. He's mad. You go to that garden. You'll find him there."

Michelle shivered. She hovered, half-sitting, half standing. Her thumbs started to move together. The man who had spoken first, fell asleep. She looked at the patient who had delivered the second message.

He nodded and repeated, "He's in the garden."

Michelle straightened up and pulled her hands

apart, bringing them to her sides. She walked decisively.

When she passed the nurses' station, one of the nurses waved at her, "That's right dear, he's out in the garden. He'll be pleased to see you."

Ed was sitting on a bench in the warm winter sunshine.

"Oh Poppy!" Michelle ran towards him and threw her arms around his shoulders. "I couldn't find you."

"You've found me now," he smiled at her, and smoothed the hair around her face. "I'm coming home very soon. Now, what d'you think of that?"

"Oh, Poppy, I'm so happy." Michelle sighed and rested her head on his chest.

After a few moments she sat on a bench next to Ed. "Billy's moved to Yoo ... roo ... ga." Michelle spread the word out, and nodded as she said each syllable.

"And, where is Yoorooga?"

"Um ... I don't know. It's a house. There's three others. I'm going to meet them tomorrow."

"He's going to live with strangers ... that's very brave."

"He knows Tom and Hal. They go to Eden House. The other ... I don't know."

The following day when Billy and Michelle left Eden House, they started walking to Yoorooga, which was only a few kilometres away.

Josie had heard them discussing their plans earlier in the day. "Where are you two going?" She'd waved an accusatory finger at them.

"Michelle's coming to see Yoorooga."

"Stupid name. Stupid house," Josie said, then

wandered off.

The journey to Yoorooga didn't take them long. They walked by the side of the road, swinging hands. Here and there, the pavement gave way to a broad strip of grass. They turned into a cul-de-sac. Yoorooga overlooked the road where they were walking. Behind it was a garden, and beyond that a small clearing and much bush.

Billy raised himself up onto his tip toes. "There it is!" He waved towards a brand new brick house, on a hill at the end of the road.

Michelle looked at it and then at the other houses in the short road. They were all brick, with a generous space around each yard. All the gardens were tidy. Trees were clipped and the grass was mown.

Clean cars stood in driveways. She looked wistfully at the house next to Yoorooga. "It's like my house, in Sydney ..."

"You don't live in Sydney," Billy shook his head.

"Not now. We did ... before Poppy broke his legs."

"I'm glad you live here," Billy swung their clasped hands hard. "I couldn't see you ... if you lived in Sydney."

Michelle stopped and processed the information. Then she laughed and flung her arms around him, repeating, "I couldn't see you, if I lived in Sydney."

As Michelle disengaged herself from Billy, Hal plodded behind them. He waved, a small slow movement that seemed to come from the elbow only. He puffed slightly, "I couldn't catch you."

Billy struck the heel of his hand on his forehead. "Sorry Hal." Then he asked, "Where's Tom?"

"Probably home already," Hal nodded. "He walks fast."

When they arrived at Yoorooga, Billy went straight into the kitchen and put the kettle on.
Michelle laughed, "That's what Mum always does."
"Dad taught me to do it."
Billy showed Michelle around the downstairs area. He proudly opened doors to the laundry and deck at the back. He grabbed her hand and ran upstairs to show her his room. They stood in the open doorway.
Billy looked at the bed and drew Michelle towards him.
Si walked up the stairs. He extended a hand, "Nice to meet you Michelle. Billy's talked about you a lot." Then he turned to Billy, "Bring Michelle downstairs now she's seen your room. Guests don't go into bedrooms, remember?"
"Oh," Billy gave his bed a longing look. He squeezed Michelle's hand, "Come on downstairs. I'll make us a cuppa."
Ryan came through the door as Billy and Michelle were nearly at the bottom step.
"What youse been doing?" He leered at Michelle. "I know youse been doin' it." He prodded a finger towards Michelle, "I'll take you up there and an' do it too." He jerked his hips forwards and backwards.
Michelle shrank behind Billy.
As she did so, Si arrived at the bottom of the stairs, "Stop that, Ryan. Michelle is Billy's guest. Billy's been showing her around, and they both know guests don't go into bedrooms."

When Michelle got ready for bed that night, she stood in pyjamas and dressing gown, brushing her hair. She thought about Billy at Yoorooga, and wondered what it would be like to live in a house full of people who were not her family. Part of her was frightened. She remembered how much she'd hated the little cabin on the caravan park when they'd first moved. She walked back into the living room, where Trish and Neville were watching television.

Neville looked up, "Hey, what's up Princess?"

"Billy's house. Yoorooga. I was thinking …"

Trish switched off the television. She sat upright, "No, Sweetie. Absolutely no."

Michelle looked confused, "No, what?"

Neville reached out for her hands. He held them lightly and guided her to the sofa. "Tell us what you were thinking."

"Billy," she tried again. "At Yoorooga … only strangers … no family … must be lonely." She burrowed her head in Neville's chest and hugged him tight.

Trish let out a long-held intake of breath, "Sweetie, I thought you meant … "

The following day Trish sat at the dining table and wrote a letter, to her one-time best friend.

> Dear Francine,
> I know it's been ages since I've written, but we've been so absurdly busy, I haven't even had time

to scratch my head. The new holiday park is up and running. No more caravans! Think of that …

I'd love you to come and visit us now that we can offer you somewhere comfortable to stay.

Neville and Gareth are in the process of building a new restaurant where the old amenities block was. Since all the cabins are luxurious we don't need a separate shower block.

We still have a rather bizarre caravan – almost at the water's edge. It's become a sort of work in progress for Michelle, who makes quite quirky mosaics. One side is almost completely finished. I think you'd like it.

Do come.
Lots of love
Trish

Trish posted the letter on the way to collect Ed from hospital.

Michelle was torn between going to the hospital and missing a day at Eden House. In the end, she put a 'Welcome Home' posy and card in Ed's house before going off to the day centre.

Ed saw Michelle's flowers and card as soon as he entered the house. Next to Michelle's card was an envelope addressed to him in Lola's handwriting.

He smiled as he read Michelle's carefully-worded

message. He loved the big childish handwriting and knew it would've taken her a long time to write her short welcoming paragraph. She'd drawn a big heart and added a message that Billy sent his love too.

Ed put the card on the centre of the table and opened the envelope from Lola.

Lola wrote that she had given Trish some food to put in the fridge.

> ... no more muffins, I'm afraid. It's healthy food from now on. My friend Dot, gave me a few recipe books endorsed by the Heart Foundation, and Neville has been very helpful, too. I hope you enjoy the snacks I've prepared for you ...

Ed got up and went to his fridge. He saw a tub of home-made hummus and a small box with sticks of carrot, celery, capsicum and cucumber. It wasn't food Ed would normally have eaten, but Lola had been kind. He decided that he would at least try it. He dipped a carrot stick into the hummus, then tasted it. It was all right, but he craved something more substantial. He looked in a cupboard for a chocolate biscuit. In place of them, were a packet of oat biscuits and a note from his daughter.

> Sorry Dad, but these are much better for you.
> Love Trish.

"Hrumph," he tore the packet open, snatched a biscuit and plunged it into the hummus. It tasted better than he expected.

Ed walked slowly towards the coffee van. He wanted to thank Lola. He decided not to tell her that he didn't really like raw vegetables. As he approached, he could see a few people at tables outside. He scanned faces. None of them was familiar.

Lola saw Ed before he saw her. She broke into a huge smile. Her eyes reflected the sparkling sea as she came out of the van and wiped her hands on her apron. "How are you, Ed? Sit down. I'll make you a coffee."

Ed thanked Lola for the hummus and vegetables, then sat down.

Lola busied herself tamping coffee into the filter holder. "Are you going to have soy milk, or will it be black?" she asked.

"Soy, I guess. I can't stand black coffee." Ed gave a small chuckle, "I didn't expect you to know so much. There'll be no hiding, will there?"

"None whatsoever. It's all about looking after your heart from now on.

Chapter 21

Michelle wasn't as relaxed visiting Yoorooga as she had been at Billy's home. She was nervous of Ryan. Once the carers got to know everybody's work schedule, Coral suggested that Billy invite Michelle to lunch on a day when Ryan was working.

Billy went to the caravan park to collect Michelle.

Trish greeted him, "I'm sorry Billy, she isn't ready yet. Have a seat."

"Didn't she get the time right?" Billy rubbed one toe along the calf of his other leg. He didn't want to sit down.

Stella came into the room, "Michelle wanted to finish one of her mosaics. She didn't notice the time." Stella, too, indicated a chair.

Billy sat but he felt uncomfortable. He felt that Stella was staring at him. When Michelle came into the room he grabbed her hand and rushed off.

Billy was quiet on the bus. He could feel Michelle's hand creep towards his. He let his hand be taken but he stared straight ahead.

"What's wrong, Billy?" Michelle's voice was timid.

"You weren't ready. I had to wait with your mum and Stella. They don't like me. I felt all …"

Billy didn't talk anymore for the rest of the bus journey.

Michelle bit her lip and looked out the window. When they got off the bus they walked slowly along the road. Billy still didn't speak. Michelle's steps slowed down even more, until she was barely moving.

Billy stopped and turned towards her, "Come on. You're walking like a snail."

Michelle looked at a pebble on the ground in front of her. "I don't want to come, if you're like that." She rolled the pebble under her foot.

"Like what?" Billy walked back towards Michelle and tried to look into her eyes, but she still hung her head.

"You didn't talk on the bus," Michelle swallowed. I don't want to come if you don't talk to me."

"I felt uncomfortable with Stella. I don't think she likes me."

"She doesn't like me, either," Michelle cried.

"She's your sister."

"She still doesn't like me. Sometimes she can be nice." Michelle's eyes moistened as tears began to form, "but mostly …" Her lips trembled with the effort of not letting them fall.

Billy instantly forgot his own discomfort. "Oh, Michelle, I'm sorry. Make up?" He wrapped his arms around Michelle's heaving shoulders.

Michelle slowly stopped crying and nodded through her tears.

Billy dabbed her eyes with the corner of his tee shirt.

When they arrived at Yoorooga, Tom was chopping carrots.

"Soup. I'm making soup," Tom peered at Michelle through heavy lenses.

Michelle grinned, "I like carrot soup."

"Not you. You don't live here. Billy can have some. He lives here."

"Oh." Michelle looked at Billy, and her lips started trembling.

Billy put his arms around Michelle's shoulders. "We're going out."

Coral walked into the room, "What's this, going out? You've just got in. You've invited Michelle for lunch."

"Tom's making soup. He said not for Michelle. We're going out."

Coral turned to Tom, "Michelle is our guest. We invited her to lunch."

Tom stared at the carrots. "I didn't invite her. I don't want her here. I'm Billy's friend, not her."

Hal interrupted, "Michelle's his girlfriend," he emphasised the first part of the word. "It's different." He nodded a few times. "Girlfriends are different." Hal put his hand on Billy's arm, and craned his short thick neck to look up into Billy's face, "I'd like a girlfriend."

Billy's arm was firmly around Michelle's shoulder, and he squeezed her shoulder as Hal spoke.

Michelle smiled at Hal gratefully, and Billy scowled at Tom.

Tom refused to look at Billy. He savaged a carrot.

"We all pay for food. She doesn't."

Billy took his arm from Michelle's shoulder. He put a hand in his pocket and drew out a ten dollar note. "I'll pay for Michelle."

Coral looked at Billy's ten dollar note on the kitchen counter. "Put it away Billy. Michelle's our guest. This is not a good way to begin. We'll find a better way."

Over lunch Coral discovered that Michelle's father was a chef. She probed Michelle to find out what cooking skills she had.

Michelle smiled at Coral, "I can make an easy pizza … next time … I can bring things."

"Great, Michelle. We'll all look forward to that."

> Dear Trish
>
> It was lovely to hear from you. How interesting that your daughter is doing mosaics. You're right I would very much like to see them. I've never forgotten my wonderful year in Barcelona and those breathtaking, though rather mad, mosaics that seemed to be everywhere.
>
> It was kind of you to invite me to stay. I would love to take you up on the offer. My hectic work schedule comes to an end soon, so I'd love to come and stay at Pelican Bay next month.
>
> Love from Francine

Trish read the letter while perched on a stool at the kitchen counter. She put it down, thinking how lovely it would be to see Francine again. She began to plan small outings.

Billy discovered a short cut from the bus stop to Yoorooga. A large open park bordered with pines was a popular place for dog owners to exercise their pets.

A few weeks after Billy had moved in, he saw his next door neighbour, Roger, with a large pale Labrador. The dog jumped up at Billy, his paws scrabbling at Billy's chest.

Billy grinned and stroked the Labrador's head.

The neighbour remonstrated, "Down Boyo, down."

The dog obediently brought his feet to the ground, and continued wagging his tail.

Billy said, "It's all right. I like dogs."

"Boyo likes you too," Roger laughed.

"I wish I had a dog," Billy said, "But I don't think we're allowed at Yoorooga."

"You can walk Boyo sometimes if you want, Billy."

"Can I?"

" Sure. I often work long hours and Ingrid's so busy with the kids she sometimes doesn't have time to do much more than take him up and down the road." Roger looked into the distance. "The trouble is, a big dog like this, needs more exercise than we can give him."

"Can I throw the ball for him?" Billy asked.

"Sure," Roger handed Billy a long handle with a depression.

"What's this?" Billy turned it over.

"It's a ball launcher. Put the ball in this dip, then you can throw it a long way."

Billy launched the ball.

Boyo ran off yelping and brought the ball back to Billy's feet.

Billy repeated this a few times, each time with a bigger grin.

After a while, Roger smiled at Billy, "I have to go now. Just ring on the doorbell anytime, and ask Ingrid if you can take Boyo out."

Billy reached down and stroked Boyo's moving flank. "Bye Boyo. I'll be seeing you."

Michelle and Lola cornered Neville. Lola said, "We both need a bit of culinary advice. I hope you can help us."

"Of course, but I doubt it's the same advice." Neville smiled.

Lola shook her head, "Oh no. I want to take Ed to a Healthy Heart cookery course. It's a one day special up at Falconville Community College. Look, here's the brochure. He needs the idea to come from somebody other than me. D'you think you could suggest it?"

"Easy—done," he laughed accepting the brochure from Lola. He turned to Michelle, "… and what can I do for you, Princess?"

"I want to cook a pizza at Billy's house … What … to put on it?" Michelle's fingers were interlaced and she was turning them through a range of different angles.

"Good choice Princess. You know how to do that. I'll help you make the dough."

Michelle shook her head. "It's too hard. Can I start with that lav … you know that flat bread?"

"You can do that too, Princess. It won't be a real pizza. But hey, why not? You can take lots of different things to put on top; some tomato paste, bocconcini, basil, tomatoes, a bit of garlic and olive oil… a feast for kings. D'you want me to write it down for you?"

"Yes please." Michelle unknitted her fingers.

Billy rang Roger and Ingrid's doorbell.

Ingrid half opened the door. "You've come for Boyo. That'll be great. I'm up to my ears with the children today. He hasn't had any exercise." She passed a lead out to Billy.

Billy and Boyo spent half the morning playing in the park. Boyo was used to Roger, Ingrid or the children throwing the ball for a few minutes, but one by one, they usually got bored.

Billy, on the other hand, didn't tire of throwing the ball.

Eventually Billy looked at his watch, "I've got to go to work, Boyo. I'll take you home now."

Ed surveyed his fridge and various new packets, boxes and jars. He didn't know what to do with some of the items Trish had put in his cupboards. She had emptied them while he was in hospital. New, unfamiliar things stared at him. Lola had been helpful, but he felt he should try to work out what to do with some of them. "If I don't," he muttered to himself, "I'm going to have very boring meals."

He decided to take a few packets to Neville. He thought his son-in-law might be able to suggest something interesting to do with them. As he was thinking of this, Neville arrived at his house.

Neville brought a brochure. "Aha," he looked at the array of packets in front of him. "I think I have the very thing."

Ed looked at the brochure. "I'm not going to a cookery course. It'd tie me up for a whole term."

"This is just one day."

"Hrumph. Trish put you up to this. First, she emptied my cupboards and put strange things in them. Now she wants me to go off and do a cookery course. I'd feel a Pansy." Ed looked disconsolately at the packets in front of him. "Why can't you just tell me what to do? You're a chef."

"Yes Ed, that's the problem. I cook with butter and cream. They're no good for your heart."

"Mm," Ed grumbled. "Alright. You can leave it there," he waved towards the table. "I'll think about it."

Neville put the brochure down and left Ed's house feeling that he'd failed. *I'll have to tell Lola*, he thought. He sighed, remembering that Trish's friend Francine was due for the weekend. He'd hoped she wouldn't come until the restaurant was finished, but she'd written back almost immediately. It looked as if he would have to be dividing his time once again. He wanted to spend every minute on the restaurant, but he knew Trish wanted to give her friend a proper weekend away.

As he walked towards his own house he saw Michelle and Billy walking up the from the beach. Billy waved. Huge windmilling movements were accompanied by a wide grin.

"Where are you two off to?" Neville stopped and waited for them.

"The movies." Billy and Michelle chimed

together.

"That's good. What are you going to see?"

"Um. Don't know yet. I want to see the one in Italy …" Michelle answered.

"It's a girlie movie. I want the adventure movie," Billy said

They laughed, then looked at each other and shook their heads.

Neville joined their laughter, "Well, have a great time. See you later."

He watched them walk through the holiday park towards the bus stop. He realised with a jolt that Michelle had blossomed in confidence in less than a year.

Chapter 22

Billy and Michelle walked through the car park on their way back from Falcon Court. Two men were hitching the mobile blood unit to a truck. They worked quickly and efficiently, jumped inside their vehicle and drove off.

Michelle stopped. "Oh look, Billy, they're going. I wanted to …"

Billy followed her gaze. "Yeah. My dad gives blood. I can't though."

"Why not?"

"They make it too hard. Long forms. Fussy people. Not worth it." He shook his head and grabbed Michelle's hand.

Michelle smiled up at Billy's face and repeated, "Fussy people. Not worth it."

They arrived at Yoorooga, carrying green bags of groceries. Si greeted them. "This was Coral's idea, but we're the ones that gets to eat the pizza. I'm looking forward to this."

Ryan was lolling on a sofa. "You gonna cook?" He leered at Michelle. "I got better things to do with you—"

Billy moved towards the sofa. He towered over Ryan. "We're cooking." He spoke slowly. "You ... shut ... up ..."

Ryan opened his mouth, but said nothing.

Si nodded towards Ryan, "You deserved that."

Tom sat by the window with a word search book. He took his glasses off and polished them on his tee-shirt. When he put them back on, he shrank into a corner and glowered at Michelle.

Billy and Michelle were taking things out of bags at the kitchen counter. They didn't notice Tom.

Hal plodded into the living area. He stood a small distance from Michelle and Billy, and held his elbow tightly at his waist as he gave a small wave. He watched Billy for a while, then trudged over to the sink. He washed his hands carefully and said, "I want to help."

Billy looked at Michelle who raised her shoulders and dropped them quickly. She grinned at Hal and gestured to the food laid out on the kitchen counter. "You choose ... put on your base."

Hal looked at the food laid out on the kitchen counter. His forehead creased. There was much more than the cheese, tomatoes and basil that Neville had suggested.

Billy had rushed around the supermarket picking up ham, salami and anything else he had ever had on a pizza. He pushed a Lavosh bread across to Hal. "Here, you put on what you want and I'll put it in the oven."

Hal continued to look at the array of food. He took a small pinch of everything and put them in small heaps on his bread.

Michelle looked at him, "You …" she mimed spreading it out.

Si came and stood next to Hal, "What Michelle means is that you have to spread it out, or you'll just get little lumps."

Hal shook his head.

"Have a look at mine," Si took a piece of bread. He spread some tomato paste over it, then sprinkled cheese and tomatoes on top. "See. I've spread the tomatoes around and put the cheese everywhere."

Hal shook his head again, but began to put topping on his pizza base.

Ryan opened the fridge door and pulled out a jar of peanut butter. He spread the peanut butter over his bread, then plonked anchovies and olives top. He pushed his tray across to Michelle, who put it in the oven.

Tom looked at Billy's pizza. He carefully replicated all the topping ingredients. He saw Billy had chosen three black olives and three strips of anchovy. Tom carefully copied the layout on his pizza before handing it to Michelle.

At the end of lunch Si said it was the best pizza he'd ever eaten.

Billy grinned and agreed.

Hal's plate had small pieces of uneaten pizza, one with a mound of basil and one with a small pile of chopped garlic, but he too nodded, and put a hand tentatively on Michelle's arm. "Best pizza, Michelle."

Tom looked at his empty plate but remained silent.

Ryan sulked, "Yukky pizza. Peanut butter's no good on pizza."

Si said, "Well, you've only yourself to blame. You put the peanut butter on."

Ryan's chin jutted forward, "She didn't tell me not to." He brought his eyebrows together and stared hard at Michelle.

Billy reached for Michelle's hand under the table.

"It's not Michelle's job," Si said. "You chose peanut butter. You've learned something today. You've learned you don't like peanut butter pizza."

Trish received a brief letter from Francine who wrote that she was coming to stay the following weekend. Trish hurried to tell Neville … She found him and Gareth in the new restaurant, looking at lighting plans. They looked up and Trish told them the news.

"That's fine," Neville said, "but you girls will have to amuse yourselves, I'm up to my eyes in all this."

Gareth winked at her, "You never know Mum, we might be finished by then. If so, you can show her around."

Trish left them, wondering what she would actually do with Francine. Although Francine had been her closest friend at art college, they hadn't really seen much of each other over the years since then. Francine had a high powered job and had never married or had children.

Trish wandered down towards the coffee van. There was only a sprinkling of customers. Trish smiled at Ed, "C'mon Dad, sit with me while I have a coffee." When they sat down she told Ed about her misgivings concerning the weekend.

"Show her around a bit. She lives in the city doesn't she? Let her just experience this beautiful place. Take her for a bush walk at Squiggly Gums, or up to Heron's Point."

"Mm, thanks Dad." Trish scooped up small teaspoons of froth. She looked into the distance. "It would be nice to do something a bit different, like take her out on a boat or something. D'you have any boats left, Dad?"

"None that are safe in the water."

"What a pity." She continued scooping froth. "You ought to get them repaired, Dad. It's a waste, having them just sitting there. Will I get Neville or Gareth ..?"

"No," Ed was sharp. "I know you mean well. You've taken over the caravan park. Leave me my boats."

When Trish left, Ed let out a long breath. He hoped Michelle and Billy's secret hideaway wouldn't be discovered and taken from them. He picked up the coffee cups. As he straightened and turned, Michelle and Billy emerged from the Norfolk Pines at the south end of Pelican Bay. Billy had one arm around Michelle's waist and her head lay on his shoulder. They waved to Ed.

Billy pumped Ed's hand, "I'm going to work. The grass ... at the sports oval." He turned to Michelle, "You stay here with your poppy, I'll get the bus. See you tomorrow." He pecked her on the cheek and walked off through the holiday park.

Michelle looked at the tables. "D'you want any help, Poppy?"

"Not at the moment ... everybody's gone now.

I've even done the washing up. How about your mosaic? You could spend some time on that. You could have it finished by the weekend."

Michelle's feet were planted solidly, but her shoulders windmilled.

Ed watched her for a moment, "What is it, Princess?"

"It need something else ... I don't know what." She interlocked her fingers and stretched her arms out in front of her, then turned her hands palms out, and pushed away. She stood, with the upper part of her body swaying and her outstretched arms swinging.

"How about, you show me?" Ed held his hand out for Michelle, and together they walked around to the back of the coffee van.

The mosaic sparkled in the sun. Starfish, seahorses, octopuses and a variety of fish flashed and twinkled in the bottom third of the picture. Buckets, spades and beach umbrellas glimmered lazily from the sand section in the middle, but the top third, the sky, was simply the bright stark turquoise that Joe had left it the day he painted it.

Michelle waved to the top. She wailed, "I can't reach."

"Mm. We'll have to think about that, but there must be an answer. Let's ask your mum. Let's go back home and ask her now."

When they were a few yards away from the house, a smart silver car draw up. The door opened and a pair of sleek nyloned legs swung out.

Michelle gasped as red stilettos landed gently in the dust of the unmade road. She grinned at her grandfather.

Following the legs, came a small dainty figure in

a red polka dot dress. Perched on a slim neck was an elfin face framed with a sleek dark bob.

"I guess you're Michelle," the newcomer dazzled, an open smile showing even, pearly teeth. She turned to Ed, "And you must be Trish's dad. How lovely to meet you both. I'm Francine."

"Ah yes," Ed smiled. "Pleased to meet you. Trish is expecting you. Come ... let's go and find her."

Trish and Francine shrieked with excitement when they saw each other.

Over lunch, Francine talked to Michelle about her mosaics, "I can't wait to see what you've done to the coffee van. Trish wrote to me that you'd transformed it. Will you show me?"

Michelle nodded.

Trish said, "We can take Francine after lunch. We can show her the rest of the holiday park too."

Michelle jiggled on her seat. She wanted to show this elegant person her mosaic on the coffee van. She wanted desert and coffee to be over.

The girls walked towards the coffee van. Trish said, "It doesn't look much from the front."

Francine giggled as they approached the sand, "Oh dear," she kicked off her stilettos and slithered out of her stockings. "That's better," she wriggled scarlet-painted toenails in the sand, and carried her shoes carelessly.

The winter sun struggled to cut through the cool, crisp air. Shafts of light caught the shiny glazed pottery, shells and inset beads. Michelle's seascape gleamed.

Francine hugged Michelle. "You've done a great job. That's magnificent. Will you leave the top?"

Michelle started to cry.

Francine was shocked by her reaction, and Trish put her arm around her daughter's shoulders, "What is it?" she asked.

Michelle wailed, "I want things on the top but I can't reach."

"There are ways around that," Francine's voice was airy. "But I think it's quite effective as it is; the ocean with its abundance, the sand with those exuberant buckets and spades, and a big expanse of empty sky."

Michelle swivelled her head and looked at Francine, whose long words were not easily understood, but she did understand that Francine liked it as it was. Michelle's lips quivered, "You think ..."

"Absolutely."

They walked back towards the house. Trish said, "I'm taking Francine for a trip around the sights. D'you want to come?"

Michelle shook her head. "I'm going to see Lola," she grinned and pushed herself up so her bodyweight rested on her heels.

Trish and Francine drove off, and Michelle found Lola burrowing in the seat space under the built-in sofa in her caravan.

"Hello Michelle. Look at this!" Lola struggled with a bag full of golf clubs.

Michelle looked puzzled. "They're golf clubs. I didn't know ..."

"I didn't play. Not much anyway. These were Henry's. He played golf a lot."

"Um ... are you ..?"

"Goodness me, no. I'm going to give them to Ed. The doctors want him to get some exercise."

Michelle looked from the golf clubs to Lola. She processed this slowly, then said, "Golf means lots of walking."

"Yes, he could go up to the golf course at Heron's Rise. It's so beautiful there, people don't think they're getting exercise. They just think how glorious it is."

Lola examined the clubs. "My friend, Dot Barker, looked after them for me. She knew they'd rust if I kept them here. I went to get them back last month."

Michelle looked with surprise. "They're all greasy!"

"Yes. Henry was always very careful. After a game, he used to spend a long time cleaning, drying and covering them with grease. The grease stops rusting."

They wiped the Vaseline from the clubs, and wrapped each one in a clean towel, then Lola made mugs of hot steaming tea, and they munched winter radishes.

Michelle said, "Billy likes radishes. D'you think they could grow them at Yoorooga?"

"Of course. I'll see if I have any spare seed packets," Lola smiled. "I could put together a small box so you can take them to Billy. It could be a sort of house-warming present from us."

Trish and Francine arrived home late in the afternoon.

Neville said, "It's good to see you so happy, Trish. These last few months have been tough for you." He put an arm around Trish's shoulder and rubbed his cheek against hers.

Trish leaned against him and held the hand that was on her shoulder. She smiled at Neville, "We've had a wonderful time."

Francine looked away from the small demonstrations of intimacy. She said, "Trish has given me a marvellous guided tour of Falconshire. Maybe someone will give me a tour of the new restaurant …"

Neville said, "We'll do that after dinner. I need to get going in the kitchen, to make a dinner to remember for our lovely guest."

"Will I meet the rest of the family?" Francine asked.

Neville shook his head. "Afraid not. Gareth and Stella are in Sydney for the weekend. They arranged it a long time ago …"

During dinner, Francine commented on how much she admired Michelle's mosaic. "What's going to happen to it when the van goes?"

Michelle's mouth dropped open "Where's the van going? She looked anxiously from Trish to Neville.

Neville said gently, "Michelle, the coffee van was only ever going to be temporary. When the restaurant is completely finished, Gareth's team are going to come and build us a new café."

Michelle's trembled. The corners pointed down, and her thumbs rubbed each other slowly.

Francine looked brightly across the dining table, "You know what? I think it would be awesome if your brother could cut it out, when the time comes. It could become a feature somewhere … maybe even in the restaurant?"

Michelle's drooping mouth recovered, and she sat up, still trembling. Once more she looked from parent to parent.

Trish got up and put her arms around Michelle, "I don't think Dad's got as far as thinking about the art work. Give him time to think about it, Sweetie."

Neville nodded. "I'll need to measure walls, Princess."

After dinner Trish said to Neville, "I'll clear the dishes. You show Francine around the restaurant."

Neville took a torch, "Coming Princess?" he looked across to Michelle who was moving dishes into the kitchen.

"I've seen it. I'll help Mum clear up."

Francine and Neville walked across to the almost-completed new restaurant.

"Why d'you need that?" Francine waved towards the torch.

"The electricity isn't completely finished yet. The electricians underestimated the load needed in the kitchen."

"Some electricians!"

"I know. Gareth's team had been booked in somewhere else. We used a local company, but they refused to listen to me … and they overloaded the kitchen," Neville said. He opened the door and continued, "Don't take any notice of the ground floor. That isn't part of the restaurant. There are separate plans for that." He broke off and laughed, "That'll be Trish's baby."

Francine looked around the large bare room. "She wrote to me about that. But I believe it has to wait awhile."

Neville jiggled the keys, "We have to concentrate on the restaurant. When that's running smoothly, we can afford to start on her art studio. She told me she thought you might be interested in doing the occasional guest workshop."

"Mm. Possibly. It might depend ..."

They heard a scuffling sound behind them. Neville turned, "Hey Princess, What are you doing?"

"I brought you this." Michelle held out a tape measure.

Her father laughed, "Sure thing, Princess. Thank you."

After Michelle left, Francine feigned surprise. "Are you going to do that now?"

"Oh yes. The Princess won't forget. Anyway I'm here now, apart from showing you around, I'm not doing anything else."

Francine lowered her eyelashes. She murmured, "I can think of other things we could do."

Neville didn't hear her. He was looking at the largest wall. "Here, hold this will you?" He indicated the tape measure.

Francine put her hand lightly on his. It was an almost imperceptible stroking movement, barely begun before deftly moving to hold the tape measure down.

Measuring the wall took longer than Francine had expected. "Are you going to show me the kitchen?"

"Of course," Neville picked up the torch and they walked into the kitchen area. He shone the torch around, illuminating it bit by bit.

A small dark shape darted out into the centre of the room.

Francine jumped. She clung to Neville.

Neville laughed and disengaged himself awkwardly. "It's only a cockroach. We don't even have any food in yet, and the buggers have managed to find their way up here."

Chapter 23

Golf became part of Ed's weekly routine. Sometimes he grumbled that he didn't really enjoy it, but every Tuesday Joe called for him, and they generally stayed for a drink after their round.

A few weeks after Ed had started playing, he and Joe stood beer in hand at the bar. Joe said, "I caught a real good snapper, yesterday."

"I don't fish anymore, remember?" Ed growled. He hunched himself over his drink.

"Okay, then … what d'you want to talk about?" Joe stared into his beer. He'd forgotten Ed was so touchy. "We've done a thorough post-mortem on your diabolical game."

"It wasn't that awful. Better than last week, anyway." Ed could feel his voice getting petty. He needed to change the subject. "What have you been up to, apart from fishing?"

"I've been looking in the property pages. There are some good houses coming on the market."

Ed wasn't interested in the property market, but it

was better than talking about fishing. When he talked about houses he didn't feel the same yearning. He'd feign an interest.

Joe continued, "Yeah, two units up in Seaview Street, behind the chemist."

"Units! Who'd want to live in a one of them?"

"I dunno. Some people do, I reckon. There's a neat little weatherboard cottage near your place … other side of the road from your north boundary. That's for sale too. It needs a thorough reno, but I reckon it'd be a good investment for someone."

"That sounds more like it … you can show me where it is on the way back to the park."

Ed returned to the cottage later. He looked at it dispassionately. He guessed it was about fifty years old. The roof looked sound, but peeling paint and unfixed gutters gave the whole house a desolate air. The front garden had become a wilderness. Here and there patches of knee-high grass had been trampled. Ed saw the *For Sale* sign, and noted the estate agents. There was a high gate leading to the side yard and garage. Ed held on to the top of the gate and pulled himself onto his toes and peered over. Small piles of dog faeces lay on the path to the garage. The back yard was as much of a wasteland as the front.

The estate agent, Sally-Anne, wasted no time in responding to his call. She unlocked the front door of the house. Both she and Ed unconsciously wrinkled their noses at the musty odour of unwashed clothes.

Sally-Ann gave a small almost-nervous, laugh, "As you can see, the present owner is finding it all a bit much. He's going to live with his daughter in

Western Australia."

Ed nodded. He looked around the living area, which he thought might be light and airy if the windows were clean. He noticed a stained floral carpet, pointed to a corner that was loose. "May I ..?"

"Go ahead."

Ed lifted the corner to reveal floorboards. He sighed with relief. He knocked at walls, and felt the window frames and architraves. At the door to the kitchen he stopped in silent horror.

Sally-Anne began, "Yes, it needs ..."

Ed looked her straight in the eyes, "It needs to be pulled out. There is nothing salvageable in here."

Ed continued looking through the house. The ceiling looked all right, and he couldn't see any damp patches either there or on the walls. He saw two decent-sized bedrooms, and an ancient bathroom with stained red tiles and a scum lined bath. When he had seen everything he stood silently for a few moments.

Sally-Ann said, "I can tell you're interested."

Ed gave a small laugh, "You mean, if I wasn't, I wouldn't have bothered to see the whole house."

"That's it."

"I think the price is a bit high. Even you couldn't pretend it won't need a lot of work ..."

"Location, location, location." Sally-Ann's voice tinkled. "Look how near it is to the beach. Whoever buys this, will most likely knock it down and rebuild. People often pay more for a property when they can do that."

"Hrmph. Aren't the houses in this road protected? I'll check with the council."

Sally-Ann swallowed. She hadn't expected the old man to be quite so quick. She made a mental note to check. If he was right, it would definitely affect the selling price.

A helpful young girl at the council offices, confirmed that Ed was right. The houses in that road were protected. They could be thoroughly renovated, but not pulled down.

Ed and Joe were propped up in the golf club's bar the following week when Ed said, "I went to have a look at that cottage. It's a darned awful mess …"

Joe laughed, "I didn't think you were really interested. I thought you were just humouring me. So, why the interest?"

"Oh, I dunno. The family have pretty well taken over the caravan park, or 'Holiday Park' as it's now known." He shrugged, "That's all right. I'm happy for them to do it, but the next step is replacing the coffee van." Ed paused and took a long sip of his beer, then swivelled around to look at Joe. "I got to thinking … We made something of that, didn't we? It was a good feeling, making something good out of something old and beat up."

"Sorry, Mate. I don't think I know where you're going with this." Joe scratched his head.

"I'm thinking of buying the cottage as a project of my own. Nothing to do with the family. I want to do it up."

"Then what happens? You gonna move?"

"Nah. I'll rent it out, long term."

Ed found Lola sitting in front of her caravan. She was sorting through a box of seeds.

"Hello Ed. I'm trying to put together a pack of seeds for Billy and his friends at Yoorooga. Michelle thinks they'd like to grow some veggies. What d'you think of this selection?" She fanned out a dozen packets. "Or d'you think I should only give them the ones to be planted now? I could give them the others later."

Ed leafed through the packets, "Yup. Just give them the ones to be planted now. The rest would get lost. Give them in dribs and drabs."

Lola sorted them into smaller piles, and then grinned at Ed. "I was so happy when Michelle told me that you wanted the golf clubs. Did she tell you, we cleaned off the Vaseline and rewrapped them?"

Ed smiled when he saw the bag of clubs. He took an iron out and ran his fingers over the handle. "Just as well you took the Vaseline off. Most clubs call it cheating." Ed put the iron down. "I remember Henry going off to play with those. It's kind of you to give them to me Lola. I've been using Joe's spare set—they're not nearly as good as these. I'll let Joe know he can have his back. He'll be envious when he sees these."

Lola smiled at Ed's evident pleasure.

Ed continued, "I'll have to ask you to keep running the coffee van for me while I'm out on the golf course."

"Of course. I'll be happy to do that," Lola said.

Billy and Michelle waited for Ingrid to answer the doorbell. They could half-hear children running and the sound of Boyo barking, both muffled by a toddler's cries.

Billy grinned at Michelle, "Boyo knows I'm here. I took him out nearly every day last week."

Michelle held Billy's hand firmly, "I'm not used to dogs."

"You'll like Boyo," Billy said, then after a moment he added, "And Boyo will like you." He turned and kissed Michelle.

At that moment Ingrid opened the door. She was in an advanced state of pregnancy and a child hung onto her skirt. Behind her, a toddler hung on to that child. There was frantic barking behind them. Ingrid reached the lead across to Billy who tried to introduce Michelle, but Ingrid didn't seem to notice her. She said, "Boyo's really been looking forward to seeing you today, and I really need the break."

The young couple took Boyo into the park. The dog ran around Billy in circles. He jumped up and Michelle pulled back. Billy wanted to be out playing with Boyo. "C'mon Michelle, he only wants to play." There was a hint of irritability in Billy's voice as he pulled Boyo towards a park bench. He didn't see that Michelle's face was white with fear. "Look, we'll sit for a while. Let Boyo get used to you."

They sat down, but Michelle edged towards the far end of the bench. "I'm frightened," she wailed.

"There isn't anything to be frightened of ..."

Michelle recognised the impatience in Billy's voice. Her breathing became fast and shallow.

Boyo ran around the bench. He wasn't used to Billy sitting down. He yelped and pushed his nose towards the ball.

Michelle looked anxiously at Boyo. She was too frightened to speak.

Billy wanted to be out and about, playing with Boyo, but instead he held the ball out of the way and stroked Boyo's head. He said to Michelle, "You stroke him now. He's soft. You'll like it."

Michelle gingerly put out a hand and patted

Boyo's head.

Boyo moved his head out of the way.

Michelle pulled back.

Billy sensed Boyo was ready to play. He too, wanted to be running around the park instead of sitting on a park bench, but he held Boyo's head in his hands. He shook it gently, then said to Michelle, "You stroke his ears. You'll like it."

Michelle reached out for Boyo's ears. A wide smile crossed her face, "They're so soft," she breathed.

Boyo, sensing her relaxation, moved his head gently, lay down on the ground and rolled around.

Michelle knelt next to him and stroked the soft fur on his inner flanks.

Billy watched them for a few moments, then he got up and threw the ball. "C'mon Boyo."

When they returned the dog to Ingrid, Michelle said, "I was scared at first … but I liked it. I like Boyo."

The time came for the coffee van to be replaced.

Ed said to Michelle, "Everyone's going to miss your lovely mosaic. Could you make me a smaller one for the new café?"

"Oh, Poppy I will." Michelle threw her arms around Ed.

Ed's mates, Joe and Stan, moved the van out of the way and Gareth supervised the speedy building of new café. A tongue-and-grooved wooden decking area spread out from the café in a wide semicircle facing the ocean, and smart new tables and chairs gave the café a chic, though welcoming, new look.

The length of Michelle's mosaic from the coffee van was just right for the long wall in Neville's restaurant. It was, however, too tall.

Michelle wailed, "Where can it go?"

Gareth said, "You said the top was boring. How about we cut the top off? You don't have any mosaics on that bit, so nothing will be missing."

"Yes, please." Michelle rubbed the palms of her hands together, and make small clapping movements.

Neville looked at her carefully, "Are you sure Princess? Once we've cut it, we can't put it back."

Gareth said, "Look, I'll take a photo, then you can cut the top off the photo, and see if you like it."

Michelle nodded.

Gareth printed a few copies of the photos. He marked one copy to show the maximum height the mosaic could be. Michelle cut off the part above it. She looked at it for a few moments, then took another picture and ruled a line lower down. Again she cut off the top section and compared the pictures. She continued doing that until she had used up all of Gareth's photos.

Eventually she pointed to the photo with the least amount of sky, "I like this one best."

"Good choice, Princess." Gareth set about cutting into the caravan wall. Several of his team assisted and the process took longer than anyone expected.

Michelle returned as the men had just freed the mosaic.

Gareth said, "D'you want it like that, or d'you want a frame?"

Michelle looked at the jagged edges. "A frame."

"That's fine, Princess. I can do that, but it'll take a while. We'll store it safe and sound downstairs until

I have time to think about how to do it. Is that okay?"

Michelle nodded. "No problems."

The holiday park had begun to pick up custom. The initial newness had worn off and the quality of the cabins was evident. The gardens were elegant, which added to the feeling of understated luxury. The wealthier clientele had commented on how much they were looking forward to a proper restaurant. Gareth and his team worked long hours on the final push to get it finished. Neville had wanted a stylish spiral staircase, but Gareth knew it wouldn't pass building regulations for disabled. Their compromise was a flamboyant conservatory, which featured Neville's longed-for spiral staircase together with a curved lift, encased in glass bricks.

Trish decided it was time to tidy away many of the magazines and brochures the family had used while deciding on various aspects of the holiday park. She picked up a large glossy magazine which flopped open. She noticed an advertisement for *Master Builders Australia* award nominations. She read the article and looked at the calendar. There were three weeks until nominations closed. She put a post-it-note in the magazine and closed it. She looked out the window at the lush gardens surrounding immaculate cedar wood cabins.

Over the day, Trish's thoughts kept returning to the awards nomination form. She phoned Francine, who said that she thought the holiday park was splendid. She wondered, however, if building awards were for building, not for installing ready-made cabins.

Trish thought of the restaurant, so carefully set to make the whole park look stylish. That wasn't preconstructed in any way. She filled in the form and posted it.

Ed told Sally-Ann about his visit to the council offices. "All the houses in North Boundary Road are protected." It was hard for Ed to keep the triumph out of his voice.

Sally-Ann smiled weakly, "I know. I also did my homework." Since that news, she had had no other interested buyers.

Ed bought the cottage for a good price.

Roger answered the door, and smiled at Billy and Michelle, "Come in. Meet Una, the newest member of our family."

Ingrid sat in a chair holding a tiny baby. The two other children were on the floor by her feet. The eldest played with a train but the toddler sucked at a small piece of blanket and held his mother's leg.

Michelle took an involuntary breath, "Oh, she's so … so tiny."

Ingrid looked up, "We only came out of hospital this morning. I've tried to keep Boyo from being too jumpy around her. He really needs his walk today."

Billy asked, "Can we take him a bit further than the park?"

Ingrid frowned slightly, but Roger asked, "Where were you thinking of?"

"If we keep him on a lead on the road, we can go over to Cabbage Tree Reserve. Then he could run on the beach."

Ingrid's face was tense, "Are dogs allowed on the beach?"

"Yes, if we have bags for the poo," Billy grinned.

"I guess it would be all right then … " Roger agreed.

When they reached the beach, the young couple took Boyo off the lead. Michelle carried small blue plastic bags, and scrupulously collected Boyo's faeces when necessary. They took it in turns to throw the ball as they walked north. Boyo always returned with the ball in his mouth and his tail wagging.

An angry man ran over a sand dune and right up to Billy. A shiny bald patch on the man's head gleamed with ill temper. He shook a finger in Billy's face. "What d'you think you're doing? Clear up that mess at once." He gestured to a small pile of hardened dog faeces.

Billy looked at the man's red face, "Why?"

"Can't you see it says, 'Clean up after your dog'?" the man shouted, gesticulating to a sign.

A small woman came up behind him. She put a hand on his arm, "No need to get so cross, dear," she said. "They probably can't read."

Billy's eyes widened in anger. He took a deep breath. He was about to speak.

Michelle pointed to the faeces in the sand, "That's old poo," she waved the small blue bag she was carrying. "Boyo's poo's in here. It's still warm. Feel it, if you like."

Billy glared at the woman. "That's little dog's poo, anyway. I bet that dog belongs to old people."

Michelle and Billy walked home quietly. All the joy had gone from their day.

Michelle dropped the little blue bag in a bin at the end of the beach as they put Boyo on the leash for the journey home.

Boyo walked resignedly. Every now and again he tugged at the leash half-heartedly, but sensed that he wasn't going to be played with.

As they got nearer the house, Billy said, "Let's not tell them about …"

"Why not?"

"They might not let us take Boyo again." He looked at Michelle wistfully. "I'd like a dog. I'd like one just like Boyo. They won't let us have dogs at Yoorooga. I asked Coral."

Michelle said, "I'd like a baby, just like Una."

Billy stopped walking. He put his arms around Michelle. "We'll have a baby. It will be ours. No one can stop us."

Michelle buried her face in Billy's chest, and Boyo sensed the change in mood. He ran around them, and his lead bound them tightly together.

"Hey, you two are very quiet," Roger said when they handed Boyo over. "You haven't had a fight have you?"

Billy held Michelle's hand firmly. They smiled at each other, then shook their heads.

Chapter 24

An unopened letter lay on the breakfast table. Trish reached towards it.

Stella looked up from buttering her toast. "Don't even think of it, Mum."

"Look, the envelope says it's from the court house. Michelle isn't going to want to know about letters like that."

"You are a hypocrite, Mum. You were the one that drummed into us that Michelle should be treated like everybody else. All through our childhoods, that's what you always said. Would you even think of opening anyone else's mail? And anyway, whose fault is it, that she's even on the electoral roll?"

"Oh, Stella we've been through this a hundred times. It's important Michelle has as normal a life as possible."

"Yes, so you made her fill in that form. We sat around this table, and it took hours, if I remember rightly, and now the pigeons are home to roost, you want to undo it all." Stella stared at her mother across the breakfast table.

Trish looked away and sighed. "You're right of course ... "

Michelle read the letter slowly. Her lips moved and her brow furrowed. "Jury service," she looked at her mother. "That's when someone's in court because they've done something bad, isn't it?"

"Well, yes and no. It's when the police think they've done something bad. The person goes to court, and the jury decides if they have done that bad thing, or if they haven't. You'd be one of the people on the jury." Trish reached across the table for her daughter's hand. "You don't have to do it, you know. We can go to Dr Grey and get a certificate ... "

"I want to talk about it with Billy."

"Why?"

"You talk about important things with Dad. I want to talk about this with Billy."

Stella rolled her eyes and Trish took a deep breath. She bit her bottom lip before answering, "Sweetie, it's not quite the same."

"I want to talk to Billy about it." Michelle got up and put the letter in her bag.

"You've come on cleaning day," Coral laughed when Michelle arrived at Yoorooga. "We're all having a tea-break and sitting around outside."

Michelle went through to the deck at the back.

Billy almost collided with her at the door. "I thought I heard your voice." He rocked back with his weight on his heels. "I'll get you a cuppa?"

Tom looked at Michelle accusingly. "Why are you here today? Billy didn't say you were coming."

Michelle looked warily at Tom. "I want to talk to Billy about something."

"What?" Ryan stood next to her chair, towering over her.

She inched away.

Coral looked at him sternly. "Give Michelle some space Ryan, you're practically pushing her against the wall."

"The wall. Against the wall, eh? Yeah. I know what I'd like—"

"That's enough." Coral's voice was firm.

At that moment Billy came out with a mug of tea. He glared at Ryan. "I heard that. You stop!" Then he turned to Michelle. "What do you want to talk about?"

Michelle opened her bag and took out the letter. "It's jury service. I've got to be at the court house at nine o'clock on Thursday morning."

"Oh ... Um ... Gosh. That's when someone's done something very bad. Urr."

"Well, the person *might* have done something bad, or... or they might not. I think that's it."

Hal tapped his hands on the table. "Maybe you can find me a girlfriend at the courthouse, Michelle."

Billy looked at Hal crossly. "She isn't going there to find you a girlfriend, Hal. She's going to do jury service. It's important. Civic duty. We learned that at Eden House." He grinned. "Don't you remember, we had to pretend to have a court session?"

Billy looked around to see if anyone else remembered.

"I think it was before I went there," Michelle said in a small voice.

Hal was silent. Tom wanted to say he'd learned

about civics at school, but was afraid someone might call his bluff.

Ryan leered at Michelle, "You could get a nice juicy murder." He rubbed his hands together. "You might even get a rape. That would be exciting."

"Oh," Michelle started to hit her thumbs against each other. Her eyebrows crept together.

Coral spoke directly to Michelle. "I don't think you'll get anything like that. Murders and things like that aren't really very common. I did jury service last year. It was a very boring case … someone who'd tried to cheat the taxman."

"Ah," Michelle relaxed. Her hands lay in her lap.

Billy took her hands in his. "What did you want to ask me?"

"Mum said I didn't need to do it. She said Dr Grey would give me a certificate … but I thought … it's what adults do, isn't it? I want to do all the things grown-ups do."

Billy nodded. "You do what you want to do." He looked into the distance then back at Michelle. "But only do it if you want to. Don't do it 'cos it's what adults do. Lots of adults do really stupid things."

The next day seemed very long to Michelle. She talked to Lola about the jury summons. Lola gave her much the same advice as Billy, then she talked to Neville who said he thought Trish was probably right, but said it was after all Michelle's decision. She really wanted to talk to Gareth, but he was in Sydney. She thought about asking Stella, but remembered the rolling eyes.

She tried talking to Ed who simply said, "I'm not going to make your mind up for you. That's what you have to do for yourself, but if you do want to go, I'll drive you there."

The next day was Sunday. Michelle got up and ate her breakfast without her usual chatter.

Trish tried to make eye contact, but Michelle refused to look at her. Eventually Trish broke the silence. "What are you doing today, Sweetie?"

Michelle put milk and butter in the fridge and returned to the breakfast table. "We're going to walk Boyo, then we'll watch a DVD at Yoorooga."

Trish nodded. "Well, have a nice time … and don't forget your sunscreen."

Trish smiled at Michelle as she arrived home. "Did you have a good day?"

"Yes. Look, no sunburn."

"That's good. What DVD did you watch?"

"It was called Twelve Angry Men. It didn't help much."

"Twelve Angry Men. Isn't that about a court case? It's a classic. How did you ..?"

"Grant told us about it. He thought it would help, but I didn't really understand it. I don't …" Michelle looked at her mother and her bottom lip began to quiver. "I wanted to …" small tears began to roll down her face. "I don't think I want to do jury service. "

Gareth tugged at the uncomfortable black tie. He hadn't wanted to get dressed up like a penguin but his family had insisted it was de rigueur. They'd told him that if he was to accept a prestigious award at a posh hotel, he had to look the part.

He took a glass of champagne from a passing

waiter and looked around the room. He saw Max and Adrian, owners of the company he'd worked for when he was starting out. Gareth recognised the girl by Max's side. Bethany had been a young receptionist when he'd worked for Max nearly ten years earlier. She hung on Max's arm and a plain gold band shone from a finger on her left hand.

Max clapped Gareth on the shoulder, "Congratulations, Mate. We were sorry to lose you, but hey, look what you've done in the last eight years ... and now this! I reckon it was that clever conservatory that really swung it."

Adrian added his congratulations and said, "I used to know the old caravan park. My family stayed there when I was a kid. I never dreamed it belonged to your grandfather."

"Thanks," Gareth smiled. "You'd be surprised how many people say that to me."

Max put his arm around his wife, "You remember Bethany, don't you?"

Bethany flashed a smile of expensive dentistry. She presented her cheek for an air kiss, "Max has been talking about you ... ever since we knew you'd won the award. He also told me about ... er ... Fliss." She looked down for a moment. "The only reason I'm mentioning it, is because she's here tonight."

Gareth felt as if he'd been hit. "Wh ...why?" he stammered.

Adrian lifted his glass, "You're being fêted big time. I think she wants a piece of the action."

Gareth ran a hand through his hair, "But we're no longer together. She ditched me nearly six months ago."

"I didn't know ... " Adrian looked at Max and

Bethany, who glanced away. He continued, "Looks like she's here for you tonight, so you'd best think how you're going to deal with it."

"Thanks for the warning."

The awards were made and Gareth forgot about his earlier conversation with Max and Adrian. As he left the stage he found himself face to face with Fliss, who reached forward and kissed him on both cheeks, leaving small red blotches on either side of his face.

Fliss giggled, then delved into an elaborately decorated handbag and produced a tissue. She proceeded to furiously rub Gareth's cheeks. "Sorry, babe," she simpered.

Gareth tried to step back, but the stage was in his way. He couldn't move forward as Fliss was too close. He thought of trying to sidle sideways, but knew she would close in and brush against him.

"I'm not going to eat you," Fliss laughed. "I'm just here to congratulate you. Isn't it great that you got that award? Maybe we should get back together again."

"Fliss, you ended it, remember?"

"Yes, but now you've got the … " she hesitated before the next word, which she pronounced slowly and carefully, "park," Then she continued normally, "up to scratch, you'll be coming back to Sydney, won't you? We can pick up where we—"

"No, we can't. Not in a million years."

"Don't be like that, babe," Fliss pouted.

"Like what? Once upon a time, we were engaged. You broke it off. There's no more to be said. Now, if you'll excuse me …" Gareth tried to edge around Fliss.

Fliss, obstinately twirled her champagne flute.

"My glass is empty, Gareth. Would you fetch me another drink?" She held out her glass.

Gareth took the glass and walked past her. When he saw a waiter, he gently slid both his glass and Fliss's glass onto the tray, and made for the door.

Trish made an appointment for Michelle to see Dr Grey.

"You've been on the pill for six months, Sweetie. Dr Grey said that about now, she'd want to see how you're doing."

Michelle remembered the fight they'd had when Trish took her initially. "I'm seeing her on my own!"

"That's fine, Sweetie. I can drop you off tomorrow morning. I've got some shopping to do. I'll pick you up later."

"No, it's okay, Mum. I'll get the bus."

Michelle phoned Billy. "I'm going to see Dr Grey tomorrow. I want to see you after. I can get the bus to Yoorooga."

Billy made whoops of delight, "Great. See you then."

Michelle thought about telling Dr Grey that she didn't need her prescription, but Dr Grey had been called away that day, and there was a locum instead. Michelle sat tongue-tied and allowed the young locum to take her blood pressure. She mumbled answers to questions she didn't understand, guessing the replies she thought the locum wanted to hear, and left the surgery with her prescription.

When Michelle arrived at Yoorooga, Billy was

sweeping the floor. He greeted Michelle and said, "Ryan always has Coco-Pops for breakfast. He eats them dry and they go everywhere." He looked at Michelle brightly, "but now you're here I can stop. We'll have a cuppa."

They took their tea into the yard at the back, and past the deck, to the end of the garden where a table, chairs and a padded swing were set up in the shade of large she-oak.

Michelle and Billy sat in the swing, their mugs on a nearby table. Michelle thought about two young mothers she'd seen waiting in Dr Grey's surgery. One of them had said she was cross with herself, because she'd forgotten to take her pill and had become pregnant. As they swung gently, Michelle told Billy about the two young women.

Billy said, "It's easy. We want a baby. You can just stop taking the pill."

"We could have a baby like Una."

"Mmm. Might not be a girl. Don't think we can choose … "

Michelle cuddled up to Billy. "Doesn't matter. Any baby would be nice."

When Michelle returned home, she tried to tell her mother that she didn't want to take her pills anymore, but Trish was preoccupied with the restaurant and her own plans.

As the restaurant neared completion, Trish concentrated on her art studio and her aim to attract wealthy Sydneysiders to her art courses in beautiful and luxurious surroundings. Although the space below the restaurant had originally been earmarked for Trish's project, she started to worry that Neville might want to expand the restaurant. She decided to confide in Ed.

Trish walked down to the new café and saw Michelle wiping tables and tidying the small containers of sugar and stirrers. "Hello, Sweetie. I need to talk to Poppy. Is he out the back?"

Ed made Trish a coffee, which she sipped facing the ocean. "I've been thinking," she said.

Ed waited. "What's on your mind?" he asked at last.

"If the restaurant is really successful, Neville might want to use downstairs too. I'd need somewhere different for my studio. I wondered about your old boatshed."

Michelle stood, cloth in hand, behind Trish's chair. Her mouth dropped open in horror.

Ed pretended he hadn't seen Michelle's reaction. "I'm afraid not, Trish. A man likes to have a shed, you know."

"Ah, but it's so well located. It would be wonderful … I'm sure Gareth would build you a new shed somewhere else."

"No!" Ed's voice was definite. "It's mine. Leave it alone."

Trish felt hurt. That was the second time he'd warned her off. She reminded herself that he was seventy-eight and entitled to be a bit cranky if he felt like it.

The glorious summer turned to autumn. The holiday park was becoming known among affluent city dwellers in search of privacy and luxury. Stella had postcards made of *Pelican Bay Holiday Park*. She'd used a photograph of cabins screened with glossy-leaved climbers, on pretty wooden trellises. The surrounding gardens featured architectural plants and exotic flowers. The sparkling sea glinted in the background.

Trish took one of the postcards and wrote to Francine.

> Dear Francine,
> Life should be very exciting right now, but I feel sort of let down. Neville's restaurant is beginning to take shape. As you know, I wanted to have an art studio underneath it, but crazy as it sounds, Neville has been talking of expanding, even though he hasn't even opened yet! I think he might want the downstairs space.
>
> This morning, I asked Dad if I could use his old boat house for my studio. He not only refused, but nearly bit my head off.
>
> Please write back and cheer me up.
>
> Lots of love, Trish

Francine phoned a few days later, full of sympathy. She promised to visit for a few days, so they could have some girly outings together.

Francine's visit coincided with the beginning of work on the new art studio beneath the restaurant.

Trish greeted her enthusiastically. She pulled Francine along to see the progress that was being made. "Oh, Francine, it's so wonderful."

"But I thought ..?" Francine picked daintily through the rubble.

"So did I ... but I was wrong," Trish spread out her arms. "I got to keep this lovely space for my studio."

Francine looked around the light airy room. "How will you advertise? It'll be costly."

"I'm leaving that to Stella. She still does the occasional bit of freelance work in Sydney. She stays with friends these days, because we don't have a house there anymore."

They all sat with drinks in the early evening, and Francine asked about Michelle's coffee van mosaic.

Neville said, "Yes, we got it cut out and put up. It's a huge feature on one wall."

Gareth added, "It was quite a mission. We had to add battens to strengthen it, and then there was the problem of a frame."

"Why was the frame a problem?"

"We quite liked the look of it cut rough, but Princess said it was untidy. Now it's got a proper frame."

"I'd love to see it *in situ*," Francine murmured.

Trish put a hand on Neville's arm, "Why don't you show Francine? There's time before dinner. You're off duty. Gareth's promised to do a barbie, remember."

Neville got up. "Okay." He turned to Trish, "Are you coming?"

"No. I'll set the table and attend to dinner. With luck, Gareth will have the meal ready when you come back."

Trish watched Francine in her high-heeled boots.

She remembered the red stilettos of her first visit. The shiny city footwear looked just as out of place as the red stilettos had done, but then Francine had always looked immaculate. Trish sighed and tucked a wisp of hair behind her ear. She couldn't remember when she had bothered to wear anything more exciting than a tee shirt with jeans.

Francine stepped over the threshold of the new building, and exclaimed, "But it's not much further on than it was last time I saw it."

"Tell me about it," Neville groaned. He leaned against an unfinished cupboard and smiled at her, "Anyway, it wasn't very long ago, that you were here, was it?"

"It seems a very long time ago," Francine murmured softly ..."but do go on. Tell me what happened?"

"The electricians finally sorted what they had to do, but by the time they'd done it all, our eight week plan was out the window. Then we had to wait for half the kitchen equipment, which had been ordered from overseas ... then the wrong lot came and ... " Neville stopped and pushed his fingers through his hair.

Francine had edged closer to him, "You poor man," she gently touched his shoulder, and brushed her cheek along his upper arm.

Neville didn't seem to notice. He stood up and shook his head. "What a whinger I've become." He gave a small laugh. "It's sort of back on track now. I think we've only got another eight weeks, then the restaurant really will be open." He turned towards Michelle's mosaic and said to Francine, "This is what we're here for. What do you think of it?"

"It's stunning. Is it going to have spot-lights on it?"

"Don't think so."

"How about those theatre lights set in the frame?"

Neville laughed. "The Princess wouldn't appreciate that. She agonised for ages about the frame. We couldn't desecrate it."

Francine smiled up at Neville through thick inky lashes. She put her hand on his forearm, and he could smell her perfume. She was disturbingly close.

"Well, thank you for showing me," she purred.

As they left the restaurant, Neville removed her hand from his arm.

During the next few weeks, the remains of the kitchen equipment arrived. Neville said to Trish, "I reckon we're ready to resume our opening plan."

Trish put her arms around Neville's shoulders, "Great! Do you have an EDD?"

"What's that?"

"Well," Trish laughed, "When a woman's expecting a baby, the medical profession refers to an expected date of delivery. I just felt … "

Neville laughed, "Yeah. I guess about six weeks from now."

They looked at the huge plan they'd started months earlier. They selected a date and marked it in the plan, then ticked off the things they'd already done.

"We've achieved more than I thought. Licences, suppliers and so on. It looks really good," Trish said.

"We'll need to get Stella on to publicity."

Stella created a grand-opening schedule. She set up interviews with the local newspaper, carefully timed for just before and after the opening day. She bombarded Neville with questions regarding details of every deadline imaginable. "I'm not committing to a definite date until I feel sure you'll be ready by then."

Neville produced a spread sheet with all the steps covered. Both of them worked closely, covering as many eventualities as possible.

"You do know, Dad, that the worst thing that could happen is for all of us to be prepared and then have some big-news disaster crop up. The media would leave us cold, and follow the trail of blood."

"How very cynical of you, Stella."

"That's just one of the things I was taught as business school," Stella shrugged.

Trish and Stella shared the day-to-day organization of the holiday park. Running the office was fairly straightforward, but the new cabins needed cleaners, and a reliable laundry had to be found. Gardeners had to be employed to keep the park in order. This, together with planning the new studio, kept Trish's days long and busy. She barely had time to run Gareth to the airport for his Gold Coast visit, where he was to help design an upmarket holiday complex for a big consortium.

Ed was still officially running the new café, but he didn't find it as satisfying as the old coffee van. He had more customers, even some who drove regularly from nearby towns. They all called it 'the café with the best view in Australia'. He also had to employ staff; two young Vietnamese girls and a student nurse who wanted to supplement her income.

About the same time that the café became more

successful, Ed took possession of the cottage he had bought. He and Joe began renovations.

Michelle was left on her own for much of the time. The café wasn't much fun for her without her grandfather. Neville and Stella were always poring over the spreadsheet for the grand opening and Trish was constantly either advertising for a new employee or interviewing one. Lola was away in the south, visiting a sick relative.

Michelle and Billy continued to spend as much time together as they could. Nobody seemed to let her get a word in edgeways when she attempted for the second time to announce that she and Billy had decided they wanted to have a baby.

Chapter 25

In the weeks preceding the restaurant's opening, Michelle and Billy delivered flyers. They walked for hours, covering the areas around Eden House, Yoorooga, Grant's house and finally the immediate vicinity of the holiday park.

When they walked along the row of cottages to the north of Pelican Bay Holiday Park they came across Ed and Joe working on the dilapidated cottage. The roof and gutters had been replaced. All the carpets had been removed and Ed was supervising a man who was sanding floorboards. The young couple stood on the grass at the front, looking at the working men.

Billy pumped Ed's hand.

Michelle looked through the dust to the sander, "Why are you doing that, Poppy?"

"We all like to have something special to do, Princess. You've got your mosaics, Gareth's got his building. Your mum and Stella are running the park and helping your dad. He's got the restaurant. This house is my special thing."

Michelle thought about it. "When you finish it ..?"

Before Ed could reply, Billy interjected, "Are you going to live here?"

"Nah. I'll rent it out," he grinned. "I guess I'll have to have a new project after that, eh?"

Billy and Michelle waved 'goodbye', and continued on their way. They'd delivered the day's flyers so they walked along the beach until they came to the south end of the bay. When they reached the boatshed, they looked around, then opened the door, closed it quietly and slid onto a pile of doonas.

The restaurant opened with a fanfare of local publicity. Stella had mobilized the local press and radio station. Neville had been persuaded to join the local Chamber of Commerce, and even had an informal pre-opening for family and friends the week before. Turquoise and white balloons fluttered at the entrance to the holiday park. Pelicans Restaurant was open for business.

Small magnetised cardboard fish in a glass tank waited for guests who would be given rods with string and magnets to catch them. A one meal special offer was written on each fish ... for free coffee or desert or fifty percent off their return visit.

The initial big night was a huge success, but after that the local custom slowed. Trish could see the disappointment on Neville's strained face. She said, "It's a bit of a letdown after so many months of preparation."

Neville put his arms around Trish's shoulders, "We can only afford the wages bill on the basis that business will pick up. We said that to start with we'd only open on the weekends in winter." He gave her a brief hug, "It's not as bad as it could be."

Trish hesitated then said, "This might sound odd, but would you be able to do a sort of limited opening in the week? I mean, we have a few guests who would love to eat out, but I there aren't really enough people to warrant opening the restaurant."

"Mm, in theory you're right, but just opening the kitchen eats away the money. We wouldn't cover our costs."

"That would be enough though, wouldn't it, if we could just cover our costs … the beginning, I mean. We don't have to make a profit. Right now, it would just be a matter of getting custom, and a name."

Michelle stood in the doorway. She'd just arrived home from Eden House. She looked at her parents, "What about the café?"

Neville didn't seem to have registered her appearance.

Trish answered, "What about it, Sweetie?"

"It's smaller. You could do weekday, easy meals in there."

Trish got up and hugged her daughter, "That's a great idea … We'll have to give that serious thought."

Neville rubbed the back of his neck. "We'd have to think very carefully about the menu, about how many people …?"

The next day they placed a blackboard outside the café announcing that it would have evening openings on Wednesdays and Thursdays.

Neville offered a limited menu. He cooked and the family helped. Pelicans Café was not going to be part of Pelicans Restaurant.

It flourished, and soon Neville had to call in the girls who worked in the café during the daytime. The café led to greater interest in the restaurant, which began to fill up at weekends.

Francine paid a midweek flying visit. She arrived in the evening and ate at the café. She was the last person eating. She looked up at the girls serving her. "It's getting late. Why don't you go home now? I can help Neville clear up."

The girls happily skipped off.

Neville came out of the café, "Where are ..?"

"I sent them home. It's my fault they're here so late, so that was the least I could do. I'll help you clear up."

"Help me? You've just landed me in it. I usually go home and leave them to do it," he said irritably.

"I'm so sorry, Neville. Here, let's sit and have coffee, then I'll do it all." Francine patted the seat next to her.

"I don't think you quite understand what you've opted for," he laughed.

"Oh, I think I do," Francine's voice was soft and throaty.

Despite Neville's tiredness, he understood the implicit invitation in Francine's voice, her physical proximity, musky perfume soft hair that brushed against him as they washed up.

He edged away, locked up and bid, 'Goodnight' to Francine. He couldn't wait to tumble into bed next to his sleeping wife.

The family didn't have time for one event to be fully appreciated before another project was under way.

The restaurant had picked up and reviews were good. Neville didn't even notice when Francine's visit was over. He was juggling weekday nights at the café with weekends in the restaurant, and worked frantically to keep them both running smoothly. Trish began to finalize her new studio. Husband and wife hardly saw one another.

About a month after Francine's visit was over, the restaurant suddenly received a visit from a prestigious food writer. Neither Neville, nor any of his staff noticed him in the dining room. As it happened, this particular famous food writer liked to be incognito if he possibly could. The anonymity in Pelicans Restaurant suited him. He wrote a glowing account of his mouth watering meal at a newly designed holiday resort. The article was written in a magazine read by wealthy Sydneysiders, who began to book small weekend retreats at the holiday park and special celebratory dinners at Pelicans Restaurant.

The favourable review brought unexpected excitement from Stella. "Look, he's called our park Pelicans Resort, instead of Pelican Bay Holiday Park. That sounds so much better!"

The family considered a name-change. Trish said, "I don't know Stella, we've spent a lot of money on rebranding already."

"Well, in a few of our recent bookings, people have actually queried Pelicans Resort? The cost of the initial rebranding wasn't really much ... Let me do the costings to see what we could do."

The café was doing too well to be closed down, but Neville knew he needed to spend his time at the restaurant. One of the chefs, agreed to work in the café during the week to reduce the pressure on Neville. This meant shorter hours for the chef and complete control over the kitchen, so he was happy with the deal.

Gareth came back from the Gold Coast for the weekend. Stella helped Trish with publicity for the art studio as well as trying to work out the cost of the rebranding. The afternoon before Gareth was due to go back to the Gold Coast, the family decided to have a conference about the possible renaming. They sat in the family living room with sheets of figures.

"I'm still not sure about this," Trish said.

"I think Sis is right," Gareth replied. I know it's a lot of money, but we must get away from the 'Holiday Park' image. So far, it's been okay, because our guests have understood that things are in a state of flux."

Neville added, " I think the young with money will come to a resort, whereas they might not come to a holiday park."

Stella looked from parent to parent, "I've done some mock-ups. They're in the office. Gareth, come and help me bring them in."

Gareth and Stella went into the office, and Neville said he had something to check in the restaurant. He promised not to be long. Trish sat poring over columns of figures. She knew that if she concentrated really hard, she would understand them. Anything to do with figures in columns gave her a headache. Nothing that Michelle could say at that particular moment would break her concentration.

Michelle came in and put her arms around her mother's neck, "Billy and I want to have a baby."

Trish gazed at the figures. She thought she'd

understood that first column of numbers.

"Umm, Sweetie." She put her hand on Michelle's. It seemed a long time since Michelle had put her arms around her neck. Trish smiled at the warmth of her daughter's arms, feeling sure that Michelle was only giving her news of her day. She said absently, "That's good," then returned to the numbers in front of her.

During the following weeks, the decision to change the name to Pelicans Resort went ahead. Attention was turned to Trish's art courses.

Stella lined up all the magazines she thought Trish should use for advertisements. She and Trish had designed brochures for the artistically inclined of Sydney's wealthy population.

Michelle walked into the office where Stella was working. She looked at the brochures, "They're pretty."

Stella smiled at Michelle, "Yes, they have to be perfect. This new project is like Mum having a new baby."

"Billy and I want a baby." Michelle felt sure she had her sister's attention.

"What?" Stella spun around in her chair and grasped her sister's wrist. "Don't be so stupid and thoughtless!"

Michelle tried to wriggle her wrist free but Stella held it firmly.

"Why?" Michelle struggled free. She rubbed her wrist and stuck out her bottom jaw. She looked angrily at Stella.

Stella released Michelle's wrist, ran her fingertips over her forehead and gestured her sister to a chair,

"Look, just think about it. Who would look after the baby? Mum. It would be Mum, wouldn't it? You'd be trotting off to Eden House and doing your mosaics and it would be good old Mum, with too much on her plate as it is. No Michelle, seriously, don't even think about it."

Michelle knew she wasn't expected to answer. She rubbed at her wrist again, then left the room. She wanted to go to see Lola, but remembered that Lola was still away. Michelle walked across the road to the cottage that Ed was still renovating. Nobody was there. A tear trickled down her cheek as she walked back to Pelicans Resort, and through the screening of pine trees, to Lola's caravan.

The familiar table and chairs had been packed away, but Michelle knew Lola had left one chair around the back. She sank into it and looked out across the vegetable patch. Guiltily, she remembered she had promised Lola she'd weed it while she was away. She wiped away the tears with the back of her hand, and stooped down to feel under the caravan for the small container in which Lola kept trowels and various small gardening tools. Starting at the back of the vegetable patch, she weeded methodically down the rows until she had finished.

Chapter 26

Francine arrived to help with setting up the art studio. Over fish and chips, she, Trish and Stella discussed different ways to present art packages,

The following morning Trish said, "Neville, I'm sorry Darling, but I won't be able to get to the bank. We need to get the takings in."

Neville groaned. "Do I have to? It's my only time off before the weekend rush."

Francine looked from wife to husband. "Come on, Neville, you know how much Trish took on when you were trying to set up the restaurant. It's only fair you do the same for her, now. Anyway I've never been to that new big shopping centre. I could do with some retail therapy, while you go to the bank."

"Okay," Neville grumbled. He got up and pecked Trish's cheek. "Bye Darl."

"It's not a very big shopping centre," Francine laughed as they arrived at Falcon Court. "Michelle told me it was enormous. I thought it would be at least as big as East Gardens." Black inky lashes fluttered, and she ran her tongue over immaculate scarlet lips.

"Well, Michelle does have limited horizons as far as shopping centres are concerned. She's never been very worldly. Trish used to buy all her clothes at some chain store. Michelle only discovered this place when Stella brought her here after the knife attack."

"Knife attack! Are you serious? When was this?"

Neville frowned. "I thought you girls told each other everything. I find it hard to believe Trish didn't tell you about the yobbos who threatened Michelle."

Francine's silky bob swished as she shook her head.

"No, Neville. We don't tell each other everything," she purred softly.

"It was a couple of years ago, not long after we moved up here. Michelle wasn't hurt, but her clothes were wrecked and she was very frightened. We got rid of the hoons. Luckily their tenancy agreement was up."

"And Stella brought her here?"

"Yes, and got her a whole new wardrobe. That's why she thinks of the place as Santa's grotto."

Francine laughed, a full deep throaty laugh.

"I see. London, Paris, Milan. Falcon Court, here we come." She opened the door and swung long sleek legs out of the car on the hot tarmac.

The shopping centre was bordered by cafés and pubs. As they passed a noisy country-themed pub, a young man fell out the open door, spilling his beer over Francine's dress.

"You clumsy oaf!" she shrieked.

The man blinked into the sunlight. He wobbled back towards the door and stood in the entrance staring at Francine. "Hey Girly, you got beer all over your dress." He lurched towards her once more, "Here, let me—"

Neville grabbed his wrist. "I think you've done enough. Just go back in there, sit down and sober up.

Francine started laughing. "Well now, I'll just have to buy a new dress, though I'm not sure going into a shop looking and smelling like this is my ideal way of shopping."

Neville met Francine at the agreed time after he'd been to the bank and she'd been shopping.

"Wow! That's some dress."

"You like it?" she twirled around. As she completed her turn, Neville saw eyelets from hem to neckline. Crossed ribbon fastened the top of the dress which was scooped low. "Come let's celebrate my dress. Let's go to a bar ... not that nasty one." She shuddered and they walked along the outside of the shopping centre, appraising all the cafés and pubs.

They sat in a dim bar with old fashioned jazz drifting from the speakers. Francine perched on a bar stool sipping a cocktail.

"That suits you. The dress, you sitting with your drink, the whole thing."

"I've always had a penchant for things like this. It's rather like bondage. I like that too." She ran her tongue over her lips and lowered her lashes. "Don't you think you should phone Trish?"

Neville got out his mobile. "Hey Darl, you'd hardly credit it." He told Trish about the drunk ruining Francine's dress. "Yes, yes, well what d'you expect ... yes, she's a bit shaken. Look we'll just stop for a couple of drinks then we'll be right back."

"D'you think she believed you?" Francine put a soft hand on his arm.

"Why on earth not? A drunk did spill beer all over your dress." Neville shook his head.

"Ahh ... We *could* have been doing something completely different." She reached out an elegant toe and stroked his ankle. Francine tilted her head to one side, letting her hair swing.

Neville saw the glossy bob, the faultless makeup and mischievous smile. He thought how long it'd been since Trish had smiled at him in that way. He couldn't help looking at the ribbon tied so carelessly at the top of her dress. Francine leaned over and kissed him. It was a long time since Neville had been kissed like that.

"C'mon, outta here," he held her wrist and dragged her towards his car.

He pushed her roughly into the passenger seat and drove silently south with set lips, intently watching the road.

Francine wriggled down in the seat. She looked up at Neville from under her lashes.

Neville could sense the smoky eyes next to him. He remembered the long luxurious lashes, and swallowed hard.

Francine watched his Adam's apple move. She looked for the Pelican Bay turn-off. As Neville drove past it, she inched herself up the seat and her breathing became audible.

Neville didn't look at her, but he could hear her

breathing. He could sense movement next to him, but he refused to look.

After a few kilometres, he swung the car into a small side-road leading to a reserve. He drove the car to the edge of a tiny rough hewn car park and stopped. He inhaled musky perfume and took in the perfect makeup, the shiny hair, and the low scooped neckline. The top few eyelets had been opened and the ribbons were in Francine's hands. He swivelled round and looked squarely at her. "Okay. So now we really could. Is this what you want, or have I got it wrong?"

"You're very masterful, Neville." A sleepy sensual smile spread over her face. "I like that. Of course you haven't got it wrong."

Francine resumed untying the ribbon at the top of her dress.

When Francine and Neville returned, Trish was just finishing the layout for a brochure she was planning to use locally. She looked up briefly, "I'll be with you in a minute."

Francine's dress was demurely tied at the top, and she had made a rudimentary effort to tidy herself up. She'd wondered about a quick shower, but decided it would look suspicious. Instead she combed her hair and applied fresh make up.

Neville jumped under a shower then wandered over to the art room.

Trish looked up distractedly. She didn't notice the wet hair and different shirt, "How's Francine, now?"

"What d'you mean?" Neville spoke quickly.

"Oh, I thought you said some drunk poured beer all over her. I expect she was fuming. I'm sure she'll need to have a shower and get all that beer off her."

Francine arrived in the art room, "Oh, I just freshened up. I'll shower later."

After Francine's visit, Neville's mind was often involuntarily drawn back to that afternoon of heady senseless passion in her arms. He told himself it was a one off, it would never happen again, and yet … He found himself thinking about Francine's soft yielding body.

Natasha flew down from Queensland again. Her friend Lizzy was opening another salon, and she'd asked Natasha to help organise the opening party.

Grant phoned and asked Billy to go home for Sunday lunch.

Billy shook his head at the phone, "I'm going out with Michelle."

"C'mon, Billy Boy. She's only here for a few weeks. She'd like to see you."

"Can I bring Michelle?"

"It's a deal."

The boatshed was dark and cool. Michelle and Billy held hands as they adjusted their eyes from the bright sunlight outside. They walked over to the makeshift bed in the far corner. Billy sank onto a seashell patterned doona. Natasha had bought him several new covers. Since he was at Yoorooga, she hadn't noticed when the old ones disappeared.

Michelle, still holding Billy's hand, knelt down on the doona and spread the other hand over a picture of a starfish.

"It's pretty. Like the ones I make out of clay."

Her fingers traced a zigzag pattern on each arm of the star. "This is my favourite one."

"Mm … mine too …" Billy was interested in Michelle's mosaics, but at that particular moment he had other things on his mind. He gently eased Michelle out of her tee shirt.

She turned and put her arms around his neck. She said dreamily, "It's so nice here. So special."

Billy buried his head in her soft flesh. "Mm, talk later, yeah?"

Michelle started to unzip her skirt.

Afterwards, Billy drew two cans of soft drink out his backpack.

Michelle scrutinized the label, her finger under each word. She read it laboriously, then said, "I'm not supposed to have this. Too much sugar."

"Me neither. Now Mum's staying with Dad, she wants me on a diet," Billy laughed and patted his stomach, which he pushed out as if to validate his mother's concern.

They drank in small sips, making the cans last. Michelle snuggled up to Billy. "There's something else I did that I'm not supposed to." Her eyes shone in the dim light and she sought Billy's fingers. She clasped both his hands so that their fingers were entwined. She looked into his pale blue eyes. "I think maybe we just made a baby."

"That's cool. It's what we wanted." He grinned at her. Dark curly hair fell over his face.

"Don't you want to know how?"

"I know how babies are made. It's what we've both just done." Billy laughed again. Big bellowing sounds reverberated around the boatshed.

"No, I mean about the pill. Mum's got flu. She's very sick. Dad said to leave her alone. She doesn't get out of bed. She doesn't watch me every day." She paused waiting for Billy's reaction.

He looked at her waiting for her to finish.

"The pill. I said Mum doesn't watch me!" Michelle was excited.

"Oh." Billy scratched his head. "You mean you didn't take that pill today?"

"Nor yesterday," Michelle grinned and she started small jumping movements on the doona. Her eyes danced and she tried to grasp Billy's hands again but this time he reached instead for her belly. Michelle stopped bouncing as he started stroking her abdomen.

"Hello, Baby. Hello. Are you there?" he asked softly.

Gently, he laid his head on Michelle's abdomen. She stroked his hair with smooth rhythmic movements. They stayed, lying on their favourite doona, revelling in the thoughts of possible future joys as the sun sank towards the horizon.

Two weeks of virus left Trish tired. It took all her energy to drag herself out of bed, shower, dress and lay on a lounge chair on the decking.

Michelle tidied and cleaned the house. She cooked simple meals and planned a new set of mosaics.

She and Billy walked through a reserve to the north of Pelican Bay.

"I want to do some bush mosaics, you know, plants and things."

"I thought you liked doing seashells."

"I do. I've done lots of those. I'm going to do a new range." Michelle savoured the word. She'd seen an article on clothes designers in a magazine. She'd read that designers often referred to their work as being in different ranges. Before Trish's flu, Michelle had asked what it meant. Trish had explained well.

"I'm going to do wattle, and flannel flowers, and of course the war … war … thing flower!"

"They'll be good. You've got talent." Billy leaned over and kissed her.

Michelle giggled. "Nice kiss, but let's wait, hey?"

Ed had had a hold-up with some supplies for his cottage and was back in the café for a few days. The girls were confused. They were used to running it without him. There didn't seem to be enough for everyone to do.

"Just make me coffee for today. I'll sit and talk to the customers. Catch up a bit."

Michelle wandered down, her sketch book was tucked under her arm. She sat down next to him. Ed ordered a pot of tea for her and grinned.

"I missed it ... this place. Doing up the cottage is all right, but I missed the people."

Michelle looked around the familiar faces. She told Shirl and Dave that she was going to do a new range. She explained about the plants she wanted to start doing.

Shirl contacted a friend who ran a small shop called Images.

Michelle went to visit the gallery owner. She brought a photo album and her sketchbook.

Cecile smiled at the photos of fish mosaics,

especially the huge mural that was in the restaurant.

Together they leafed through Michelle's sketchbook. Cecile looked back to the earliest pages, noting the fish, and other aquatic life. "Have you done any bush plants before?"

Michelle shook her head. "Mostly seashells and things. Once. After the fire ... I did ..." Michelle looked away and Cecile saw Michelle's thumbs rubbing against each other. She smiled at Michelle, "Your work sounds like just the ticket for my shop. Tell you what ... Why don't you make one, and bring it in to show me?"

Michelle took her materials onto the decking where Trish lay resting. She told Trish about meeting Cecile.

"That's nice Sweetie." Trish who hardly ever used the word 'nice', couldn't summon the energy to think of a better word. "I'd like to see you working here. I get so bored. I can't even read."

"Poor Mum," Michelle put her arms around her mother's neck.

Trish smiled again. She pointed to the sketch book. "Do that one first. I'd like to see that one."

When Michelle wasn't at Eden House, she did what was needed in the house, then spent much of her time on the deck patiently working on the first of her bush range of mosaics.

Neville had forgotten normal life. He juggled the restaurant with furtive trips to Falconville and Francine's waiting arms. Solicitously, he asked Trish how she was and praised Michelle for the help she was giving. Generally he was gone for hours at a stretch.

Trish didn't register when Neville wasn't there. She slowly regained her strength but wasn't yet well enough to be fully involved.

When Michelle's first bush mosaic was finished, she labelled it 'Bush 1'. She took it to show Cecile.

"I'll definitely buy that," Cecile said happily.

"I have to show my friend first, then you can have it. Lola's been away a long time. She's coming home soon."

Michelle and Billy arrived at Yoorooga with bags of shopping. Hal had asked them to help him make a Bolognaise sauce for spaghetti. Michelle lined up chopped onions, garlic, tomatoes and a bag of mince in front of Hal. "You do it in this order." She pointed along the line.

Hal gripped his top lip with his teeth as he concentrated on getting the onions and garlic in a pan with some oil.

Billy passed him a wooden spoon. "You have to stir it."

Hal gripped the spoon vertically, using his whole arm to stir. He called out, "Look at me, Coral. I'm cooking."

Coral walked over and stood with Billy and Michelle. "Good cooking, Hal. What goes in next?"

Hal looked at the pile of chopped tomatoes. He pointed, "Those."

When the meal was ready, everybody sat around the large dining table. Hal served Michelle first.

Tom glared at Michelle, "She doesn't even live here."

Coral said, "Michelle was kind enough to bring the ingredients, and just remember, she's our guest."

Michelle's hand sought Billy's. She said, "It's all right. I'm not … hungry."

Ryan rocked back on his chair, "I bet she's up the duff."

"Shut up." Billy sprang to his feet to tower over Ryan.

Michelle had not heard the expression before, but only understood that Ryan had said something rude. She squeezed Billy's hand and looked at Coral, who was watching her quizzically.

The following day, when Coral was handing over to Si before his shift, she said, "Something happened last night … it made me think that Michelle might be pregnant. It's only a hunch …"

Si shrugged, "I thought she was on the pill."

"I thought so too, but now I'm not sure ... As you said, it's only a hunch. Michelle's not directly under our care. I don't think we should interfere."

"That's a relief. I didn't want to be the one to tell her family."

Kessie sat talking to the staff, after the clients had gone home.

One of the new helpers said, "I overheard a bit of conversation between Tom and Hal today. Tom seemed very angry about Michelle."

Kessie said, "Oh, Tom's always angry about Michelle. He wants to be Billy's friend and he thinks Michelle takes up too much of his time."

"I just got the feeling something's different though. He was really vitriolic, then Hal said, 'Don't be mean. She's having a baby.' Is Michelle pregnant?"

"I didn't think so, but thanks for mentioning it.

We can keep an eye out. It wouldn't be the first," Kessie sighed. "If she is, we'll contact Burnside, and work with them on a parenting program."

Chapter 27

Lola arrived home the following week.

Billy and Michelle took her a welcome-home meal of dips and salads.

Michelle told Lola of all that had been happening since she'd been away. She told of the restaurant's full bookings and good reviews, of Trish's first successful art course, and of her subsequent flu and post viral fatigue.

Michelle showed Lola the mosaic she'd finished and told her that Cecile was going to buy it. Then as the late afternoon sun began to sink, she told Lola that she was pregnant.

Billy beamed. He held Michelle's hand and looked expectantly at Lola.

Lola didn't break into the big smile they'd hoped she would.

Michelle and Billy looked at each other. "Aren't you pleased?" Michelle said.

"Are you?" Lola's voice was neutral.

"Of course!" Billy was offended. "We want a baby, but Michelle's mum kept making her take the pills. Now Trish is sick, she doesn't make her do it anymore." He let go of Michelle's hand and reached towards Michelle's abdomen, which he rubbed gently, "and now there's a little baby in there."

"I see," Lola said slowly, "and have you told your mum, Michelle?"

"Not yet."

Lola said gently, "Don't you think you should?"

"I wanted to tell you first," Michelle's lower lip started to tremble. She looked from Lola to Billy and back. "Mum'll want to spoil it," she said. "She always wants to spoil things between me and Billy. Remember when she …"

Billy put an arm around Michelle's shoulder, "It's all right." He stroked her forehead. "Lola's right. She'll have to know sometime."

Weeks passed, but Michelle never felt it was the right time to tell Trish about being pregnant.

As Trish's fatigue lessened, she inched her way back to normality.

One Sunday morning, when Neville had gone to the restaurant to start his busy schedule, Trish stretched out on the garden lounge chair and took in a big gulp of fresh sea air. She contemplated a second cup of coffee which she hoped would give her the boost she needed to begin her day. Some of Michelle's skirts were looking a bit tight. She wondered about taking Michelle shopping for some new clothes, then remembered how much better Stella had done that. She wondered if Stella would have the time and would take them both. Maybe she could learn from her older daughter. Perhaps that would make up for the previous frantic months when she and Neville had been so wrapped up in their own problems. She got up and walked lazily from the shady veranda into the kitchen, enjoying the calm and quiet of the morning. She contemplated her 'to do' list, poured coffee and sat at the kitchen counter.

She soon became aware of retching sounds coming from the bathroom. Her eyes widened. "No, oh. No!" She walked swiftly to the cupboard where she kept Michelle's pills. Front right, that's where they should be, but no pills were there. Trish's hand scrambled around in the back of the cupboard, seeking the small packet.

"Got it." She drew out the little silver rectangle, which glinted in the morning sun. She couldn't remember when she'd last overseen Michelle's pill-taking. She realised she hadn't got back into the swing of things since her flu. She wondered how long Michelle had not been taking her pills.

The retching sounds had stopped.

"Michelle," she called. "Are you all right?"

There was no answer. Trish walked from the kitchen. She knocked at Michelle's door.

"Come in." Michelle lay on her bed. She was staring at the ceiling.

Trish walked towards the bed. Michelle moved her feet, and Trish sat down.

"Were you being sick, Sweetie? Are you all right?"

"I think so. I think it was the muesli."

"But you always have muesli for breakfast, Michelle."

"I know, but now it makes me sick."

Trish's voice was careful, "Do you know why it makes you sick Michelle?" She sought her daughter's hand.

Michelle pulled it away. "I'm pregnant. That happens, doesn't it? My magazine ... I read about it."

Trish spoke very slowly, "You read about being pregnant in a magazine ... Is that right?"

Michelle looked at her mother. "Yes."

"But you didn't think to tell me you were pregnant?"

Michelle turned towards the wall. She said in a very small voice, "I forgot."

"Oh Michelle ... Michelle. That isn't the sort of thing anyone forgets." Sudden uncontrollable tears rushed down Trish's face. She grabbed her daughter and hugged her close.

Michelle let herself be hugged, then disengaged herself and plucked a handful of tissues. She offered them to Trish. "It's all right Mum. We wanted a baby, remember? It'll be all right. You'll see."

When Neville returned later that afternoon, Trish's face was ashen. Her recovery had curtailed his trysts with Francine, but he still lived each day wondering if he'd be able to sneak away.

"Everything all right, Darl?" He wondered if Trish suspected something.

"Michelle's pregnant," Trish said in a flat voice. "We need to talk."

Neville sat down heavily beside her, "What ..? How far?"

"I don't know. The little minx told me she wanted to be pregnant. She can't ... Oh Neville, what'll we do ..?" Trish broke into anguished sobs.

"Is it too late? She could have …"

"Oh no, Neville." She threw herself at Neville's chest.

Neville tried to hold her away. The sobbing woman who clung to him seemed like a stranger. He spoke through her hair. "It's not practical. How could she possibly look after a baby? You'll be the one to do the work. Just wait and see. Bang go your art courses, and do you really want her to go through all that? How would she cope with the labour?" He seemed to run out of steam, then in much smaller voice he said, "And anyway, what if the baby ..?"

Trish started thumping his chest with her fists. Her body heaved. After a while, she simply clung to him.

He realised with a start, that her body was no longer familiar. He was used to wrapping his arms around a smaller slighter frame, in response to surges of excitement and passion. Now he barely felt compassion for his distressed wife.

Trish became aware that something was different from their previous rows. She didn't seem to fit against his chest anymore. She felt the absence of Neville's arms around her. She pulled away, "I guess I'll take her to see Dr Grey as soon as I can."

"You'll ask Dr Grey if she can … you know?"

Trish stood up and folded her arms. "We've tried to let her be as independent as possible. I suppose that's a natural progression."

Neville's eyes flashed, "No. She doesn't understand the implications of having a baby. To her it's just a sweet, romantic idea. She's imagining pink frilly cot sheets and cooing people, and in the centre a smiley happy baby who only needs to be fed, changed and cuddled."

Trish managed a wan smile, "Actually Neville, that's all newborn babies do need."

"Come on, Trish," he answered sharply "The baby isn't going to be newborn forever. It will grow, get colds, get teeth, crawl, learn to walk, get into cupboards and everything else. Don't you realise it could get into all sorts of danger?"

Trish looked at the man she thought she knew. His words seemed extraordinary. She said, "All babies do that. Not all babies have as much love as Michelle, Billy and all of us will give it."

"It'll leach the life out of you. Think how drained you were when we got Michelle's diagnosis. Suppose the baby has Down syndrome too?"

"We'd manage. We'd just have to give even more support."

"Huh!" Neville grabbed his car keys and stormed out of the house. He dialled Francine's number from the hotel lobby. His nostrils flared in anger as he listened to her voice on the answering machine promising to get back to him.

Neville left the hotel and started to walk across the car park. Francine was just on her way back though the wrought iron gates. She carried large bags emblazoned with names of expensive clothes shops. She stopped, shielded her eyes from the sun, and looked in his direction.

Neville strode towards her. He grasped her wrist, "Where've you been?" Without listening to her reply, he pulled her into the hotel, up the stairs, and into her room. She unlocked the door smiling at his impatience. Once inside, Neville took the bags and threw them to the floor. He wrenched the room key from Francine's hand and threw it towards the bags.

Francine's face shone with expectation. She reached for the zipper at the back of her dress.

Neville pushed her hand away then threw her onto the bed, "Damn the bloody zipper. Leave it on. I want you now." He pushed her dress up and unzipped his trousers. Without preliminaries he threw himself heavily onto her. He banged and thumped into her furiously for a few seconds. He gripped her hair roughly and let out an anguished roar. He fell over her and ran his lips down her neck, then lay inert, staring at the ceiling.

Francine's eyes widened. She'd thought it was going to be enjoyable, but it was over before it began for her. This was the first time Neville hadn't satisfied her. She pulled herself up on her elbow and pushed him away. She struggled out of her wet wrinkled underwear, which had been hastily pushed to one side. She caught sight of Neville in the mirror and held his gaze steadily directing her words at the mirror. "I don't know what this is about, and I don't want to, but there wasn't much pleasure in that. I think it's time for you to pleasure me."

Neville grunted, shook his head and allowed small tears of defeat to roll from the corners of his eyes towards his ears and thence onto Francine's bedding. He wanted to tell her but she'd been clear she didn't want to know, so he lay staring at the ceiling waiting or the tears to stop. When they did, he zipped up his trousers, grabbed his keys and left the room.

Chapter 28

The next time Michelle was at Eden House, she admired Kessie's dress. "That's nice. Did you dye it?"

"Yes, I did." Kessie smiled at her. "You know about tie dying? Your mum?

Michelle nodded. "But I've only done small bits." She drew a rectangle in the air in front of her. "I'd like a dress. Can I dye a dress?"

"Maybe. I guess we could give it a go." Kessie put one finger to her chin.

Billy came up behind Michelle and put his arms around her waist. "Michelle wants a big dress 'cos there's a little baby in there. It's going to get bigger."

Kessie nodded, "I think we might need to think about more than clothes—"

Billy held Michelle's hand, "Yes there's the cot too, and nappies … lots of things."

"How about you two come to my office? We need to chat."

Neville and Trish continued to argue about Michelle's pregnancy while they waited for the first available appointment with Dr Grey.

Stella put an arm around her mother's shoulder and said to her father. "Look, I know it was irresponsible of them, but it's what they want. We don't really have any say. It's her body. You can't force her."

Gareth, who'd just returned from the Gold Coast, said, "Sis is right. It's up to Michelle. We'll just have to pull together, and help. That's what we do, isn't it?"

Neville stared at them, "And what if the baby's ..?"

"We'd cope. That's what we've always done. We coped when we learned Michelle had Down Syndrome. We'll cope if the baby does."

Neville ran his fingers through his hair, "It's all very well for you. You're hardly ever here anymore. It'll be Trish who picks up the pieces."

Stella got up and stood beside Gareth, as if physical proximity would underline her position in the matter, "That's not fair Dad. Everything has been strange for the last couple of years. Yes, Gareth has been away a lot, but when he's here he'll more than pull his weight."

Trish held up her hand, "We have to stop bickering like this. It's not about us. It's about Michelle." She turned to her husband. "Don't you understand, she wants this baby. Billy wants the baby too."

"For heaven's sake, it's not as if she understands what's involved!" Neville was almost shouting with frustration.

"None of us ever do," Trish said in a small voice. "Nothing can ever prepare anyone for what is involved when they have children." She looked at Neville defiantly, "I mean everybody, from the intellectually brilliant to those who may have less than average reasoning ability."

That night when they went to bed, Trish was aware of how far apart she and Neville lay. They each seemed to be gripping their own side of the mattress. The silence roared around the room and settled between them like a third person in the centre of the bed. She wondered if this was just because of the row. She willed herself to speak, but words wouldn't come. She tried to think how long they'd been moving in different directions. She couldn't think. Her tired brain refused to work for her. She drifted into a shallow, troubled sleep.

The next morning Trish went to the café to find Ed.

It was one of his days at the café. The sea sparkled in the warm sun. She gave a weak wave as she approached. "Where have you been for the last few days, Dad? I've really needed to talk to you."

"I had to go to Sydney to collect some new kitchen units for the cottage." He noticed her pale face, and drew out a chair for her. "What's up?"

"How long have you got?" Trish slumped down in a floppy heap and wiped the back of her hand across her forehead.

"This sounds serious."

"It is. Oh Dad, it really is," she folded her arms on the table in front of her and lay her head on them.

Ed pushed some paper serviettes across the table. "Okay, tell me what's happened."

"Michelle's pregnant. She and Billy actually planned it. Can you believe that? When I was ill, she deliberately didn't take her pill."

To Trish's surprise, Ed laughed. "You gotta hand it to her. When our Princess wants something, she does her darndest …"

"Dad, it's not funny!"

Ed moved his chair closer and rubbed Trish's shoulders. "It isn't that bad either. Michelle and Billy will make better parents than many people I know."

"You haven't heard it all yet," Trish gripped one hand around the other so tightly that her fingertips grew red.

Ed reached forward and prised tense fingers loose. "So tell me."

Trish took a deep breath and spoke very quickly, "Neville thinks she should have an abortion."

"But that's inhuman," Ed shook his head. "D'you want me to talk to him?"

"No. Things are bad between us. That would make things worse. He stormed out of the house this morning, for the second time in two days."

Neville had sat in his car and phoned Francine. "I'm coming over, but we're going out. I need to be with you and I need to walk."

Francine was waiting outside the hotel. She jumped in the car nimbly, and plonked a kiss on Neville's cheek.

Neville drove south, back along the road beyond Pelican Bay where he'd driven Francine on that first occasion when she had so determinedly seduced him.

Neville turned off, onto the bumpy road towards the rough hewn car park on the edge of coastal bush.

A smile played on Francine's face, "Are we revisiting?" She ran her tongue over cherry rouged lips and stroked his thigh.

"This time we'll just walk."

The start of the bush path was wide and sandy, but after a while it became narrower and split in several directions. Neville hesitated.

"That way," Francine pointed towards the east. "We'll stay as close to the water as we can. That'll make getting back easier." Every now and then they glimpsed the ocean through the trees. Wild bomboras crashed out to sea, while nearer shore the inky swell smashed onto rocks and sprayed the air.

"I can almost feel the spray up here," Francine rubbed her hands over the back of her neck and across her shoulders towards her breasts suggestively. Again, she licked her cherry lips. "Let's go down and feel the sea-spray on our faces."

Neville looked uncertainly at her feet. He was worried about her dainty, narrow-strapped sandals, but at least they were flat. "Will you manage on the rocks?"

"I'm sure I will."

They began to climb down the rocky path towards the sea.

An inlet at the bottom was bordered with a rocky sandstone face and boulders that looked out on to the furious wind-whipped ocean.

"Here?" Francine pointed to a small patch of pebbly beach.

"No, over here." Neville took her towards a rocky ledge that jutted out over the crashing waves. He needed the danger of it to make himself feel areal. "I want the sea spray on our bodies." He began to claw her out of her clothes.

Ed stopped by Lola's caravan. He found her weeding the vegetable patch at the back. She straightened and pulled up a couple of chairs.

Ed contemplated the small patch of cultivated soil. It was soothing, looking at the once-poor earth. He thought about the loving care that'd made the soil so fertile. "I've just been told our Princess and Billy are having a baby."

Lola smiled. "I'm glad you put it that way. A lot of people would have just said, 'about Michelle having a baby'. It's good she's finally told the family. She was worried, you know. But then, most young girls who get pregnant are worried about telling their parents."

Ed studied some late-ripening tomatoes, "It's not as simple for Michelle though, is it?"

"What's not simple?"

"Well, the Down Syndrome for a start."

"You mean her syndrome affecting the way she'll be able to parent?"

"I suppose, the baby could have …"

"Or, it might not."

Ed laughed, "Okay, point taken." He looked at a maturing pumpkin, glistening in the morning sun. It was beginning to spread over the grassy area that Lola generally kept clear of vegetation. He noticed she'd just cut the grass around it, and left the plant to sprawl. In a quiet voice he said, "There've been huge family rows already. I think they might be irreparable. Neville's been odd lately. Very. He wants her to have an abortion."

"No!" Lola exclaimed. "How could he possibly?"

"I asked myself the same question. I just ... needed to tell you, I suppose."

"I'm glad you felt you could talk to me. How have the others taken the news?"

"Trish was shocked, but she didn't go along with Neville for one minute. It's caused a huge rift. Our Stella has surprised me though."

"How?"

"It seems Michelle told Stella about a year ago, that she and Billy wanted a baby. Stella laid into her, telling her it was irresponsible. None of us knew anything about this, mind you. Stella thought that was the end of it. But now Michelle actually is pregnant, Stella's been very good."

Lola nodded, "I'm glad about that. And Gareth?"

"He'd be as helpful as he could be, but he's got a job in Indonesia. He's leaving shortly. A pity that ... he always was a champion for our Princess."

"She's got you. She's got me, and it sounds as if she has Trish and Stella, and she very definitely has Billy."

Lola's hand lay on a small table between them.

Ed put a hand out and lightly stoked the back of her hand. "Thanks Lola, it always helps to talk to you."

Lola smiled, "I'm going to make a cup of tea. Stay and have one with me. I need to ask you something."

They sat with their backs to the caravan, the tea steaming gently in the morning air. Once again Lola smiled. "I wanted to ask you about that cottage you've been doing up. Are you going to be moving into it?"

"Good heavens, no. It started as a sort of hobby, I

suppose. I needed something that was really mine. The family seemed to have taken over running the caravan park, so I made the coffee van mine ... Now that's gone too. Don't get me wrong; I'm glad really, but it left me needing something of my own."

"Good."

"Because ..?"

"Well, Dot Barker's niece is moving up here. She plans to work for three months in a local school. She doesn't have anywhere to live yet. She could stay with Dot, but I don't think that would work ... not for so long. D'you think you could consider renting it to her?"

"Yeah, that might be a possibility."

Michelle and Trish sat in the doctor's waiting room. Trish hissed, "I need to talk to her too ..."

Michelle's mouth puckered into a small tight bunch. She sat upright and kept her head square, while letting her eyes swivel toward her mother, "You can see Dr Grey after me."

Trish sighed. She knew when she was beaten.

Dr Grey listened as Michelle explained about the family row, as well as about her pregnancy. "Do you want this baby, Michelle?"

Michelle nodded, "When Mum was sick I didn't take the pills. I'm happy. Billy's happy." She smiled and rubbed her abdomen. "I think the baby's happy, too."

Dr Grey smiled at Michelle, "Can you remember when you had your last period?"

Michelle thought. "It was Christmas. I remember that. Christmas Day!" She beamed triumphantly.

The doctor looked at a desk calendar, "Mm, that

makes you about three and a half months pregnant. It'll be a spring baby, September, I think. I'll need to examine you and we'll need to get you booked into the hospital."

Michelle started shaking her head, "Not the hospital."

"Babies get born in hospitals. You have to go there for your check-ups. That way you'll get to know what it's like ... get to know the people ... the doctors and nurses there."

"Why can't I see you? You're a doctor." Michelle's thumbs began to rub against each other.

Dr Grey leaned forward, "I can see you sometimes, but you do need to go to the hospital as well. Everybody who's going to have a baby, has to go to the hospital. You need to meet the midwife."

"Who's that?"

"The midwife is the person who actually delivers the baby."

Michelle's face was blank.

Dr Grey thought for a moment, "The midwife is the person who helps the baby to be born." She tried to read Michelle's face and decided that it still wasn't registering understanding. She continued, "The midwife doesn't just hold your hand. She actually helps the baby come out of your body, into the world."

Michelle nodded solemnly, "It's an important job."

"That's right. Don't you think it matters ... to get to know the person who will do that special job for you?"

Michelle thought for a moment. "Yes. Getting to know someone ... it takes time."

"Exactly," Dr Grey relaxed.

When Michelle left her room, Dr Grey finished her notes. She thought of some of the girls she'd seen over the previous few years. Some of them had refused to even try to understand why they needed to go to hospital. She knew they'd simply not gone. She got up and called Trish's name as the next patient.

While Michelle and Trish were visiting Dr Grey, Cecile was talking to a journalist who was visiting her gallery.

The journalist picked up Michelle's mosaic. "This is a bit unusual. I really like it."

"I'd rather you didn't buy that just yet. I've only just got it in. I've ordered a series from a local girl."

The journalist looked quizzical, "and?"

"Oh, I don't know how fast she works yet, so I'm not sure how often I'll get her work. She's … special."

"How d'you mean, 'special'?"

"She has Down syndrome."

"Ahh …" the journalist let out a sigh. "How very interesting." She thought of her neighbour's son who had Down syndrome. She didn't think he was capable of producing work of the same calibre. In fact she knew very few people at all who could produce work that good. "D'you think she'd talk to me?"

"I'll ask her."

Cecile phoned Michelle who was on a bus with Billy.

"That's good," Michelle bounced on her seat. "I can see the journalist this arvo."

Chapter 29

Grant was mowing the grass at the front when Billy and Michelle arrived. He switched off the mower and went to greet them.

"Dad, we've got some news," Billy moved his weight forward, rose on his toes and bounced.

Michelle's face was one big smile.

"Nice to see you both," Grant said as he took Billy's outstretched hand. He kissed Michelle's cheek. Grant tried to remember when Billy had decided that this was an appropriate way to greet his father. He thought it was probably not long after Billy'd moved to Yoorooga.

Billy's bouncing increased.

Grant noticed that Michelle stood with her feet slightly apart, firmly planted, but the hand that wasn't holding Billy's, was making a figure of eight by her side.

"We're pregnant," Billy almost shouted.

Grant flung one arm around each of them. "Wow, that's big news. Congratulations." He refused to look beyond their smiling faces. He thought that for this one day, they would all celebrate and be happy. They could worry later about any possible difficulties.

He brought out a jug of lemonade and set it down next to the large garden swing under the awning. "Would you like me to make a cot?" he asked. "I like working with my hands, and that would be something special for me to do."

"Yes, please," they said together; without hesitation.

Michelle and Billy sat on the swing, smiling happily. They held hands and their legs swayed rhythmically.

Grant looked at them, framed by the swing, with a lemonade at each side. He knew he would always remember that moment. "Hey, this will be my grandchild … You'll have made a grandad out of me, Billy-Boy."

"Not on my own, Dad."

They all laughed.

"And Mum will be a nanna, won't she?"

"She will indeed," chuckled Grant. "I'll phone her this evening … unless of course, you'd like to do it."

Billy looked at Michelle, "We could do it together."

In the afternoon Michelle and Billy met the journalist who asked how Michelle had got started with her mosaics.

Michelle told her about Eden House, and Billy laughed and reminded her of the first day when Josie had dropped a box of tiles on the floor.

The journalist turned to Billy, "And you are ..?"

"I'm Billy, Michelle's boyfriend." He stuck his chest out. "We're pregnant."

A slow smile spread over the journalist's face. "And when?"

"September," Billy and Michelle cried in unison.

Billy's hand crept towards Michelle's abdomen. He rubbed it gently.

"You won't have much time to be making mosaics once you have a baby," the journalist said.

Michelle looked serious, "I will. When the baby sleeps, and—"

"And I can look after it some of the time too," Billy said eagerly. He turned to Michelle. "and there's Lola, and your mum and dad and your poppy, and ... oh, lots of people."

Trish drove Michelle to her first appointment at Falconville Hospital. She knew Michelle wanted to see the midwife on her own, and braced herself for a row. When Michelle's turn came, the midwife approached them in the waiting room. She smiled and sat down next to Michelle. "My name's Emily. I'm your midwife. As this is your first appointment, I need to see your mum as well."

Michelle's face lost its happy smile.

Emily continued, "I have to find out all sorts of things about illnesses you had when you were little."

Michelle glanced at Trish, who tentatively searched for her daughter's hand and tried to look reassuring.

Emily continued, "Most people can't remember those sorts of things, but their mothers usually can."

After they had seen Emily, Michelle and Trish

returned to the waiting room clutching a wad of leaflets and a small card on which Emily's name was printed. Some letters followed the name, as well as phone and fax numbers. Underneath, was a handwritten date and time.

Michelle pointed to the leaflets. She looked at Trish. "There's a lot to read. Billy can help me," She glanced at Trish's stricken face. "You can help me too, if you like," she added.

Billy and Michelle found that they didn't need to tell anyone at Yoorooga. "We must have told them already," Billy scratched his head.

Hal said, "Well you and Michelle are always saying you want a baby. Nobody's surprised."

Ryan stuck his bottom jaw out and ran his tongue over his top lip, "Yeah we know 'cos you're always doin' it." He got up from the sofa and jerked his hips backwards and forwards.

Si's voice cut in, "Sit down Ryan. You're embarrassing Michelle."

Hal glanced at Ryan, "Embarrassing yourself as well," he put an arm out gingerly, and touched Ryan's arm. "I know you haven't got a girlfriend, but you have got those magazines …"

Michelle looked puzzled.

Ryan got up, "Yeah, I'm going to look at my magazines."

Neville was looking at the local newspaper when he came across a reference to Cecile's gallery. He began to read out loud to Trish.

Images Art Gallery, near Pelicans

> Resort, is one of the region's best galleries for finding unique and idiosyncratic treasures. The owner, Cecile Gammer likes to foster new talent, and her newest find is a young woman called Michelle Grafton. Michelle produces beautiful work despite having Down syndrome. Michelle and her boyfriend Billy, are expecting a baby in September, but it sounds as if Michelle has a lot of family support and she assured me she will continue to make mosaics. Look out for her work, which is set to become very collectable.

Neville felt anger rising in his chest. He thrust the newspaper to Trish, "How on earth did they get to interview her? Did we give our permission?"

Trish read the article and put it down. Her voice was dull, "She's twenty years old. She doesn't need our permission."

"Hmm, I suppose you're all gloating. She'll have to go through with it now. Is that it?"

"No, I don't think anybody's gloating." Trish felt inordinately tired. The effort of talking to Neville, left her drained. She hardly noticed when he left the room. She was dully aware of the sound of his car revving up and then of him driving away.

Francine's face looked different. She sat on the edge of her bed and leaned forward. Neville couldn't miss the gleam of excitement. The shades were half-drawn and the whites of her eyes shone in the semi-darkness. "You wanted to up the danger level."

The familiar slow lick of the tongue over scarlet lips started Neville's heart racing. Did he really need the danger level upped? It had been exciting on the rocks with the sea spray threatening to consume them both before they consumed each other. He watched as she languidly dipped a hand into a bag at her feet.

Metal glinted in the darkened room. Francine dangled chains, and an open set of handcuffs above his head. "Today you get to have me how-so-ever you want. Lock me up. Indulge your secret dream."

When Neville returned home he found the family gathered on the front porch. He realised with a shock that he had forgotten about Gareth's imminent departure. He struggled to remember. He thought it was Western Australia, but he couldn't be sure.

He'd missed the farewell lunch. He wondered how he could have forgotten. He'd even arranged for the restaurant to cater and deliver to the house. He quietly slipped in behind the little group.

"I wish you'd let me drive," Trish stroked Gareth's face.

Gareth wrapped his arms tightly around his mother. "Mum, I've told you, I don't want tears at the airport. The company's happy to pay my every expense, so I'll let them pick up the tab."

Gareth barely glanced at Neville, but he hugged Michelle close. "Indonesia isn't so very far away. With luck the project will be over before the baby comes. You take good care, Princess."

Neville started. Indonesia. My God, how could I have forgotten that? he thought. He bade his son an awkward, 'Goodbye.'

Michelle, Trish and Stella stood with arms firmly around each other's shoulders, as they waved to Gareth in the back of the Indonesian company car.

Stella turned to Michelle, "I know you'd rather it was me that went, and Gareth that stayed, but that's life, Baby Sister. I'll try not to be so bossy. You don't want your baby to have a bossy aunt, do you?"

Michelle smiled at Stella. "You're not always bossy. Will you come with me when I need to buy the baby clothes?"

"You betcha," Stella raised a hand and clapped Michelle's high in the air.

Trish's energy deserted her once more. She wondered about the ever growing distance between herself and Neville. She was hardly surprised that he had missed lunch. He hadn't offered any explanation and she thought it would take too much effort to tackle him about it.

She phoned Francine, "I haven't seen you for weeks. You've been living so near. Why don't you come over? We've so much catching up to do. We could walk along the beach and get something to eat at the café. Nice and relaxed, have a girly chat."

Francine told Neville about Trish's phone call.

"You're not going to go?"

"Why not? She's my friend. She's been sick and I haven't even been to see her once." Francine saw the puzzled look on Neville's face. She lowered her voice, till it was soft and silky, "Okay, so the reason I haven't seen her is because I've been seeing to her rather dishy husband." She pulled him slowly towards herself, wrapping her legs around his back.

Afterwards as Neville dressed, Francine said, "If you can't face seeing the two of us together, just pick a time when you're working. We'll go with that." She smiled, and dropped into her soft husky voice. "Also, it won't eat into any time we might have together."

Francine arranged to meet Trish the following Sunday morning. Trish had said, "Neville will be busy at the restaurant, and Michelle will be out with Billy. We can catch up without interruption."

On Sunday morning Billy and Michelle stood outside the cinema.

Billy wanted to see the newest adventure film.

"I don't want to see that," Michelle raised her bottom lip then pouted her mouth.

"What do you want to see?"

Michelle named a film which had been dubbed the latest, 'big hit, chick flick.'

"No way. I'm not seeing that." Billy laughed.

"I don't want guns," Michelle planted her feet wide.

"Tell you what," Billy grinned. "I really, really, really want to see this film." He waved at a poster advertising a frothy romance. You can see that one with Stella. I bet she wants to see it."

Michelle looked down at her shoes. She'd wanted to spend the morning with Billy, but she knew he wouldn't change his mind.

"Maybe Stella'll see it with me," she said crossly and glared at the poster of Billy's favoured film.

"Why don't you do some of the mosaic … the one you promised Cecile? I'll come over this arvo.

Don't sulk. "

Michelle looked up from her feet. She saw Billy's smiling face. "You're right, sulking isn't any fun." She reached over and kissed Billy lightly, "Missing you already."

Billy arrived at Pelicans Resort in the afternoon. He said earnestly, "The film was good, but you wouldn't have liked it … too many guns"

Michelle smiled, "I'm glad I came home. I did lots on my mosaic, but now—"

Billy grinned. "Now, let's go to the boat shed."

"Mmm, yes."

Later they lay warm and satiated.

Michelle stretched out and ran her hands over her abdomen, "What'll we call the baby?"

"Dunno," Billy put his hands over hers. "We don't know if it'll be a boy or girl. Can't choose a name."

"Could have names in case …" Michelle traced a pattern on the doona. "If it's a boy we could call him Billy."

Billy looked perplexed, "How'd you know which was me and which was the baby?"

Michelle giggled, "You're bigger."

Billy laughed too, "No, I mean, how'd people know who you're talking about?"

"I've thought it all out," Michelle was excited. She splayed her hand out in front of her, "There'd be Big Billy and Little Billy."

"Umm. Maybe. What if it's a girl?"

Michelle turned on her side. She caressed Billy's face, "D'you want to call her after your sister? It's a nice name, Grace."

"I'd like that," Billy stroked Michelle's hair, but his eyes lost focus and he gazed through her. "I don't really remember Grace. I mean sometimes I think I can remember, but really it's only things Dad's told me." After a few moments Billy said, "We won't tell anyone, will we? I don't want anyone to know until the baby's born. Just us, right?"

Michelle nodded solemnly, "Our secret."

Trish and Francine walked along the beach. Francine held her sandals and paddled through the water. She had frantically skimmed the local papers, and talked of neighbourhood news. She was grateful that Trish didn't ask many questions about the previous few weeks.

The two women walked along the beach at Pelican Bay. Trish talked to the person who had once been her closest friend, of her immense tiredness, but she didn't mention Neville and the ragged hole in her life. She struggled to keep up with Francine, who noticed Trish's laboured breathing.

Francine said, "Let's go back now. I can see you've had enough." They turned and walked back towards Pelicans Resort. When they reached the café she said, "Sit down here. You're shivering. I'll get you a sweater or something."

Trish nodded, "That'd be really good. I am beginning to feel cold."

Francine walked briskly to the family house and found a pale blue sweatshirt on a chair in Trish and Neville's bedroom. She picked it up as Neville walked through the door.

His face lit with pleasure, "I wondered how I

could sneak a few minutes with you, and now … " He wiggled his fingers like a pantomime magician.

"For heaven's sake, Neville, we don't have time. I'm about to have lunch with Trish. I just ran up here to get this."

"Doesn't this count in the danger stakes?" Neville's heart was racing. He took the sweatshirt from Francine and tossed it on the floor. He began to lift the hem of her dress. "It doesn't have to take long."

"You're on," Francine's eyes glittered, and she started to grapple with Neville's clothes. "I'm not doing it fully dressed again," Francine panted. "This might be a quickie, but I need to feel skin on skin, not clothing."

Michelle laid tiles out on her mosaic. She wondered about a border. She remembered the first one she'd brought home, the one she'd wanted in the living room, but Stella had made a fuss and it was finally hung in Trish's bedroom. Michelle couldn't remember what happened at the edges of that mosaic, and decided to check.

Neville and Francine writhed on the marital bed. They didn't hear the door open.

Michelle stood, frozen in horror. She let out a shrill squeal.

Francine jumped up and scrabbled around on the floor searching for her clothing.

Neville grabbed a sheet around himself as he heard Michelle start to wail. He tried to put his arms around her, but she shook him off.

Michelle looked angrily at Francine. "Go away! Go away," she screamed.

Francine picked up Trish's sweatshirt.

"That's my mum's sweatshirt. Put it down." Michelle shouted.

Michelle's shouting brought Stella running. She too, stood at the bedroom door in shock. She stared at Francine, and jerked her thumb towards the door. "Out!"

Stella took Michelle outside the bedroom and washed her sister's hands and face, and sat her down in the living room. "You know what they were doing. We can't fob you off anymore." Then she murmured to herself, "The question is, what do we tell Mum?"

Michelle rocked gently on a sofa. "It's what people do when they love each other. She shouldn't be here. Dad shouldn't …"

"Hush, Baby Sister, I know that. You know that. We just need to think."

Trish appeared through the living room door. "Whatever's going on? I thought Francine had come up to the house to get me a sweater. She's been ages, and I'm getting …" She stopped as she saw her daughters' faces.

"I'll get your sweater, Mum," Stella said. "You wait here. Oh, and don't go back to the café. Francine's gone home."

"Gone home?" Trish looked from daughter to daughter.

Michelle sat with her lips tightly shut.

Stella went back to her parents' bedroom. She picked up the blue sweatshirt, and fixed Neville with a steady stare. "Mum's here, in the house. I'm taking Michelle out. You'd better tell Mum what's been going on, and you'd better tell her it's over." She looked at him steadily, "because if you don't, I sure as hell, will!"

Chapter 30

Billy arrived as Stella was about to bundle Michelle into her car. Stella looked straight in his eyes, and said, "I'm so glad to see you."

Billy began to smile. Stella didn't usually talk to him like that, and yet her face didn't seem to look at all pleased. His smile stayed half-formed. He looked at Michelle, who sat chewing her bottom lip.

Stella said, "Michelle's had a bit of a shock. Can you take her somewhere completely different for the afternoon?"

"Um. We'll go to Yoorooga." He turned to Michelle, "Is that okay with you?"

Michelle nodded.

"Look, it's beginning to rain. I'll give you two a lift. You'll be okay to get the bus back, won't you?"

"Sure thing." Billy opened the door for Michelle, then clambered in the back.

The television was on when they arrived at Yoorooga, and Tom got up and moved so he didn't have to sit next to Michelle.

Ryan leered, "I wouldn't have moved."

There was a sudden 'PHUT' noise, then everything went quiet.

Ryan looked at the blank television screen. "Another blasted power cut. I was enjoying that."

Si grinned at Ryan. "I expect the electricity company did it just to annoy Tom."

Tom peered at Si through smeary glasses, and laughed. "Yes. It's always my favourite show."

Ryan leered at Michelle. "I bet they did it so Billy and Michelle could do things when it gets dark."

"Shut up, Ryan." Billy got up from the sofa and walked towards the games cupboard. He looked at the neat piles of games.

"We all know you did do it." Ryan stared hard at Michelle's thickened waistline and small pronounced bump. He pointed at her. "We can see."

Billy turned to Ryan angrily. "Stop it, you perv."

Hal joined Billy at the games cupboard and said, "Anyone want to play a game?"

Ryan shouted, "Cards. Let's play cards." He turned to look at Billy and Michelle. "I want to play poker. I'll play strip poker with you." He stabbed a finger in Michelle's direction.

"D'you have Guess Who?" Michelle asked.

"Yeah. Yeah, we do." Hal and Billy started searching.

"Here it is." Billy brought the game and put it in the middle of the dining table.

Ryan got up from the sofa and moved towards the table. "Looks like a stupid game. I want to play cards. Who wants to play cards with me?"

Nobody answered.

Tom looked uncertainly at Billy. "How d'you play Guess Who?"

Billy tried to explain. Michelle and Hal kept interrupting him. After a while, Billy rubbed his hand across his forehead and looked at Si. "You tell them Si. I can't do it. Everyone's butting in all the time."

Si moved a chair to the table. "Tell you what, why don't we just have a game. I'll sit with Tom and we can play against Billy, Michelle and Hal.

Ryan waved a pack of cards in the air. "Too many people for that stupid game. I want to play cards. He moved towards a small coffee table which was flanked by two arm chairs.

"Okay." Hal got up. "I'll play cards first. I want to play Guess Who, next."

Si sat next to Tom who pulled away. "I want to sit next to Billy. It's not the same now she's here. And it's going to be worse. There'll be a noisy baby. I don't want her here."

Si looked directly at Tom. "Don't be rude. Michelle's our guest. Next game we can swap around. Okay?"

Tom muttered, but settled down. Si gave him helpful hints about the questions to be asked, and he and Tom beat Billy and Michelle.

Hal moved towards the table and addressed Billy. "Can I play with Michelle now?"

Ryan looked up from his cards. "You always want to do the same as Billy. I bet you even want to do the same … " Si put his hand up and Ryan stopped. He lowered his head and looked at Si from below dense eyebrows. He threw the cards down on the table and started mumbling obscenities.

Hal put his hands on his hips and stared at Ryan.

"You're crude. That's what you are! Billy's got a girlfriend. I want a girlfriend. You'll never have a girlfriend. No one would want you."

"Yeah, I know what you want to do to a girl—" Ryan threw the pack of cards at Hal.

The afternoon wore into evening and Ryan went off to his washing up job, Tom settled with his word search book and Hal decided to cook.

Michelle told Billy about finding Neville and Francine.

Billy put his arms around her, "That's gross." He shook his head. "He shouldn't do that."

"I don't want to go home. Can I stay here with you, Billy?" Michelle sobbed.

"We'll ask Si."

Si said, "No. I'm sorry Michelle. We can't let people stay over. That just alters everything. Whatever it is at home, you need to go and face it." Si wondered how many people without learning disabilities could do that.

Neville sat opposite Trish with his head in his hands. He spoke to the floor. "I'm so ashamed, I can't even look at you."

"I don't understand."

Neville's voice faltered, "I've been so stupid ... " He shook his head, "So very stupid. I can hardly believe ... "

Trish's mouth dropped open, "Francine ... you?"

Neville nodded.

Trish rocked on the sofa. She hunched her shoulders and gripped her arms tightly around herself. She lifted her feet off the floor as she moved back and forth, and made low moaning sounds.

Neville brought his hands down from his face and looked at his wife's distressed movements.

Suddenly Trish leapt up and rushed across the room. She grabbed his shoulders and shook him, "Oh my God, just now. That's it, isn't it? Both of you, now when she was supposed to be getting me a sweater."

Trish barely noticed as Neville inclined his head. She let out a small bitter laugh, "What an idiot I've been! You two have certainly made a fool out of me, haven't you?"

"Don't be like that Trish—"

"Like what?" Trish's voice rose. "You and my supposed best friend," her voice soared, "romp in our bed, while I foolishly wait for her to bring me a sweater. How d'you expect me to be?" She brought her fists up and started hammering at Neville's shoulders.

He caught her wrists. "Trish, you weren't foolish. I was the foolish one. You were trusting, and I betrayed you. Just tell me what you want me to do now."

"I don't think I want you to do anything, but I know one thing. I'm not going back into that bedroom. I'm not sharing that bed with you, ever again. I'll take my things into Gareth's room. I don't know if we will ever … "

Neville threw himself into work. He was relieved when he noticed that Shane had picked up on many details that he'd let slip. Shane had also taken to overseeing the rest of the staff. The standard was still as high as it had been when he opened the restaurant.

He ran his eye along chopping boards of perfectly prepared baby carrots and asparagus. Chicken sat in a fresh marinade, and Shane was stirring a pan. Neville smiled. "Yes, I'm here now, properly. Thanks for keeping everything working. I hadn't realised ... "

Shane answered his smile. "Glad to have you back, Chef."

Hal and Tom wanted to make a birthday cake for Coral. Hal said to Billy, "Ask Michelle to help. She knows how to make cakes."

Tom looked angrily at Hal. "We can do it on our own. We don't need her."

"Michelle and Billy helped me make the Bolognaise sauce. She's Billy's girlfriend. I want her to help," Hal answered evenly.

"Then I won't." Tom crossed him arms and turned away.

Billy looked from Hal to Tom, " I can't make a cake on my own. Hal can't make a cake on his own. Can you make one?"

Tom took his glasses off and polished the lenses on his tee shirt.

Billy shook his shoulder gently, "I said, can you make a cake, Tom?"

"No," Tom mumbled.

Michelle and Billy arrived with green bags full of groceries, and a large recipe book.

Tom looked at her accusingly, "I thought you knew how to make cakes."

Michelle started unpacking the bags, "Usually my dad tells me what to do ... "

"So, why d'you need a book."

"I'm not ... I don't want ..." Michelle bit her lip.

Billy said, "It's all right Michelle. We'll prop the

book up here." He looked angrily at Tom, "We can read. We just do what it says. Michelle has done it before. This is just to help her remember."

Once the cake had cooled, Hal placed candles on it. Everybody sang Happy Birthday, and Coral blew out the candles. Tom sneaked three slices, but was the only person who didn't praise Michelle.

Trish lived within a huge grey cloud that barely left her room to breathe. She tried to summon up the will to take Michelle to her appointments, but her limbs wouldn't move. She used all her energy to get out of bed and crawl into clothes. The family tip-toed around her and others filled the roles she no longer could.

Stella checked the calendar in the kitchen. She said to Michelle, "You have another appointment at the hospital on Tuesday. I don't think Mum will remember. I could take you, but I'm really busy. D'you think you could go on your own?"

"Billy'll come with me." Michelle answered.

When Michelle had left the room, Neville said, "I'm not sure about this. You know what that lot are like. They'll say we're not giving her enough support and put her into care. Is there any chance you could get a duty manager in for the morning?"

Stella phoned one of the duty managers, to see if she could work. Gabby was pleased to have the opportunity.

After the hospital visit, Trish looked at her youngest daughter through tired eyes, "Was everything all right, Sweetie?"

"Um, yes. I have a so … social person. Look … " Michelle produced a card. "She's coming here next week."

Ed visited Lola. "I'm fed up with coffee. Will you make me a cup of tea? I'd like to sit and watch your veggies grow for a while."

"My pleasure," Lola said and filled the jug.

They sat at the back of Lola's caravan on canvas chairs that flanked a small wooden table.

Ed leaned towards Lola, "How d'you think she's coping?"

"Depends on who you mean by 'she'."

"Ah ... I take it, Michelle's told you what happened."

"Yes, she came to see me the day after... She'd wanted to stay at Yoorooga that night, but she couldn't. So ... is it Trish or Michelle you're worried about?"

Ed gave short laugh. "I never thought I'd say it, but I think Michelle's okay. Stella's been acting as a bit of a shock absorber. They don't usually get on, but this time Stella really has been a star."

Lola smiled at him, "Yes, the sisters do seem to be closer. Something good to come out of ... "

"But Trish is locked inside a big wall she's built around herself."

"Didn't Michelle say a social worker was coming next week? Maybe you could speak to them about Trish. Try to get her some help."

"You don't think she'd feel betrayed?"

"From what you've told me, I don't think she's aware enough to notice. Can you manage things, so that you're there when the social worker comes?"

"I doubt it, but maybe I could bump into her as she leaves."

"That sounds like a good plan."

Michelle's social worker, Pru Smith, arrived at Pelicans Resort the following week.

Trish met Pru with vacant eyes. "I've been ill. I'm afraid things aren't quite normal. What can I do for you?"

Pru noted Trish's drawn face. "I'm really here to meet your daughter," she said. She turned to Michelle, "I need to find out what sort of support you might need."

Michelle opened her mouth, "I—"

Trish spoke quickly, "We're her support. I'm normally not like this. My husband... he's working in the restaurant. He's here too, and my other daughter, Stella. She's in the office at the moment."

Pru nodded, "Your older daughter brought Michelle to hospital for her last visit, didn't she?" Again, she turned to Michelle, "Perhaps we could talk?"

Michelle showed Pru her bedroom. "Grant's making a cot. It'll go there."

"I thought your boyfriend's name was Billy."

"It is. Grant's his dad. He likes making things."

Pru scribbled in a small note book, "And I've heard you like making things too."

Michelle grinned, "Yes, mosaics. And I like cooking. Last week Billy and I ... we helped Hal cook at Yoorooga."

"D'you like it at Yoorooga ..?"

Michelle nodded. "I can get there by bus. Billy showed me how to use the them."

Pru nodded, "D'you like it there?"

"Yes, but I can't live there. No girls ... only to visit. I can't even stay over."

"Tell me, what did you cook?"

"We made a cake for Coral. She's one of the carers, and before that we showed Hal how to make a Bol ... I can't say the word; a sauce, tomatoes and meat, for spaghetti."

"Bolognaise," Pru clarified for Michelle, "Are you cooking today?"

"Baked potatoes. Stella told me when to put them in the oven."

Pru smiled, "Lovely. I make baked potatoes with lots of cheese and butter."

Michelle shook her head. "I'm not allowed ... We'll have," she checked them off on her fingers, "tuna, yoghurt, and salad."

Pru left the house wondering about the support Trish would be able to give her pregnant daughter. She walked towards her car, deep in thought.

"Good morning," Ed stepped forward and intercepted her. "I'm Ed, Trish's dad, and Michelle's grandfather. You must be wondering about all of us."

Pru smiled uncertainly. "That's actually exactly what I was doing, but that's part and parcel of my job."

"I run the café down on the beach." Ed waved towards eucalypts, through which glimpses of sand and water could be seen. "Would a coffee be welcome?"

"I've heard about the coffee at your café, and since you've twisted my arm ..."

Ed and Pru sat in the late autumn sunshine. "Can I ask, you are here for Michelle aren't you?" Ed asked.

"Social work isn't as simple as that. Michelle is part of a family. In a way, as soon as I'm brought in, the whole family's involved."

"Ah. You'll have noticed, Trish is depressed. At the moment I'm more worried about her than I am about Michelle."

Pru asked, "Is she getting any treatment?"

"No. Neville, my son-in-law, would've taken her to her doctor, but there's been a bit of a falling out there. We're all trying to work out where to go from here."

"Would a visit from her doctor help?"

Ed chuckled, "If the mountain won't go to Mohommed ... "

"Something like that. Who's your family doctor?"

"Dr Grey at Pelican Heights."

"That's a private practice, isn't it?"

"Yes, we thought with Michelle ... "

"That's good. I'm more likely to be able to get her to come and visit."

Ed's face relaxed, "That could work. Neville certainly can't get her to do anything. Our Princess ... I mean Michelle," Ed smiled apologetically at Pru, "she's been getting to the doctor with Billy or Stella. I think everything's on track."

"What about other practical things?"

"Oh, Michelle can cook simple meals and keep on top of day to day household tasks. She's done a lot since Trish's been ill. Because of having Down syndrome, she's been taught about healthy food all her life. She's making lunch today. Come back to the house and see what she does."

"I saw her preparing baked potatoes with yoghurt and tuna. It looked very healthy. I have to say I was impressed."

Michelle was pulling the cord on the salad spinner when Ed and Pru arrived. At the sight of Ed, her serious face changed instantly. Her eyes crinkled as she smiled, "Are you going to have lunch with us, Poppy?"

"I might. What are you cooking?"

"Baked potatoes." Michelle's smile vanished. She brought her hand up to her mouth, "Oh no! I put four potatoes in the oven. That's one for Mum," she tapped her little finger, "and one for Dad," she tapped the next finger, "and me and Stella." Michelle finished tapping her fingers.

Ed put an arm around Michelle's shoulders, "It's okay, Princess, I don't want to upset the numbers."

Michelle stood chewing her bottom lip and looking at the ceiling. Suddenly she grinned again, "I know, I know," she said excitedly. "We can share."

After Pru had left, the family sat down to lunch. Trish and Neville both complimented Michelle on the meal.

Michelle smiled happily, "Healthy food for everyone. My baby needs healthy food too."

"You always say 'my baby'. Have you thought of any names for the baby yet?" Trish looked up from a plate of untouched salad.

"Umm ... " Michelle looked around the table.

Trish was toying with salad dressing and Neville seemed to have become a statue.

Stella poured out glasses of water, "Well, have you, or haven't you?"

"We've talked about it," Michelle rearranged her cutlery then picked up her knife and fork and cut her potato very slowly.

Neville said, "You can be so infuriating, Princess.

We just want to know what names you've thought of."

"Haven't decided yet." Michelle refused to look at any one.

"Well let's think of some good baby names … " Trish moved the salad from one part of her plate to another. What do you think about—"

"No," Michelle shouted.

Trish sat open mouthed. "You haven't heard what I was going to suggest, yet."

"I don't want to. It's my baby. Mine and Billy's." She pushed back her chair and left the room.

Chapter 31

Dr Grey visited Trish late the next morning. Trish was out of bed, but sitting in a frayed dressing gown and old slippers. She stared at Dr Grey though glassy eyes. She was dimly aware of questions. She didn't know what she answered. She thought she had said the right things: the things she thought Dr Grey wanted to hear.

Michelle wandered into the living area. She rubbed her abdomen and smiled at Dr Grey. "My baby's growing."

"That's good Michelle, but today I've come to see your mum. D'you think you could find your dad or Stella. I need to talk to them, too."

A little later, Michelle returned with her sister.

Stella looked at the doctor, "Dad's in the middle of something he can't leave, at the restaurant. Can I help?"

Dr Grey's eyebrows lifted slightly. "I've suggested that Trish would benefit from anti-depressants. I've explained it all to her, but I don't know how much she's taking in at the moment. Can I rely on you to get her to take them?"

Stella sat down on the sofa next to Trish. She held her mother's hand and looked into her face. "Mum, d'you understand what Dr Grey is saying?"

"Yes. I need some help to get well." Trish looked at Dr Grey, "Will I feel less tired?"

Dr Grey replied, "I certainly hope so. But it's not magic. It'll take a while."

The weather was turning chilly. Billy and Michelle snuggled under the doona in the boatshed.

Billy felt the swell of Michelle's belly with his hands, then laid his head on it. "Are you growing, Little Baby?" he whispered.

Michelle stroked Billy's hair. "I think so." She patted her abdomen gently, "Are you listening Little Billy or Little Grace? Your daddy's talking to you."

Billy wriggled his way up to the top of the doona. He poked his head out and said, "Mum's coming to stay again."

"Why?"

"Dunno. Last time her friend had a new hairdressing place. But I don't think there's a reason this time. I think she just wants to be with Dad."

Michelle laughed. "D'you think they want to be like this, like we are now? D'you think they ..?"

"Um. Not sure ... maybe ... She wants me to go and stay with them for the weekend."

"That's nice."

"Not if they're together ... like this. And we can't be."

Michelle smiled at Billy. "Ask if I can come too."

Natasha leafed through an old recipe book. She saw annotations in Grant's handwriting, together with a series of small pictures of smiley faces. She went through until she came to one with five smiley faces.

Natasha turned the page towards Grant, "Do I take it that this is Billy's favourite recipe?"

Grant chuckled. "That's rather an old book. I don't think it's his absolute current favourite, but he still likes it."

"Why don't I cook it when he comes to stay on the weekend?"

"Are you sure you want to cook? We could go to a restaurant."

"No, not a restaurant. Last time I was here, Michelle's poppy told me to try to get to know Billy. I don't think I really tried hard enough. I want to do better this time and that'll be easier here than if we're out."

"That's great, but remember to buy enough food for four. He and Michelle come as an item now. If he's here, she will be too."

Natasha smoothed non-existent wrinkles from her skirt. "She won't be here all the time, will she?"

Grant grinned. "Just for the weekend. He asked if she could come too."

Natasha's mouth dropped open, "You mean, as in, over night?"

Grant laughed, "You haven't turned into a prude, have you? She's pregnant. That should tell you they're not strangers to each other. Besides, so far they've never spent the whole night together. I think it's quite important for them. Let's not spoil things, hey."

Stella took Trish to the bathroom and waited outside. "I'm not leaving until you've had a shower. I'll help you get into some clean clothes afterwards, but you can't stay like this all day, Mum."

"My clothes are all in that … that bedroom." She waved towards the room that she and Neville had shared until Michelle found Neville in bed with Francine.

Stella suddenly realised that Trish had been wearing the same few clothes for weeks, simply because she'd refused to go into the bedroom. They were the clothes she happened to be wearing, or that were in the wash, when Neville and Francine had been caught.

"We'll get your clothes. We'll put them all in Gareth's wardrobe. I'll get Michelle to help."

Together, they took the clothes into Gareth's room and crammed them into his smaller wardrobe. Then Michelle went into her own room and returned with a cellophane wrapped bar of soap which she gave to Stella. "This smells nice. Give it to Mum."

Stella took the soap and sniffed it. "This is lovely. Where did it come from?"

"Lola gave it to me… a present. Mum can use it. She needs nice things."

Stella phoned Gabby again,. "D'you think you could come in and run the park for today?"

Gabby jumped at the chance.

Trish looked guiltily at Stella. "I appreciate what you're doing for me Stella, but it's extravagant. Surely, Dad could have stepped in."

"No Mum. It's all on the computer now. Poppy didn't have a computer before we came. He doesn't understand them. He'd be out of his depth. I'm going to spend the day with you. Among other things, we're going to the hairdressers. C'mon, let's all go."

Michelle said, "I'm going to Billy's this arvo. I need to pack."

Trish smiled at her youngest daughter, "You don't need to pack for an afternoon, you silly thing."

"I'm staying. Grant and Natasha asked me."

Trish wiped the back of her hand across her forehead. She opened her mouth, then shut it firmly.

Stella reached for Trish's hand, "Well done, Mum." She turned to Michelle. "Have a great weekend, Baby Sister. D'you have any idea what to pack?"

Michelle raised her shoulders and grinned, "My toothbrush …"

"What else?"

"Umm … Not sure. I haven't been to many sleep-overs."

"Here, I'll write a quick list for you," Stella offered.

Neville was desperate to break the ice with Trish, and took to going home at different times of the day, hoping to find a good time to talk to Trish, but whatever time he chose, she seemed unwilling to talk.

On that afternoon, the first thing he noticed was the fresh haircut, then that Trish was wearing different clothes. "That looks nice," he smiled.

Trish made the effort the talk, "Stella took me to the hairdresser. I do feel a bit better."

"Would you like me to cook something before I get back to the restaurant, or is Michelle lined up to do supper again?"

"Michelle's off for the weekend."

"The weekend! Don't be absurd Trish. This is our Princess we're talking about. She doesn't do weekends away."

Stella came into the room. "She does now."

Neville looked at Stella with surprise. "Did anyone ..?" he caught sight of Trish's face.

"Yes," Stella's voice was firm. "Grant and Natasha invited her. I've given her a list of things to pack. She'll be fine."

Michelle unzipped the small suitcase that Stella had lent her. On top of all her folded clothes was something Michelle didn't recognise; a navy blue, lace-trimmed, satin negligee.

Michelle held it against her face. "Thank you, Stella," she murmured.

Billy looked at the negligee appreciatively. He walked towards Michelle and kissed her neck. He breathed into her ear, "Put it on now."

Michelle took it and walked into Billy's small bathroom.

Billy rattled the door knob. "I wanted to see you put it on."

Michelle's voice was muffled by the door, "No—wait! I want you to see me in it."

When Michelle came back into the bedroom Billy gasped. He reached out and ran his hand on the satin over her shoulders and down her arm. He steered her towards the bed.

"It's so soft." He used both his hands to stroke around Michelle's large bump with wonder in his eyes, "Our little baby's in there."

Michelle kissed him for a long time. "Mmm …"

Grant and Natasha stayed up after Billy and Michelle had gone to bed. Grant opened another bottle of chardonnay and poured a glass for Natasha and one for himself.

Natasha sipped her wine and inched up the sofa towards Grant, "It's nice being here with you … and I think I'm a bit better with Billy this time. What do you think?"

"More than a bit, I'd say. He was over the moon when you taught him to text. He'd never told me that he wanted to be able to do that."

"Funny. I didn't think he'd be able to do it, but he saw me texting Lizzy and he was insistent. He must have seen people texting before."

"Yes, but I don't think he ever thought he had a need to do it. Now he wants to text you when you go back to Queensland."

Natasha smiled, "That makes me feel good." She reached towards Grant, "Come here, and help me keep that warm feeling."

Grant slid up the sofa. He took her gently in his arms. "Are you sure this is what you want?"

"Quite sure. Can I sleep in your room tonight?"

Billy woke with a sore neck. He'd cradled Michelle in his arms all night. He stroked her hair and watched dawn's rosy glow though the chinks in the blinds.

Michelle stirred and snuggled closer. Her warm sleepy body against Billy awoke an urgent desire again. He nibbled her ear and neck. He started whispering to her.

Michelle opened her eyes, "Oh, Billy … yes."

As they lay in a state of warm satiation, Billy's phone

beeped. He reached out of bed and brought the phone in front of his face. "A message ... from Mum. Do we want breakfast yet?"

Michelle smiled lazily, "Not yet."

Billy pressed buttons and sent a reply.

Michelle reached for his phone. "Can you teach me to do that?"

"Yes. Get yours. We'll do it now."

They lay in bed laughing and sending texts to each other. After a while Billy said, "Let's get up. You can shower first, if you like."

Michelle went into Billy's bathroom. She looked hesitantly at the towel rail. Memories of Stella's anger when she used the wrong bath towel, flooded her. "Which one?"

Billy laughed, "The pink one. Mum bought it for you. We don't have anything pink in this house."

Michelle held the towel against her face, "Your mum bought this, for me?"

"Um yes. We didn't have any guest towels. She said we were ... what was the word? Oh, I've forgotten."

The following week Billy arrived at Eden House looking glum.

Michelle hurried towards him, "What is it, Billy?"

"Boyo's gone. They've all gone."

Michelle's bottom lip trembled. "What? And Una too."

They were standing by a heavy wooden bench. Billy held on to the back of it and started pawing the ground with his foot. "When I got back to Yoorooga after the weekend, I went straight there. I wanted to take Boyo out." He kicked the bench. "They didn't even say goodbye."

"Oh Billy, we'll miss them," Michelle wailed.

Billy kicked the bench again.

Josie walked past with a tray of acrylic paints. She stopped and stared at Billy. "What you cross about?" Then she slowly smiled and jerked her head in Michelle's direction. "You cross with her?"

Billy stared at Josie. He frowned.

Josie put down the box. "I can give you nice time, Billy." She shimmied her body towards him. "I'm not big and fat like her."

Michelle lunged towards Josie. "I'm not fat ... I'm ... "

Kessie hurried along the path. "Stop it at once!" She placed her large frame between the two angry girls. Turning to Josie she said, "Take the paints to the art room. I'm going to talk to Michelle."

Kessie looked at tears coursing down Michelle's face and at Billy's angry clenched fists. "Have you two had a row?"

They both shook their heads.

Michelle said "Josie wanted ... "

Kessie nodded, "Ah, I understand. I know what Josie wants." Kessie walked towards the main building.

Neither Billy nor Michelle heard Kessie muttering to one the helpers, " ... trouble is, Josie wants it with everybody."

Chapter 32

Michelle returned home from Eden House. She tried to tell Trish about the incident with Josie.

Trish wasn't listening properly, "Josie. that's a nice name. Have you thought of—"

"No, Mum. I'm not talking about names with you. Michelle stomped into her bedroom. "I'm going to shower and get changed."

Trish thought she might do the same. She surveyed her clothes. They looked unfamiliar in Gareth's wardrobe. She sighed, thinking that things had been easier when she only had two sets of clothes. The row of different possibilities evoked feelings of confrontation. She didn't want to have to make choices. Everything looked old and dowdy. She saw a favourite tee shirt and remembered she had been wearing it the day when Francine had come to lunch the previous summer. Francine had worn that tiny white swimming costume. Trish remembered the lacing at the front. She remembered Neville driving Francine back to the hotel.

Trish clutched the tee shirt and rushed into the kitchen. She opened a drawer and grabbed a pair of scissors. She stood at the counter grinding her teeth and trying to cut the fabric. The scissors were not designed for fabric. Eventually, she made enough of a cut to tear the rest.

Her eyes glittered as she tore the fabric. She reached for the scissors and ran back to Gareth's bedroom.

Michelle stood in the doorway. Her eyes widened, "Mum … what are ..?"

Trish ignored her and continued seizing clothes from the wardrobe, cutting and ripping.

Michelle's thumbs started to rub together. She pulled her lips in so that her mouth disappeared into a thin line. Her thumbs began to beat.

Trish continued to cut and rip.

Michelle swallowed hard. She pulled her hands to her sides with great mental effort. She wanted to shout, to run and get Stella, but her voice just croaked, "Stella," and her legs wouldn't move.

Trish pushed past Michelle and ran into her own bedroom. Wild-eyed, she ran her hands along bottles and jars on the dressing table until she found the bottle of perfume that Francine had given her. She picked it up and hurled it at the mirror.

The sound of shattering glass drove through Michelle's numbness. She pushed herself away from the door jamb. Then she ran as fast as she could, shouting for her sister.

Stella phoned Dr Grey.

Dr Grey came. An ambulance arrived and took

Trish to hospital.

After Natasha returned to Queensland, Michelle's social worker visited Grant.

Pru put her bag down in the kitchen and glanced around. " As you know, I'm here to assess what sort of support Michelle will have from family, and you definitely count as family." Grant offered Pru a chair and smiled at the way she seemed to be appraising everything in his kitchen. He was glad he'd got it back the way he wanted it after Natasha's visit. "Yup. This is my grandchild that's going to be born."

Pru looked around the kitchen and smiled when she noticed the door of the laundry was open. There was a vast collection of baby paraphernalia tidily piled on shelves. "My goodness, you have everything you could possibly need."

"Oh my neighbours just moved. They had young children, who'd grown out of all the baby things. They'd kept everything, so when they told me they were rationalizing before their move, I jumped in quick and asked if I could have first refusal. I'll even have a spare cot here for when they come to stay, and a stroller and capsule for the car."

"You did well."

"Oh yes, I was planning to buy it all anyway, but this was so much easier. Also … " he hesitated, "I mean with things as they are with Trish, I think I'd better be prepared to give a lot of support. They might want to come here quite a bit."

Pru tucked her feet under the chair. "Are you in a position to give lots of support?"

"Yes, my hours are pretty flexible, and I want to help as much as I can."

Pru nodded.

Grant said, "I know you were brought in because both Michelle and Billy have intellectual disabilities, but does she really need a social worker, with a lot of us to support her?"

"The thing about us, is that we know the system. If Michelle needs anything we can probably arrange for it much quicker, and … Trish being in hospital, may alter things."

"I've never really understood what you do. I've always thought, 'If it ain't broke, don't fix it'."

Pru laughed. "I'm definitely here for Michelle and the baby, but in some ways you're right. Perhaps what we do best, is assess whether or not something is broke, and then, if it is, we know all the agencies that can help fix it."

"I've just had a few weeks with my ex-wife. We're wondering if we can fix a marriage that ended over fifteen year ago."

"Not so much fixing, more starting again, I'd say."

"Yeah. She wants to play 'happy families' but, it's too late for that. She's fixated on us as a cosy little family unit." Grant paused, "But Billy and Michelle, they're about to start their own family … only I'm not sure if they can do that properly with Billy in Yoorooga and Michelle at Pelicans Resort."

"D'you think they could make a go of it together?"

"With the right help, yes. I did think of offering them a home with me, but I don't think I can offer enough support." Grant shook his head sadly, "Billy on his own, I can manage, but two of them and a baby, that's a big commitment. I can have them for weekends and the occasional week here or there, but not full time. I have a job. I couldn't … "

"I have to tell you, we are seriously worried about whether Michelle will manage unless Trish gets better."

"There's more support there, than you might think. Stella's been training up new managers. That frees her up a lot. Michelle's grandfather, Ed, he's around every day except for a couple of hours in the morning, and even those he can shift around if he needs to."

Pru scribbled in a notepad. "Yes, I've met Ed. He has a lot of confidence in Michelle."

Grant said, "He didn't always feel like that though. When they first moved up here, he loved her to bits, but had very little confidence in her."

"What changed?"

"Lots of things … Lola's been a big influence."

"Lola?"

Grant looked surprised, "You haven't met Lola yet?"

Michelle and Lola sat wrapped in scarves and warm jumpers.

Lola washed the earth from some winter radishes. "How was the weekend?"

"Mm … Lovely. Stella lent me a satin neg…" she waved her hand in the air, "thing to wear. I wish I could be with Billy all the time." She thought for a moment. "Now I'm back home, I miss Mum. I hope she comes home soon."

"Have you seen her yet?"

Michelle shook her head, "Next week. I can go next week. But I hope she won't want to go on about names again. Billy and I ... It's our baby. We want to choose a name."

Ed's customers didn't dawdle over their coffee on winter mornings. As soon as the last customer left, he locked up the café. He wondered if Lola would like to go for a walk. The morning was cold, but crisp and sunny.

Lola was happy to walk, "Beach or bush?" she asked.

"Bush. Although I love the beach, I see it every day. Let's go to Scribbly Gums."

They walked through the banksias, gums and tall tree grasses, and talk drifted to the days of their youth. They talked of Henry and how things used to be.

Lola cut through the narrow path, as she returned the conversation to the present. "Are you asking me if I think she'll make a good mum?"

Ed pushed on at her side, "I suppose I am. She and Billy both want the baby. He'd be with her all the time if he could."

"I know. Time was ... " she looked at him sideways as they continued to walk, "When a family like yours would just have put another caravan in the park ... given it to them. That way they'd have been close by, but still together."

"Umm. The family is pretty set on not having anymore caravans. They made a big exception with you."

"Billy and Michelle could have mine. I could move out."

Ed stopped, "Move out! Where would you go?"

"Doesn't matter. They're more important than I am."

Ed turned and clasped both her hands, "That's very generous Lola. Even if I were to accept, the family wouldn't buy it. Then you'd have made yourself homeless for nothing ... but I'll never forget your offer. I know it came from the heart."

Lola shrugged and smiled, "Any time."

Pru Smith and Emily Croft had not realised that both their diaries had Pelicans Resort written in for the same day. They laughed as they alighted from their respective cars.

Pru said, "Normally, I'd regard this as a prize bungle, but actually it'll be good for us both to see how Michelle is doing without Trish.

Michelle was pleased to see Emily. "Are you going to feel my baby's heart?" I think she's growing very well."

"Oh, 'she' is it? And, yes I will feel for the baby's heartbeat, among other things."

Michelle put her head to one side, "I'd like a baby girl, but I don't mind." She put her forefinger on her chin, "A boy would be nice ... one just like Billy. I'd have Big Billy and Little Billy."

When Emily was finished, Pru smiled at Michelle. "Lucky you. You have two of us today. I'm here to find out how you are going, with your mum in hospital."

Michelle's hands were interlaced. "I miss her." She brought her hands palm up. "Stella's here and Lola's always here."

"Lola ... That's right, Grant told me about Lola."

"Lola's my friend. I want to show her my new mosaic. D'you want to meet her?"

"Yes, but could we talk to Stella first?"

Michelle took Pru and Emily to the office to see Stella. She said, "I'm going to see Lola, now. Pru and Emily want to meet you, then Lola. Will you show them where to find us?"

"Of course I will." Stella waved her out of the office door and grinned at Pru and Emily, "You've caught me at a good time. I've just trained up two new duty managers. I've been working like a maniac to do that, so I'll be around to help a bit more, especially once the baby's born."

"How d'you think you'll be able to help Michele with the baby?" Emily asked.

"Well, for a start, I can take away any domestic worries. She isn't going to have to do anything to help run this place."

Emily smiled, "What sort of things is she doing, now?"

Stella shrugged, "Up until now, Michelle's been taking on more than I ever thought she would. After the baby's born, all she will have is the baby."

Pru looked at Stella's tidy desk and her neat business like appearance, "And after that ... How will you help Michelle, directly?"

"I've offered to stay in the room with her and the baby overnight. It'll give her confidence to know there's someone else with her. You know, as long as things are fairly straightforward, everything seems to work. Even now, although she can't manage to wash the clothes yet, Lola sometimes helps her ... or if we're desperate, we give it to the laundry company that we use for the resort.

"Lola sounds like an interesting person."

"Oh, she is ... but you're going to meet her anyway, aren't you?"

"Yes, just point us in the right direction, and we'll leave you to it."

Lola greeted Emily and Pru warmly. She looked from one professional to the other.

Pru was the first to speak, "How is Michelle is managing with Trish in hospital?"

Lola turned towards Pru but reached for Michelle's hand "I think Michelle is doing very well." She squeezed Michelle's hand, "She's keeping the family fed and the household ticking over. That's a pretty responsible job, I'd say."

"Really?" Pru leaned forward.

Michelle said, "Stella gives me a list of things to do ... I do them. It's easy. Lola helps me with the washing. The meals ... I only do easy meals. Sometimes Dad cooks, or brings food from the restaurant."

"How did you find time to do this?" Pru looked at the mosaic Michelle had taken with her to show Lola.

"Not now. I did that before ..."

As Pru and Emily walked to their cars, Pru said, "I think there's an air of desperation about that family."

"What d'you mean?"

"That sister training people up so quickly. It'll cost them a fortune. I wonder if it's realistic."

"Have you seen their brochures? D'you have any idea how much it costs to stay just one night at Pelicans Resort ? It's become one of the most exclusive places around here." Emily passed Pru a brochure.

Pru gasped, "No, I didn't realise All right. I accept they have enough money, but when Trish comes home, she'll need to be looked after. That older sister will have her work cut out, looking after Trish and Michelle. When the baby actually comes, we'll have to think whether it's in the best interests for the baby to stay … "

Emily looked at Pru in horror, "You seriously think the baby will be at risk?"

"I simply said, it might be something we have to consider."

Neville and Trish walked slowly around the hospital garden. Trish allowed herself to hold her husband's arm as he propelled her past small clumps of bright white snowdrops.

She motioned towards a bench in a paved area. There was a small rectangle of earth from which grew the thorny stems of roses. Then she sat down slowly.

Neville thought she seemed much older than she was. A wave of shame ran through him as he sat down with her, and thought, I am responsible for how she is.

Trish nodded towards the rose beds, "They probably look lovely in the summer."

"Yes, you always liked roses, didn't you?"

Trish summoned a weak smile, "Yes, you said they were a pain. Always getting pests … mould or aphids."

Neville felt his wife disappearing into a place he couldn't reach. "Trish, come back to me." He started gabbling, "Come back to me, and I'll plant roses all around the house. One for every year we've been married … "

Trish turned jerkily towards him. Her voice was shrill, "But not this year. I don't want a reminder of this year." She moved herself to the edge of the bench.

Neville's eyes rested on a piece of broken paving between his feet, "There's still almost half a year left. Can we try to re-build something?"

Trish gazed into the distance, "I can't keep ignoring you, pretending you don't exist. When I come home, something has to be different."

"Is it me, that has to be different?"

Trish shook her head. "It's not as simple as that."

Grant retrieved his letters from the mailbox. He recognised Natasha's large spiky handwriting, and he wondered why she hadn't ever learned to email. Even Billy emailed him every now and then. He took the letter into the house and sat down to read it.

> Dear Grant
>
> I've been thinking about the wonderful time we had when I came to stay with you a few weeks ago. It was very special, seeing you both.
>
> Property prices are much lower up here. I have just bought a really lovely new home. We could start over—all together—as a family. There is enough room. You would get a job easily, and Mr. Carpenter up the road, has said he will employ Billy for a few hours a week.
>
> I really wanted to say something when I was with you both, but I didn't quite have the courage. That's why I'm writing.
>
> Looking forward to hearing from

you,
> love and kisses
> Natasha

Grant read the letter slowly." What planet is she living on?" he muttered to himself. He thought back to Natasha's previous visit. He had enjoyed sharing his bed with her. He had appreciated the time spent with Billy and Michelle, too. He remembered the meals, the fun, the texting. But that was a weekend, it wasn't life. He re-read the letter. There was no mention of Michelle or the coming baby.

Grant went to work. He finished edging the grass and thought that Natasha was right about one thing. He'd be able to get a job anywhere. The bowls club had difficulty getting people who would take enough care. He decided to pack up and have a beer in the bar before going home.

Ed and Lola were sitting at the bar. They beckoned to him to join them. When Grant was seated, Ed said, "It's Lola's birthday. We're going to have lunch. Would you care to join us?"

Grant smiled, "Happy Birthday Lola. Are you sure ..?"

Lola put her hand on Grant's arm, "You're very welcome, Grant."

They sat and talked of local and family events. Grant mentioned Natasha's letter. "I don't know what she's thinking of. She talked of me and Billy. She didn't mention Michelle or the baby. She can't think Billy would leave them."

Lola looked up from her salad. "From what you've told me, she's never really been one to think things through, has she?"

"You mean, 'act now, think later'. You're not wrong, there." He looked out the window, "The trouble is, she wants to cover the ground she's missed. She wants to recreate Billy growing up. She can't do that. It's too late … Billy grew up without her. Although … we could start again, just me and Natasha."

Ed said, "You could tell her just that. There's room in your house, after all."

"Oh no. That's not her idea at all. She wants me and Billy to fly up to Queensland and play happy families up there."

Ed's mouth dropped open, "What and leave … "

Grant nodded. "It's okay. I'm not even going to tell Billy. It'd make him furious, and undo all the good Natasha's been striving for."

Lola leaned forward, "There's something more to this, though, isn't there? You could simply write back and say, 'nothing doing', but I get the feeling that you would like to explore the possibility of the pair of you starting again as a couple. There's no reason why that shouldn't be possible, unless of course you're both stuck on living in your own state … "

Grant laughed, "Oh, I'm not sure I'd mind moving, if I felt Billy would be okay. And in a way he is okay at Yoorooga, but the weekend he and Michelle spent with us was pretty special. I was hoping they might do that a bit more often. We wouldn't be able to do that so often if we lived in Queensland … especially with a baby."

Grant went home and wrote to Natasha. He tried to tell her how much he would like to start again with her. He also explained how important it was for Billy to stay in New South Wales.

> … He's very happy at Yoorooga. It's good that he can come and stay here with me on weekends if he wishes. Perhaps you and I could start over here, somewhere in Falconshire?

Natasha's reply was ecstatic. She still hadn't mentioned Michelle, and there still seemed to be an assumption that Grant and Billy would be moving to Queensland.

Grant shrugged. He couldn't spend anymore time thinking about it.

Trish came home from hospital. She insisted on staying in Gareth's room. Michelle put a bunch of bottlebrush in the room. Stella had moved all of Gareth's things to a box in the garage, and replaced Gareth's plain navy doona cover with a new pale blue and white one. Sprigs of daisies bordered the cover. The room looked fresh and clean.

Trish seemed less jumpy, at least with all family members except Neville.

Neville was unable to talk to Trish without rehearsing what he was going to say. Some afternoons before he went to the restaurant, he and Trish sat on the veranda, while Neville tried to communicate.

One afternoon a few weeks after Trish had come home, she said, "You treat me like an invalid. I'm just mentally wounded. The rest of me … "

"The rest of you had flu, followed a very long post viral fatigue and depression, and that was before

I ... "

Trish's mouth began a smile. At first it was weak and uncertain.

Neville remembered that he hadn't seen her smile for a long time. He'd always liked the way her smile was uneven. The left side of her mouth rose more than the right. A few strands of hair fell over to one side. He remembered that was one of the things that had attracted him to her years before. He reached across and gently moved the lock of hair behind her ear. Trish saw his wistful face, "Lets go for a walk, just along the shore, for a few minutes."

Neville lifted Trish to her feet, "I can start to woo you all over again."

A small speck of Trish's ice thawed.

Neville was disconcerted that there didn't seem to be a smooth improvement. Although he was still wary, he found that on some days he could talk almost normally. On those days she would let him hold her hand, stroke her face, on others she withdrew.

The sisters arranged to go shopping for clothes again. Stella stood on the veranda with her car keys. "Would you like to come too, Mum?"

Trish shook her head. "I used to buy Michelle the wrong clothes. Think how completely out of touch I am with maternity wear. I'd be hopeless."

Michelle put her arms around her mother's shoulders. "Stella's better with my clothes," she nodded, "but you need new clothes too."

Trish shook her head, "You buy something for me ... just one thing, okay."

Michelle and Stella arrived home with new comfortable clothes for Michelle's expanding size.

Stella brought a smart shiny paper carrier bag to Trish. It had rope handles, and big plain lettering on the brown bag.

"I can tell before I open it, that you have spent more than you should, on me," Trish said.

Michelle stood with thumbs under her chin and her hands around her face. Her smile was large and happy. "Go on, Mum, open it."

Trish reached inside and brought out a silver-grey top. She held it up, appraising the cut and hang of it. "Stella, you shouldn't have. You've spent too much. "

"Hush, Mum. You need something nice. Just try it on."

Trish went to her bedroom with the grey top.

Stella and Michelle could hear the shower. After a while Trish returned wearing clean fitted trousers, and the new top. She was wearing makeup too, for the first time in … Stella wondered how long it had been.

When Neville came home from the restaurant he found that Trish was still up. He noticed her new smartened appearance. "That's new. Have you been shopping today?"

Trish shook her head. "Stella and Michelle went together. Stella bought me this. She's good at buying clothes. I just …"

"It matches your beautiful grey eyes. You look lovely," Neville said.

Trish thawed just a bit more.

The following morning, Neville was in the restaurant kitchen supervising a new dish. Butterfly prawns, grilled Haloumi and a rich capsicum puree sat in different dishes waiting for other ingredients, when

Neville's phone rang. He delved in his pocket and walked out of the kitchen area.

"Hello," a husky voice he recognised so well, seemed to be breathing into his ear.

Neville's heartbeat raced. He stood for a moment. He could almost inhale her musky scent. He took a quick gulp of air and pressed the little red button before returning to the kitchen.

When he finished work, he went into the washroom before walking home. The memory of that one word phone call reverberated around his head. Images he had pushed aside, flooded his being. The sleek dark bob, the feel of her silky hair in his hands … Neville stood at the washbasin and threw cold water over his face.

That afternoon Trish again wore fresh clothes and makeup. She said, "Shane told me you're trying to work out a new signature dish. How's it going?"

Neville smiled. It was a long time since Trish had shown any interest in the restaurant. "We've got a few variants on a theme, but we haven't decided anything yet."

"What's the theme?"

Neville sat back comfortably, "Well everyone who comes here, comes because of the fabulous location. We have to keep it seafood based, but we're not sure about which one or ones. We've got a new rich capsicum sauce and … "

"I love hearing you talk about food. You get so animated."

Neville reached for her hand, "We used to talk about our plans a lot. Your art studio is still there. When you're … When you feel like it."

"You mean 'when I'm better', don't you?"

Neville wanted to kick himself. "I suppose so. You wouldn't feel up to running an art course yet, would you?"

Trish gave a small lopsided smile, "We both know I'm not ready to do that yet."

"I want to help, Trish ... truly I do. But I need some guidance. What comes first?"

Trish squeezed his hand, "We do, Silly."

Michelle and Billy sat on the bus. When it stopped at Falconville Hospital, Billy helped Michelle out. He heard sniggers from some boys near the door. Once safely on the pavement, he turned and poked his tongue out at them. The boys looked taken aback for a moment, then the bus moved off and their faces were lost to him.

Michelle held Billy's hand as Emily felt Michelle's abdomen.

Emily laughed, "Look at that little foot. How long has the baby been kicking."

Billy looked proudly at Michelle, "He kicks for Australia. He's going to be a footballer, you see."

"You're certain it's a boy?"

Billy shook his head. "We don't want to know. We like to wait and see ... "

"Like Christmas ... " Michelle smiled. "Just sometimes we imagine things."

Emily nodded and continued with the routine tests. "Everything's fine," she said. "Not long now ... I know it's early, but I think Stella should help you pack your bag soon."

"The baby's coming next month."

"The trouble is, babies don't know when they're supposed to come. Sometimes they're early.

Sometimes they're late. A packed bag is a good idea."

"It will be you ... when I have the baby." Michelle looked imploringly into Emily's face. "Last time I came you weren't here. I saw Mary. I didn't like Mary."

"I'll do my very best, Michelle. Mary saw you because I was away. I had to go to a conference. If I'm here I will deliver your baby, but if the baby decides to come when I'm not, like the middle of the night, I might not be here."

Michelle's bottom lip trembled.

Billy reached over and stroked Michelle's abdomen. "Did you hear that, Little Baby? You have to come when Emily's here. Don't come in the night."

Michelle relaxed.

When they left the hospital Billy said, "Let's go to Yoorooga next. We've got new neighbours. Roger and Ingrid's house was empty. I saw a van this morning. I want to see them."

Michelle said, "I'll phone home."

"Why don't you text?"

"Good idea."

They sat on the bus while Michelle tried to text. "Too hard," she passed her phone to Billy, and watched his thumbs hitting keys. After a while, he passed the phone back to her. "Easy. Now they know you're having lunch with me."

Michelle held Billy's sleeve. She laid her cheek on his arm. "You're so clever Billy. I can't always do texts."

Trish looked at the message on her phone. When she had been in hospital, the first text from Michelle had been a surprise. She remembered how pleased she'd been, to get the small messages with smiley faces.

Trish told Stella about Michelle's text. Stella opened the fridge door. "That's good. I bet they have pizza though. I'll do a quick salad. Is that okay?"

Neville came into the kitchen. He put his keys and phone on the side and looked at Stella slicing tomatoes, "Where's Michelle?"

Stella looked up from the chopping board, "It's all right. She and Billy texted to say they'd be having lunch out. I don't mind doing it, providing you can cope with my simple fare."

Neville's phone beeped. Trish laughed, "I bet that's from Michelle. You'd better look at it. Maybe she's changed her mind."

Neville grabbed the phone. Colour drained from his face when he read Francine. A small pulse at this temple throbbed.

"What is it?" Stella grabbed his phone. "Dad. How could you?"

Neville ran his hands through his hair. "In case you hadn't noticed, I didn't open it. I wasn't going to."

Trish looked alarmed. "What is this?"

Stella pursed her lips and passed Neville's phone to Trish.

Trish read the header. Everything inside her wanted to hurl Neville's phone through the window. She gripped it so tightly that her knuckles went white. With trembling fingers, she pressed 'open'.

Why haven't you returned my calls? Francine x x x

Trish let out a long breath. She passed the phone to her angry daughter. "Read it, then pass it to your father. I think you should let him read it."

Neville's eyes looked fearful. "I really don't want to."

Trish put her arms around him gently. "It was a bit of a leap of faith … opening it, I mean. And now, I'm glad I did."

There were no new neighbours for the Yoorooga residents. The van that Billy had seen in the morning, had been sent to collect some things from Roger and Ingrid's garage. Billy's mouth drooped. "I wanted new neighbours."

Si laughed, "You wanted new neighbours with a dog. What if we had new neighbours, and they didn't have a dog? Have you thought of that, Billy?"

Billy shook his head.

Hal said, "You want a dog and a baby. And you've got a girlfriend. That's greedy."

Si said, "My mum's about to have a new hip, and she won't be able to take her dog, Dewy, for walks for a while. I was going to walk Dewy, but if you'd like to, I'll bring her over tomorrow. You have to promise me you'll be reliable, though."

Billy puffed his chest out. "You can count on me."

"I'm sure I can."

As Pru and Emily were discussing Michelle's family dynamics, Michelle went back to the office.

"I like Emily. She's going to help me with the baby, but I don't know why Pru keeps coming."

"It's just her job, Michelle. She has to make sure you can look after your baby properly and that we can look after you."

"Of course I can look after my baby. I don't need

Pru. It's a silly name anyway." Michelle ran her toe along the bottom of a filing cabinet and gave it a small kick.

"Ah is it, now? And what would be a good name, d'you think?"

"I think," Michelle's eyes lit up momentarily. She caught her breath and looked suspiciously at Stella. "You tried to trick me! You want to know what Billy and I will call our baby. I'm not telling you."

"Oh well, it was worth a try," Stella grinned. "Don't think I'm going to give up so easily, Baby Sister."

"All right Star Sister, I'll just have to be very careful." Michelle laughed.

Chapter 33

Neville returned from the restaurant and found Trish was still up. She was leafing through some brochures for the art studio.

Neville said, "That first art course you ran, it went very well, and you enjoyed it. D'you think you'll feel up to doing another one soon?"

"I was thinking about that. It's difficult with Michelle right now. It's only another month before the baby is due. Even if I felt completely well, I couldn't schedule in a course with a new baby in the house."

"Let's wait and see. Gareth's due home for a bit. His contract will have finished and he won't be working. Maybe, if all goes well, he could hold the fort and you could do a weekend course."

"That might be possible. As you say, we'll wait and see."

Neville reached for her hand, "It's a long time

since you used the word 'we'. It sounds good. Will you let me cook you a special meal? Not a family meal, but one just for us?"

"Busman's holiday?" Trish laughed.

"Something like that." Neville started kissing her neck.

"I think I'd like that ... but I'm not sure I'm ready. "

The next day, Trish took the brochures to Stella. "You did a brilliant job for me all those months ago. D'you think I will have lost all the contacts because of my illness?"

"Some, but not all. When you're ready, we'll do a new drive. We'll have to fix it around Michelle though." Stella doodled on the pad in front of her. "I've got it! Why don't we do a special midweek package, say two or three nights at Pelicans Resort, with two dinners in the restaurant and two days in the studio? You could invite a local artist for one of the days, a different one each time. That way you only have to do one day."

"That could work. We'll discuss it with Neville later."

Stella smiled, "I'm glad Dad's included in things again."

"Ah ... He wants to cook a special meal for me. I'm not sure I'm ready for that yet."

"Why pass up the opportunity of a Neville Grafton dinner?" Stella laughed. "Go for it, Mum. The thing with Francine is over."

Trish winced and looked down.

In a softer voice, Stella said, "You need to try to move on. "

Billy loved Dewy. He reached down to her animated little body and tried to stroke her. She was so excited she yapped, wriggled and licked his hand. He phoned Michelle, "I'm going to take Dewy to the park."

"Who's Dewy?"

"Si's mum's dog. I'm walking her."

"Can I come too? Dad's cooking Mum a special meal tonight. Not for me and Stella. We have to do something else."

"We can eat here. Come now, and you can come to the park too."

Soft music played as Neville served Trish the same menu he'd cooked for her, on the evening that he had proposed to her, many years previously.

Trish reached for the small vase of spring flowers on the centre of the table. She brought it to her nose and smiled at Neville across the table. "The music, the flowers, redolent with memories of happier times. I feel … special."

"You are special. I just had a time of madness, when I didn't see it. We've finished the meal. The music's still playing. I would like to dance with my wife."

Trish tried to look at Neville, but found herself addressing her lap, "I'm still raw and untrusting. Everything reminds me of … "

Neville walked around the table. He knelt on the floor next to Trish, "Nothing here can remind you of anything other than us. I didn't want to spoil this evening by talking about her, but for what it's worth, Francine and I didn't do the romantic bit … ever." He stood up and gently lifted Trish to her feet. Trish allowed herself to be carried into the room which had become hers.

In the dawn sunlight, Neville smiled at her sleeping face. He propped himself up on one elbow and watched the rise and fall of her chest as she breathed easily in her sleep. When she woke he said, "I'm going back to my room for a shower."

Trish rolled over so that she was looking up at him, "So now it's 'my room'?"

Neville caressed her face. "Well, since we don't share it anymore, I guess it must be."

A shadow fell across Trish's face. "I don't think I can ever ... go back there. I'll always remember ..." she started to weep.

"You don't have to," Neville gathered her in his arms. "We'll do it however you want." He kissed her tear-stained face and held her till she stopped crying.

Natasha phoned Grant to say she was planning to visit again. She didn't give any excuse or reason, but she did request that Billy should come and stay for a weekend again.

"Same deal as last time. If Billy comes, Michelle comes too," Grant said.

"Oh, all right then, but I want some special time, with just you and Billy."

Grant could almost hear her pout at the other end of the phone. He smiled to himself, but decided he needed some allies. He phoned Billy at Yoorooga, "I'm in need of some of that coffee that Michelle's poppy makes. D'you want a lift to Pelicans Resort?"

"It's a long way to go for coffee."

"That's the coffee I want. D'you want a lift, or not?"

"Yes, please."

Grant found Ed at the café. "I hope you don't mind, I've come to bend your ear again."

Ed tamped the coffee down, "Talk away."

"Natasha's coming to stay. She wants ... to play happy families with me and Billy. I really would like us to be back together, but she doesn't seem to realise Billy's grown up. He's twenty-two now. If she moves down here, instead of this crazy plan of hers that we move to Queensland, maybe we could get a bigger house. Maybe Billy, Michelle and the baby ... I don't know ... am I just clutching at straws?"

"I don't think that'd be what she wants at all." Ed gazed out over the ocean, "I think I have a plan. I have something in mind. You have to pretend to go along with it all, that'll keep the peace. Just make sure Billy doesn't get to hear her plans."

"You sure?"

Ed nodded vigorously, "Absolutely."

The next time Pru came to visit, Ed came up to the house, "Do you have a few spare minutes? There's something I'd like to talk to you about."

Ed and Pru walked through Pelicans Resort.

Ed took her arm and started crossing North Boundary road.

Pru looked at him questioningly.

"It's just over there." Ed waved towards his cottage. "I bought this little house some time ago. It's been let, but only for six months. I've just got it back. I've been thinking; d'you reckon our Princess could live here with Billy and the baby?"

"Maybe ... I'd need to see it inside at the very least."

"Come in and see."

As Ed was about to unlock the door Pru said, "It isn't just a matter of how good the cottage is, there are other considerations ... You do know that, don't you?"

Ed nodded, "Let's go in. You can see it first"

Pru and Ed walked into the recently vacated cottage. Dot Barker's niece had left it immaculate. Pru walked through all the rooms, admiring the new modern bathroom and kitchen. "I'd be happy to live here, but the question is, would it be suitable for Michelle, Billy and the baby?"

"I haven't said anything to the family, but I think Michelle and Billy could manage here with the baby... if we gave enough help."

Pru leaned against the architrave. "Billy's already living pretty independently. This cottage is only a stone's throw from Pelicans Resort, but we have to remember there is a carer at Yoogrooga all the time and that's just with the four boys. I don't think I'd be happy about Michelle, Billy and a new baby here all on their own."

"Well how about if one of the family stayed over? We could take it in turns."

"Hmm ... there are three bedrooms. I wonder, would you be able to sustain it, do it consistently, I mean?"

"I don't see why not. And don't forget Lola. I'm sure she would stay sometimes ... and Grant of course."

"I won't rule it out, but I'd better run it by the office."

Ed's face shone. "Don't tell the rest of the family. I want it to be a surprise."

Gareth was due home. Stella offered to collect him from the airport.

Neville remembered with guilt, how he had hardly noticed Gareth's leaving. He said, "It's my day off. I'd like us to do that." He asked Trish, "Would you like to come too? Gareth's flight isn't due till mid afternoon. We could have lunch somewhere in Sydney."

Trish looked anxiously at Michelle. "Are you okay with that?"

"Go on, Mum. You and Dad have a nice lunch. The baby isn't due till next week."

That evening Michelle and Stella heard on the radio that Sydney was gridlocked. Stella said, "How awful. Mum, Dad and Gareth will be stuck in that."

Michelle reached across the dinner table for salt. She sat back suddenly, trailing her arm ... She clutched the top of her abdomen. "Ah ... " She let out a small involuntary sound. Her hands went to the top of her bump.

Stella looked up quickly. "Was that a contraction?"

"I think so," her fingers remained on the top of the mound. She looked at her watch.

Stella looked at her, sharply this time, "That is the first one, isn't it Michelle?"

Michelle shook her head.

Stella moved to the chair next to her sister. "When was the first one?"

Michelle pursed her lips.

"You have to tell me. I must know. If you've been having them all day, it's very different, from if this was the first one."

Michelle leaned away from Stella, "I know," she muttered through barely parted lips.

Stella shook her head, "When did they start?"

Michelle stared at her sister, "This morning. When I woke up."

"This morning! You let Mum and Dad go off to Sydney."

"I thought Mum would be back. I didn't know about the traffic hold-up." Michelle clutched at her abdomen again. She held her hands there for a while before dropping them.

Stella watched Michelle carefully, then shook her head, "Well nobody knew there'd be a traffic pile-up that would have the entire freeway clogged for hours." She looked at the clock. "That contraction wasn't long after the first one. When was that first one you had just now?"

Michelle looked down. "It was half past," she barely whispered.

Stella's eyes widened, "That's only five minutes ago, Michelle! I don't believe this. You've been having them all day, and you didn't think of telling me."

"I wanted to wait for Mum to come back."

"How many times have I told you, there's a gridlock around Sydney? They're stuck in traffic. It's the worst traffic jam for seven years. It's a good thing it's Dad's night off and Shane's in the restaurant tonight."

Michelle's face crumpled, "But Mum's going to come to hospital with me."

Stella's face softened. She took Michelle's hand, "Darling Baby Sister, we need to get you to hospital soon. I'm afraid Mum won't be here in time."

Michelle's bottom lip trembled. "But … "

"But nothing, Michelle. Your bag is packed. I'm going to phone the hospital and take you in."

Michelle shook her head. She felt a sudden gush of water, and she opened her mouth.

"That settles it," Stella said, "Your waters have broken. We'll get you changed, and to the hospital."

Chapter 34

Emily picked up her car keys. She stretched. It'd been a relatively easy shift but she was looking forward to a shower and a relaxed evening. She walked towards the automatic doors of the labour ward.

The doors burst open and Michelle's creased face beamed at her. "Emily! My baby's coming."

Emily's thoughts ricocheted around her brain. She knew that Michelle was almost due. She walked back into the ward forcing her mind to recall the previous clinic appointment, when the baby had been active. She pulled various other relevant bits of information into her consciousness.

Emily bit her lip. She knew she couldn't say, 'I'll just stay and settle you before I go … ' She sighed inwardly, but her voice was bright. "Let's get you settled then … " She washed her hands, thinking of the times she'd spent with Michelle discussing the 'Special Day'. She remembered how anxious Billy had been to take part, and wondered where he was.

In the labour room, Stella held Michelle's hand. Emily set up monitors and reassured Michelle as she heard her moan.

Michelle turned to her sister, "Did you phone Mum?"

"No point. They're on the Sydney side of the Hawkesbury. She'd go mad with worry. You'll be fine. I'll stay with you." Stella used her free hand to stroke Michelle's forehead.

Emily asked, "D'you remember the all-fours position that we did in antenatal classes?"

Michelle tried to nod, but her groans turned to yells and screams.

Emily continued smoothly, "Stella and I are going to help you get into that position." Then midwife and sister manoeuvred Michelle until she was semi-kneeling on the bed.

Michelle gasped as they turned her around.

Emily said, "Just put your arms around this beanbag. Hug it tight. Remember how we practised at the classes?"

After a while, Stella looked at her watch. She realised they'd been in the labour room for four hours. Emily had been in the room most of the time, but Stella had hardly noticed others walking in and out.

Michelle yelled again and Stella said, "C'mon Baby Sister. We can get through this together, let's take some deep breaths. One, two, three … That's right … Well done."

Stella was only dimly aware of the sweat coursing down her own forehead.

Emily looked at the two sisters. "You're both doing very well." She thought Stella looked almost as exhausted as Michelle. She turned towards her patient, "I'm going to give you some gas and air. D'you remember, we talked about this too at the antenatal classes?"

Michelle nodded and grabbed at the mask. After a few moments she thrust the mask away. "I don't like it … I can't breathe. I want Billy," she screamed. "Why isn't he here?"

"I'm sure he's on his way," Emily soothed. "I'll take the mask away, you can just use this," she gave Michelle a simple mouthpiece.

Michelle took it and held the tube. She inhaled deeply with the next contraction.

Michelle's contractions were regular for a while. Emily left the room and the sisters barely noticed.

"Did you phone Billy?" Michelle panted at her sister.

"Yes, but he didn't answer. I've left a message."

"What about Yoorooga?" Michelle shouted.

"Coral answered, but Billy isn't there. I'm sure he'll phone when he gets my message."

Michelle breathed more easily with the gas and air. After a while, Emily re-entered the room. Stella was trying to calm Michelle as she moved around, calling for Billy. Emily said to Michelle, "I can tell from your voice, you're going into the next stage. It's really important that you listen to me."

Stella interrupted, "Sorry, I don't understand."

Emily spoke softly, "It's called transition. It's a kind of panicky stage. Michelle will want to push, but we mustn't let her."

Michelle screamed, "I want to push the baby out.

Now!"

"No. Don't push Michelle. You have to wait. We'll help you move into a different position. That'll make it easier."

Stella and Emily helped Michelle onto her side. Michelle panted. Sweat ran into her already-drenched hair.

Stella resumed synchronised breathing with Michelle. "C'mon Baby Sister, you can do this. Just keep breathing with me." She squeezed Michelle's hand rhythmically. "Take a big calm breath now. That's right … nice and slow. Let go now … that's right, and another one … " Slowly her breathing eased.

Emily watched closely as the gas and air started to take effect. In a low voice, she said to Stella, "It should be easier now, but don't be surprised if she seems a bit high."

"High?" Stella queried.

"Yes … the gas and air, it'll make her a bit light-headed."

Billy burst into the room, "Where's Michelle?"

Michelle panted, "Our baby's … com … ing."

Stella beckoned to Billy, "C'mon Billy, hold her other hand. Mine needs a rest." She took her aching hand from Michelle's and wriggled her fingers and wrist for a few moments. We've been breathing together. You can take over for a bit."

Billy looked bewildered.

"There is something really important you could do, Billy." Emily's voice was calm, "Could you massage Michelle's back for her? That'll really help her relax. That's what she needs most of all, right now."

Michelle grabbed Stella's hand again as Billy stood behind her and began to rub her back with slow rhythmic movements.

"That's nice, Billy," Michelle's voice was soft.

"Hey, don't relax too much," Emily's voice seemed to be drifting from far away.

Michelle gazed into the distance sleepily.

"What's happening?" Stella looked up sharply. "Why's she gone all quiet?"

"It's all right," Emily soothed. "It's only the white noise from the gas and air. It's helping her to focus. It's quite normal, I promise you." She turned to her patient, "Michelle, your contractions are slower again, but you must stay with us."

Michelle squeezed Stella's hand ferociously, "I want to push again." Stella looked at Emily questioningly. Emily shook her head.

Billy said, "No. not yet, Michelle."

Stella looked into Michelle's eyes. "C'mon let's do our breathing again."

Emily said, "It's really important that you don't push yet, Michelle."

Michelle sobbed, then gradually resumed breathing with Stella.

Emily soothed, "Everything's just as it should be. It won't be long now."

Michelle shifted her position, "I want to do a poo."

"I don't think we could get you to the toilet in time," Billy looked at Emily for guidance.

Emily said, "That's all right. We always get excited when we see poo. It means the baby's coming soon."

Michelle's small iron fingers gripped Stella's hand again. Stella tried not to wince.

"Okay Michelle," Emily said. "You can push with the next contraction. Make it a nice big push."

Michelle's body was wracked with a long hard contraction. Her groans became long screams, "Uh ... uh ... ahaaa ... "

Emily said, "The head's coming. Michelle, that's great. Keep pushing."

Michelle panted, "I can't. I can't."

Stella used a face cloth to wipe Michelle's brow. "Come on, Baby Sister, one more push. We'll do it together ... come on, one, two, three ... p-u-u-u-sh."

Stella made a groaning sound and Michelle gathered all her strength and pushed again.

A small glistening head appeared. It was followed by red shoulders. Then with lightening speed, the rest of the body slipped out.

"A girl. You have a baby girl, Michelle. Congratulations!" Emily laid the baby on Michelle's chest.

Michelle felt the baby's soft wet skin on hers, "Hello, Baby."

The baby nuzzled into its mother's chest while Michelle stroked its back. Emily clamped the cord and gave Billy the scissors, "Now, Dad, you get to do the important job of cutting the cord." She smiled at him as she held each clamp and said, "Cut between my fingers."

Billy screwed up his face in concentration, and cut the cord. He breathed out, grinned at Michelle and handed the scissors to Emily. He moved up the side of the bed towards Michelle. "Our own little girl." He gently touched the soft tiny face.

Michelle inched over and Billy sat on the bed, one arm around her shoulders, the other hand stroking the baby.

Trish, Neville and Gareth arrived home way past midnight. Stella half-dozed in a chair.

Trish exclaimed, "We thought you'd have gone to bed hours ago." Her voice penetrated Stella's semi-consciousness.

Stella jumped up and hugged her mother. "It's all right, Mum. Everything's fine. You have a perfect little granddaughter."

Trish's mouth dropped open, "Michelle's had the baby!" She put her hand over her mouth, "Without me there … "

Stella laughed. She said gently, "The baby wouldn't wait for the traffic jam to sort itself out."

Trish managed a smile, "Of course." The words tumbled out, "Is she okay? How did she cope?"

"Relax, Mum," Stella put her arms around her mother. "Everything's fine. It was a textbook birth … well that's that Emily called it. Michelle did really well. You'd have been proud of her. Billy's with her now. Dads are allowed to sleep in the same room as mothers and babies now."

Neville turned to Gareth, "Wow, that makes us grandparents, and you're …"

"Yes, I'm an uncle … Uncle Gareth." He rolled it around to see how it sounded, then turned to his sister, "And you were there with her all the time. Well done, Sis." He paused then said, "Goodnight, Auntie Stella."

Later in the morning all four grandparents arrived at the hospital at the same time. They took huge bouquets of flowers. Trish thrust her flowers into Neville's arms and said, "I want to have a few precious moments of 'mother and daughter time', if that's okay." She hurried on ahead of the others.

Billy had spent the night in a large armchair next to Michelle's bed. He'd been down to the hospital shop as soon as it had opened and had returned with a large bunch of pink roses. He was half-sitting, half-sprawled on the arm chair with his upper body on the bed and one arm around Michelle.

Trish's face momentarily showed disappointment, then she smiled quickly and rushed towards Michelle who was sitting up. The baby was in a small transparent cot next to the bed. Trish flung her arms around her daughter and started sobbing. After a few moments she disengaged herself. "My little girl's a mum, now." There were tears in her eyes as she looked from Michelle to the baby, "Oh, she's gorgeous." She reached towards the baby, "May I ..?"

"Yes. She likes being cuddled. We've just put her back in the cot."

Trish reached over and picked up the small warm bundle. She held the baby next to her face, "You're perfect ... just perfect," she murmured.

The remaining new grandparents entered the room. They rushed to admire their granddaughter and made a fuss of Michelle.

Trish hugged her daughter for a long time. "What are you going to call her? We're all dying to know this secret name."

Michelle reached for Billy's hand, and smiled at her mother, "We're going to call her Grace."

"That's a beautiful name," Trish said.

Billy buried his head in Michelle's shoulder. He hugged her fiercely. When he released Michelle, Trish noticed glistening tears at the edges of his eyes.

Tears also gathered in Grant's eyes, but Natasha looked away. She walked towards the window, and stood with her back to everybody.

Billy wiped the back of his hand across the outsides of his eyes. "My sister, you know … "

Trish nodded, she remembered Michelle telling her about Grace not long after she had started going to Eden House. "It's lovely that you're going to call her Grace." She noticed the tears in Grant's eyes and Natasha's hostile back. She hugged Grant and quietly said, "It's the best name … "

Grant grabbed a tissue from Michelle's table and quickly dried his tears. He mouthed "Thank you," at Trish then said, "There are too many of us in here. We'll go and have a cup of coffee and come back in a while." On the way out he sneaked a look at the large vase of pink roses on the bedside table. A small card attached simply said, for Michelle and Our Baby, love from Billy. He smiled.

Billy looked at the flowers Trish was holding and said, "There's a flower room over there," he waved towards the door of the ward. "You can find vases and water … "

Trish smiled as she remembered visiting Ed in a different part of the hospital, a mere three years earlier. She'd used almost the same words to Michelle.

When Grant and Natasha returned Trish and Neville moved towards the outside of the little group.

Neville said, "We might just grab a coffee too. We'll come back later." Trish blew a kiss from the door and they disappeared.

Grant stretched out his hand and shook Billy's, then threw his arms around his shoulders, "I didn't get to congratulate you properly Billy B ..." he stopped. "Perhaps now you're a dad, I should stop calling you Billy Boy."

"It's okay, Dad," he waved towards the baby lying in Michelle's arms, "She'll always be our baby. I understand. I'll always be Billy Boy to you."

Grant laughed. Natasha moved towards the flowers. She said, "I think I'll rearrange them. There are too many is these vases."

While Natasha was rearranging flowers, Billy said, "Dad, we want you to drive us back to Pelicans Resort when Michelle and the baby are allowed home. Will you do that?"

"It'll be my pleasure." Grant grinned, looking at the shining faces of the young parents. "I'll be happy to drive you."

Later, when all the grandparents were together outside, Grant said, "Billy and Michelle have asked me to drive them to your place, when Michelle's allowed out of hospital. Billy wants to come too, if that's okay with you guys."

Trish said, "But we were going to ..."

Natasha looked surprised. She opened her mouth and reached towards Grant, who stepped back and refused to meet her gaze.

Neville gently put his hand on Trish's arm, "It's all right, Darl. If that's what they want. It's their decision." He turned to face her and tucked a stray wisp of hair behind her ear, " ... their baby ... not ours." He put an arm around her and she nodded and then rested her head on his shoulder.

As they left the hospital, Natasha hissed at Grant, "Why did you say that?"

Grant spoke evenly, "Because that is what they want."

"But when we ... "

"These are two entirely different things. You and me, and Billy and Michelle. They are a family now. You and I have the chance to start again if we want to but Billy isn't a child anymore. We can't have him along with us. I'll put the capsule in the car tonight. "

Natasha nodded, but her eyes glittered with anger.

In the family home at Pelicans Resort, Gareth was catching up with his parents and sister over lunch. "Now Michelle's actually had the baby, I suppose the bedroom swap makes sense."

Stella tried to kick Gareth under the table, but she got her father's ankles instead He winced, but said nothing.

Trish looked at her plate, "It wasn't just planned that way, with Michelle in mind. I know our room is much bigger than yours or hers, but when I was ill I moved into your room ... " She forced herself to look at her son, "When you left, I was tired, ill ... Things got worse. I know Stella told you about it all."

"It's all right Mum. You don't have to tell me anything you don't want to. I think Dad and I should go out ... wet the baby's head, and all that."

The pub was large and brash. It reminded Neville of the pub he'd passed with Francine that day when a drunk had fallen out and spilled beer over her dress .... the day he'd allowed her to seduce him. With a huge effort he pulled himself together. He wondered how long he would find reminders of Francine everywhere around him.

Gareth arrived at the table with their drinks. "I think this is one of those times when father and son should get thoroughly smashed and end up talking about life, the universe and everything." He raised his glass.

Neville half raised his glass in return. "I'm not sure about the getting sloshed bit, Son. Your mum's taken a bit of an emotional bashing. I don't think she'd like me arriving home weaving and singing." He looked levelly at Gareth, "and as for 'life, the universe and everything', I think you mean Francine, don't you?"

Gareth shrugged. "Sure. Sis told me what happened. I just thought we should clear the air."

"You know all there is to know. There's nothing new. Middle-aged couple, too busy to make proper time for each other. Wife's best friend throws self at husband, who behaves irresponsibly and idiotically."

"But Mum was depressed. Didn't you care about that?"

"Not at the time. The thing with Francine was a relief from the dreariness of living with a depressed person."

"That sounds so callous."

"It was an all-consuming madness, but it's over now." Neville put his glass down firmly.

In that moment, Neville knew his words were

true. It was finally over. There would be reminders but they would be fleeting. They wouldn't drag him back to that hungry longing.

Chapter 35

Grant and Billy picked Michelle and the baby up from the hospital and drove them to Pelicans Resort.

Billy asked, "Where's Mum?"

"She's at home. She thought it was a special time for just the three of you." Grant lied, as he remembered Natasha's silent fury.

At Pelicans Resort the family gathered around to admire Grace, who started to whimper.

"I think she needs feeding," Michelle reached over and picked her up. "They showed me how to feed her, but … " Michelle looked at Trish, "Will you come … and help?"

"Of course, Darling."

Michelle took the baby into the bedroom that used to belong to her parents.

Trish stood in the doorway. She hesitated, then her eyes rested on the white cot in the corner. She let out a breath that she hadn't realised she'd been holding. Her refusal to go into the bedroom suddenly seemed foolish and petty. She followed Michelle, and held the baby while her daughter sat down and unbuttoned her blouse.

Trish watched as Grace nuzzled around Michelle's full breast. The baby didn't take long to find the nipple and start to suck.

Billy came in as the baby fed contentedly. "She's a good eater, isn't she?" He grinned at Trish, who smiled at the happy parents and their new baby. He sat down on the edge of the bed. "Some of the new mothers in the hospital … they cried 'cos they couldn't feed. Our little baby likes her milk. No worries."

At the end of the feed, Michelle passed Grace to Billy who held her against his chest. He rubbed her back and murmured to her, stopping every now and again to kiss her soft face. After a while he said to Trish, "Do you want to cuddle her?"

Trish took the small warm bundle and looked into wide blue eyes. The remaining ice in her heart began to thaw.

Later, in the living room, Stella said to Michelle, "Would you like your bossy sister to stay with you and the baby for the night?"

"I'd like Billy to stay over tonight. It's our first night. That would be all right, wouldn't it?" Michelle looked from parent to parent.

Trish opened her mouth, "Ah," there was slight pause. "I think that's a lovely idea, but you must call us if … "

"Of course." Billy and Michelle said together, then giggled as they realised they'd both spoken at once.

That night when Trish and Neville settled in Gareth's old bedroom, Trish babbled about Grace. "I know she's our granddaughter, but she really is very beautiful."

"Almost as beautiful as her grandmother," Neville rolled over and stroked Trish's face. "Her skin might be softer, and she has her life before her, but each of these lines tells me about you … "

The next morning Michelle took Grace to the dining area. She said, "Our first night at home. It was nice. Nicer than hospital. I'm glad Billy was with me. Grace only woke once. It was easy."

Trish exclaimed, "Lucky you. When Gareth was born, he woke me every three hours for what seemed like years."

Stella reached for the marmalade and said to Michelle, "If you like I can stay with you tonight."

"Yes please."

Trish said, "We can take it in turns. I can stay with you tomorrow, if you'd like that." She held her breath waiting for Michelle's reply.

"That would be nice. I don't want to be on my own just yet."

Ed was practising on the golf course when he noticed Gareth walking towards him. He blinked in surprise, "I thought you didn't like golf." He nodded towards Gareth's bag of irons. "That looks like a pretty serious set of clubs."

"The CEO of the Indonesian company insisted I played. I was hoping we could play nine holes. They gave this to me as a farewell present when I left them. I don't suppose I'll play much, but was hoping we have a short game."

They walked and played and talked. As they covered a particularly long stretch between holes, Gareth stopped and said, "I've been wondering about our Princess. She's doing really well, isn't she?"

"Yes. I think the thing is that she and Billy really wanted a baby. Grace isn't some awful mistake."

"Stella's been sleeping in the same bedroom with Michelle and the baby, but she thinks Michelle could manage without her soon. I've been wondering … "

"That's the second time you've said that. Out with it! What is it, that you've been wondering?"

Gareth stopped and looked out over the fairway. "You remember when I built the cabins at Pelicans Resort?"

"Of course I do. Only it wasn't Pelicans Resort then. It was just the Pelican Bay Caravan Park."

"Yes, but I'm talking about the cabins. If I can find the right spot, I could build a cabin for Michelle, Billy and the baby."

Ed's voice shot out across the grass, "No. Don't even think of it."

"Hey, can't we just … "

"No," Ed thundered. "I want you to put that idea right out of your mind." He crossed his arms. "You have to promise me not to mention that to anyone, you hear me?"

Ed stormed off.

Gareth paused then caught up. They walked on in an uneasy silence. Gareth had been sure he would have had an ally in his grandfather. He wondered if he could just sneak in a smallish cedar-wood cabin somewhere. Then he remembered that Pelicans Resort still belonged to his grandfather.

In the coming weeks, the relationship between them was strained. Gareth couldn't understand why Ed had been so adamant, and Ed wished the conversation hadn't taken place.

Ed wanted to take Gareth into his confidence about the cottage, but he also wanted it to be a surprise. He wanted to hug the secrecy to himself until the time was right. He accepted Gareth's curtness as the price he had to pay for holding his secret.

The next time Pru visited, Michelle tip-toed into the bedroom and pointed to Grace sleeping peacefully in her cot. "I think she'll wake soon. My breasts … they're full. That's when she wakes."

As if on cue, Grace stirred and cried. Michelle lifted her up, gently kissed the top of her head, slowly unbuttoned her blouse and started to feed her.

Pru sat on the bed talking to Michelle as Grace sucked contentedly. She looked at the shelf of soft toys and baby books and noted the ordered piles of nappies and baby clothes.

When the baby was fed, Michelle changed her. She smiled as she saw Pru looking at the change mat on the carpet next to the cot. Michelle knelt and methodically dealt with the changing routine. "The floor's easier. She can't fall off."

When Grace was clean and fresh, Michelle hummed as she tidied away the dirty nappy and wipes. Finally, she washed her hands and picked up Grace.

"Lola told me about the floor. We practised

before Grace was born. Lola bought me a doll. We put everything out … just like this."

"D'you see much of Lola?"

"Every day. She helps lots. I'm going to ask her …"

Chapter 36

Ed felt Gareth's coolness more than he cared to admit. He nursed his frustration over what he saw as his grandson's obstinacy. After a few days of being ignored by him, Ed jumped into his car and drove to the nearest fast food outlet. He arrived back at Pelicans Resort with a distinctive brown paper bag in his hand.

Ed opened the car door as Lola was walking over to see Michelle.

Lola looked at Ed's wild appearance then slowly her gaze rested on the brown paper bag. "Ed Farmer, how could you?"

"Easy. I've had a crap day, and if I feel like eating crap, I will." He refused to met Lola's gaze, and stared ahead belligerently.

"So, you've had some kind of family argument, and you punish them by putting your own health at risk. I suppose another heart attack and spell in hospital will punish them quite effectively."

"Hah," was all Ed could manage. He clutched the paper bag with unnecessary fierceness and stomped off towards the beach. He walked faster than he would normally have done. He felt this heart thumping. He would have slowed down, but he wanted to get far away from Lola as soon as he could.

He felt a slight grinding at the top of his legs. He'd never been able to walk fast after he'd broken his legs. Normally it didn't matter, because he didn't want to walk fast, but the grinding had become very uncomfortable. When he reached the sand his heart pounded and his forehead was sweaty. He continued to clutch the bag, but his hands started to tremble.

Walking on the soft sand was harder than on the bitumen roads and paths of the resort. He started to puff. He remembered the heart attack. Surely he wasn't having another one. He sank to the ground, allowing the soft sand to support his body weight. The bag slid from his hand.

Ed lay half-slumped on the sand and watched as a hungry seagull alighted on his bag. It's beak quickly hacked and tore at the paper and began pecking at the hamburger and chips. Soon other squabbling seagulls joined it, shrieking and fighting. The first gull was driven off as other more aggressive birds swooped down on the unexpected feast.

A young couple grasping water bottles walked past.

Ed sat up dizzily, "I haven't drunk all day."

The girl looked fearful. She took in Ed's dishevelled state and the torn remains of his paper bag with scattered chips and parts of bread roll. She assumed he was responsible for the litter. "I don't think you need anymore to drink." She was about to walk on.

Ed reached his hand out, "Water … "

"Oh!" She bent down, "I'm sorry I thought you were … "

Ed finished the water in both their bottles. "Thanks. That feels better. I should … " he gestured to the litter-strewn beach and managed to sweep food remains into an undamaged corner of the bag.

The girl looked concerned, "Will you be all right?"

"Yes. I don't live far away."

Natasha surveyed Billy's room. She knew that most of his belongings were at Yoorooga. She tried to remember the room as it had been before he left. She cast her mind back to the large house she had bought in Queensland. She imagined Billy's things laid out in the room she had mentally labelled as his.

In her head, she made a list of things that would be moved interstate, but she didn't mention it that evening when Grant returned from work. Instead she cooked dinner for two, and laid the table with candles and strewed flower petals over the tablecloth.

Billy phoned Natasha the next day to ask why she hadn't been to visit Michelle and the baby since they'd been home.

"I'll come this afternoon," she said. She arrived with armfuls of pink baby clothes and a solid silver Tiffany teething rattle. She cooed over Grace and smiled indulgently at Michelle, whom she thought of as a child playing with a doll.

Michelle was enchanted with the gifts, and Billy

beamed.

Natasha was pleased to have made Billy smile. She returned to Grant's house fully believing that her gifts of baby clothes had bought Michelle off. She was sure Michelle would be so happy with a wardrobe of pink frills that she wouldn't mind Billy going to live in Queensland. She even persuaded herself that Michelle would hardly notice Billy's departure.

Ed arrived sheepishly at Lola's caravan. He held the corner of the bag. "Gulls ate it," he grinned. "Got some healthy Baba Ganoush and veggies for an old man who doesn't want another heart attack?"

Lola laughed, "I can manage the veggies, but Baba Ganoush takes about an hour to make." She looked at her watch. "Let's go to the bowls club for lunch."

"Sure. Just the two of us, or d'you think Michelle would like to bring the baby."

"I think, just us. I don't know if Michelle would be able to handle feeding the baby in public. I'll go and ask though, she might be glad of the opportunity."

When Lola returned to Ed, she said, "Michelle's having some special time with Trish. That's more important than lunch with us."

"You mean because of ... "

"Yes," Lola nodded, "Trish was ill for so much of Michelle's pregnancy, it's good she's able to re-establish her relationship with her daughter, and of course to bond with the baby."

Over lunch, Ed told Lola that it would be Michelle's twenty-first birthday the following month.

Lola's eyes danced, "And, if I'm not mistaken,

it's your eightieth birthday as well."

"How did you know that?"

"You're two weeks older than my Henry was. Don't you remember the joint parties you used to have?"

For a moment they sat reminiscing, then Lola said, "So what are you planning?"

"I'm planning a party for Michelle … and me … well, all of us. Of course you have to be there too. We've had a tough year, and now we've a lot to celebrate. Billy and Michelle most of all." Ed thought of the new little family and he smiled as he hugged his secret.

Lola asked, "Will you have it at the house or take over the restaurant?"

"Even though it's her twenty-first, I think Michelle would be overwhelmed by the restaurant … and I'm not sure we could take the loss of an entire evening's takings. I was thinking of opening the café. It's been idle in the evenings since the restaurant picked up. Michelle and Billy can bring the baby down in the pram. She'll be warm and snug."

"Will Michelle want an evening party?"

"You bet ya. An evening party signifies being grown-up far more than a lunchtime one."

Lola nodded, "You're probably right."

Natasha had stayed on at Grant's house to help her friend Lizzy in the salon at Falconville. She stopped mentioning her plans for an interstate move. When the party invitations arrived, Grant was rearranging his tools in the garage. Natasha said to him, "I think I'll stay until after the party. We can tell him then."

Grant didn't hear the last sentence. He had heard

'stay' and 'party'.

"That's good. I like having you around. You'll get to see a bit more of Grace too … "

Natasha wandered out of the garage, but Grant didn't notice. He continued, "We can have Billy, Michelle and the baby over again soon."

Billy asked Grant when he could bring Michelle and Grace for the weekend.

Grant said, "Ask your mum, Billy. She'll be the one to organise things now."

Billy asked Natasha, but there was always a reason why it wasn't convenient.

Everyone had come to accept that Billy usually stayed over at Pelicans Resort for the weekends. During the week, Stella and Trish took it in turns to stay the night in the same room as Michelle and Grace.

The baby began to sleep through the night and after she had done so every night for a week, Trish said, "It's probably time Grace had her own room. We've got five bedrooms after all, and we could link up the baby alarm."

Michelle looked anxious.

Stella said, "Look, we use it during the day. You always hear it if you're in a different room."

"Yes. It'll be the same as in the day, won't it?"

They moved the cot and baby paraphernalia into the spare bedroom.

Neville thought about Michelle on her own in the biggest bedroom and wondered whether he and Trish might reclaim their bedroom, but he still didn't dare mention it to her.

Lola looked after Grace one afternoon while Michelle and Billy wrote invitations to the party. They couldn't decide whether to ask everybody from Yoorooga, or whether to leave out Ryan and Tom.

"Tom isn't nice to you. I don't think you should invite him," Billy said.

"But he's your friend."

"He only says he's my friend." Billy crossed Tom's name off the list.

The next name on the list was Ryan. Both of them picked up their pens and crossed off the name.

When Michelle got dressed for the party she asked Stella, "D'you think it would be all right if I asked Lola to be Godmother?"

"Great idea!"

"You don't mind?"

"Mind what? I'm Grace's only aunt. I don't need to be her Godmother too. I think Lola would be the perfect choice."

"We'll ask her now. When Billy comes, we're going to walk down to the party together ... We'll take the pram to Lola's caravan on the way."

Stella watched as her younger sister finished getting dressed. "You look great Baby Sister, but I think you just need a little something else to finish the effect."

"Oh," Michelle's mouth drooped.

Stella held out a small present wrapped in blue tissue paper, "This."

Michelle took the gift. Her fingers pulled at the sticky tape and she gingerly unwrapped a large silver locket. She gasped, "Oh, Stella ... "

"Open it," Stella smiled at her.

Michelle's fingers trembled as she opened the locket. Inside were two photos. One was of Michelle, Billy and Grace, and opposite was a picture of Grace when she was a few days old.

Michelle wrapped her fingers around the locket and hugged her sister. "Thank you, Stella. Oh, Thank you."

Billy arrived, with his present in a tiny flat box.

Michelle clapped her hands and flung her arms around Billy, when she saw dangling amber ear-rings. She put them on and shook her head gently, feeling the earrings move with her.

Billy looked at her shyly. "I'm glad they're right. I asked Coral. She said you liked her big amber necklace. We went shopping."

The couple wrapped Grace, put her in the pram and walked to Lola's caravan.

Michelle bounced eagerly on her toes, "We came a bit early 'cos we wanted to ask you something."

"Ask away."

Billy and Michelle grinned at each other then started to speak. They giggled and Michelle continued, "We want you to be Grace's Godmother."

"What a beautiful thought. I'm very ... " Lola brought her hands to her heart. "I'm honoured. I'd love to be her Godmother." She stroked the tiny face in the pram, "I promise to do my very best for you, Darling Baby." She straightened up, "What a lot of things seem to be happening at once. We mustn't forget it's your birthday." She picked up an envelope and gave it to Michelle. "Here's your card and there's something else inside, too."

Michelle drew out the card with a tiny clay

flowerpot. Lola had drawn a plant with a smiling face growing out of the flowerpot. A voucher lay in the card, and inside the card Lola had written,

> Dear Michelle,
> Many Happy Returns for this special day. I hope you enjoy a beauty treatment at Heron's Retreat.
> Lots of love from Lola.

Michelle gasped. "Thank you, Thank you. I've never been to Heron's Retreat."

Most of the family were already at the café. They gave a loud cheer as the trio arrived with the pram. Ed lit tea-lights in small oriental lanterns. Other lanterns, already lit, hung decoratively from poles and the awning. Pastel balloons fluttered in the breeze, along with streamers from the café. Pale tablecloths were laid with silver, and jars of sugar almonds sat among strewn frangipani petals.

The evening was warm and balmy. Guests fussed over Michelle and Grace, who smiled sleepily at cooing faces.

Waiters on their day off from the restaurant had been given an extra evening's work. They walked around with platters of tiny canapés and miniature tartlets.

When Natasha and Grant arrived, Gareth pulled Grant to one side because he wanted to talk about the bowling club, which had been considering a complete revamp.

Natasha moved quickly. She found Michelle and Billy at a rare moment when others were refilling glasses or in search of something to nibble. She presented Michelle with a pale pink angora cardigan.

Michelle smiled and thanked her.

Natasha said, "It'll be something for you to remember us by when we go to live in Queensland."

Billy looked surprised, "What, you and Dad ..?"

"And you of course, Silly. I wouldn't move without you. We're going to be a family again."

"This is my family now." Billy put an arm around Michelle. He spoke to his mother over his shoulder, "Michelle and Grace and me."

Natasha's smile was varnished onto her face. Her gritted teeth glittered in the dusky light. "Now, don't be difficult, Billy. I know you'll miss her for a bit, but we can have a wonderful life ... "

Michelle started to cry. Small sobs grew louder, until people started to notice.

Grant was the first person to reach them. He stood next to Billy. "What's the matter?" He looked suspiciously at Natasha. "What have you been saying?"

Natasha shrugged. "I told him, that's all."

"Told him what?"

"About us moving to Queensland."

"Who's moving? You already live there. I live here, just outside Falconville. Billy lives at Yoorooga. Michelle lives here. Nobody's moving."

"But we are going to start again ... as a family."

Grant shook his head. He spoke not to Natasha, but to Billy. "I don't know how your mum got that idea. We did talk of getting back together as a couple, but never ... " He turned to Michelle and held her face gently in his hands, "And you Sweet Girl, are the best thing that's ever happened to Billy ... you and my beautiful granddaughter."

Lola was standing near Gareth, "I could be wrong, but I think you'll find this is where you get to heal the rift with your grandfather."

Gareth frowned. He was still angry about Ed's non-compliance over the cabin he wanted to build.

"Look Lola, I respect your opinion over many things, but this … well, I'd have thought that you, of all people, would be backing me."

Ed cleared his throat. "Friends … Family … Everybody … welcome to this special occasion. Our Princess is twenty-one, and I'm … well, I'm a year older than I was yesterday."

The crowd laughed.

"I'm not going to be long, but I have one announcement. I haven't given Michelle my birthday present yet, so I want to do that now." He put his hand in his pocket and drew out a small bunch of keys tied to a piece of cardboard on which was written,

2 BOUNDARY ROAD

Michelle looked puzzled, "A bunch of keys, Poppy. What for?"

Lola's hand was on Gareth's sleeve. "I think you'll find … "

Gareth's face was transformed. He spoke as if to himself, "Why Poppy, you sly old dog!"

Michelle and Billy looked bewildered by the swell of excitement. The buzz and chatter made it impossible for them to get anyone's attention for a few minutes.

Silence descended on the gathering as people became aware of Michelle's baffled face. Everyone looked at her as she asked, "What ..?"

A huge grin spread over Billy's face. He

squeezed Michelle's hand hard. He opened his mouth, but he couldn't get any words out.

Trish moved forward. She put her arms around Michelle's shoulders. Her cheek was close to her daughter's, and she beckoned to Billy. "Remember the cottage that Poppy bought and did up? He did it for you, for both of you and for Grace. That's your birthday present." She slid away quickly.

Billy swallowed hard. "I wanted to say … " He grasped both Michelle's hands and spun her around. They each released a hand and grabbed Ed.

"Oh Poppy, Thank you, Thank you," Michelle blurted out.

Ed put the keys into Michelle's hand and took hold of the pram. "I'll come with you," he said "But you and Billy go on ahead. You can open the door and go in without me."

END

Printed in Great Britain
by Amazon